'My Side of the Ocean is a riveting read that opens with a dramatic shark attack and traces the after-effects of trauma on a woman's life, art and marriage. Profound and unputdownable, it's a novel of great empathy and insight, exploring essential questions about what it means to live, and love, when the secure foundations of a life have been ripped away.'
– JENEFER SHUTE, author of Life-Size

'I couldn't put this novel down. It is filled with the majestic, but troubled, beauty of Cape Town today and it shimmers with a quiet, unrelenting passion emerging from the fragility that haunts us all, providing a deeply touching reminder to find some way to choose the truths of what we unexpectedly discover about ourselves.'
– HAMILTON WENDE, author of Red Air and House of War

'There are few places more seductive and turbulent than Cape Town, South Africa, the tip of a continent where two oceans meet. My Side of the Ocean brings us the story of Stella Wright, an American artist in love. It's a powerful novel about art, sharks, longing and the exquisite pain of making a decision that will change your life forever. I loved it.'
– AMANDA EYRE WARD, New York Times bestselling author of Forgive Me and The Jetsetters

My Side of the Ocean

Jax Pax

My Side of the Ocean

A Novel

Ron Irwin

MACMILLAN

First published in 2023
by Pan Macmillan South Africa
Private Bag X19
Northlands
2116
Johannesburg
South Africa

www.panmacmillan.co.za

ISBN 978-1-77010-833-2
e-ISBN 978-1-77010-834-9

© Ronald Irwin 2023

All rights reserved. No part of this publication may be reproduced, stored in or introduced into a retrieval system, or transmitted, in any form, or by any means (electronic, mechanical, photocopying, recording or otherwise), without the prior written permission of the publisher. Any person who does any unauthorised act in relation to this publication may be liable to criminal prosecution and civil claims for damages.

This is a work of fiction. Any resemblance to actual events, places or persons, living or dead, is purely coincidental.

Editing by Nicola Rijsdijk
Proofreading by Jane Bowman
Design and typesetting by Nyx Design
Cover design and text illustrations by Ayanda Phasha
Author photograph by Valentina Nicol

'Recent research suggests that sharks virtually disappeared from the ocean during the early Miocene Epoch, around nineteen million years ago. We cannot say why, but the early Miocene was clearly a period of massive change for open-ocean ecosystems. From one perspective, the shark went extinct long before the first ancestors of the human tribe appeared.'

– PRELIMINARY REMARKS ON THE MIOCENE DISAPPEARANCE OF SHARKS, PROFESSOR ANELE GWAMANDA, UNIVERSITY OF CAPE TOWN DEPARTMENT OF OCEANOGRAPHY

The slave heart all alone
Strives timelessly
To go where you are gone–
Whether to vaults of air
The imponderable nowhere,
Or the pellucid sea–
The regions that are fair
Beyond heart's mastery.

– FROM 'THE ANABASIS', ALLEN TATE

There are over 440 known species of shark on the planet.
The coastal waters of South Africa are home to over a quarter of them.

– THE COMPREHENSIVE BIOLOGY OF SHARKS AND RAYS

Two Seas

Table Mountain (3,558 feet or 1,086 meters) is famously flat-topped and forms a prominent landmark overlooking the coastal city of Cape Town in South Africa. Parts of Table Mountain are estimated to be over 500 million years old. The original name given to the mountain chain by the indigenous Khoisan people of the Cape is *Hoerikwaggo* (Mountain in the Sea).

Table Mountain sits close to the meeting of the Atlantic and Indian Oceans.

Pencil Drawing from Stella Wright's Private Collection, Cape Town

The sea brings in the change of weather over Cape Town. Clouds roll in from the Atlantic and hang over Table Mountain, then blow inland. Looking back, I recognise that I'd been heading toward a crossroads for quite some time but the day we met became a defining point for me. Since then, whenever I reflect on my life, I always think of it in terms of Before and After the day that brought me Ben. You have to have experienced a watershed moment to truly understand its power. A friend of mine once tried to explain how her world had turned upside down the moment her daughter was placed wet and mewling on her naked chest. It was a cosmic shifting, she said, a total and absolute reshuffling of her values and priorities that took place in a matter of seconds, the time it took her to feel and hear and smell and see her baby girl. I cannot have children and I remember being alarmed by the intensity of her conviction. In truth, I did not believe her. I dismissed what she was saying as some kind of postpartum sleep-deprived, hormone-fuelled craziness.

But now I know.

I understand exactly.

I'm not saying things were better or worse after that traumatic afternoon. Just completely, inexorably changed.

Great White

The great white shark is the largest species of mackerel shark and is found in all major oceans. They are notably common off Cape Town, the American artist's South African home.

It is deemed impossible to keep a great white shark in captivity.

Charcoal and Graphite Pencil Drawing, One of Ten by Stella Wright
Collected in University of Cape Town Main Gallery, Cape Town

The wind pushed against the outside walls hard enough to rattle the pots and pans over the stove. That's how it blows off the sea here. It slams doors and sucks air out through the chimneys. Anything not wedged or weighted down outside is shaken; it howls and moans and wheezes while you shelter inside. The wind can continue for days; it casts grit in your eyes from rocks of smoothed and hardened sandstone. It is an ancient, ceaseless lifeforce that has, in the long past, ripped sails from caravels, galleons, clippers and dreadnaughts and blown thousands of sailors to forgotten depths. These days, cargo ships and fuel tankers are not spared, and every few years a whale appears on the beach, bloated by cetacean gases to be cut up and hauled away in trucks. The heavy smell of the carcass is unforgettable. It lingers in the sand. Over a few white-horse mornings that week it had tossed onto these close shores cans, flip-flops, paint tins, oil drums, fruit crates, dolls, bottles, fish, seabirds, frayed lines from freighters.

Water has moods – I learnt that in New York. You look out at a morning-grey ocean and wonder how far the mood goes, how long it will last.

Capture this with your eyes, your mind, tuck it away for later. Over a decade ago, Demetrius told me this on one of our walks. He was my studio mate in the loft in the West Village, and we used to walk to get away from the smell of paint and the close, steamy heat of the studio. Gazing over the Hudson River on a much colder day, squinting into the steel sky and iron water, he told me, *Keep this. Even this. Especially this.*

That day in Cape Town, my morning consisted of an early studio workshop at the university, marking papers in my office and then a drive around that magnificent mountain back toward Camps Bay and my tiny hamlet of Bakoven. The university nestles against the ominously named Devil's Peak, and beside it is the sandstone behemoth of Table Mountain; a stately beacon older than the Himalayas, the only mountain with a constellation named after it: the Mensa. The modest suburban houses of Camps Bay face a long swipe of beach, beside which is Bakoven, easy to miss, tucked away from tourists but sharing the same sea, boasting a small, discreet beach that is really only visited by those in the know. Granite and lava fingers jut out from the land and our house was perched upon one of them.

So I would be home early enough in the afternoon to swim, the afternoon to swim, make notes and paint. I had the house to myself; my husband, Jack, was back in New York closing up our lives here from afar. 'Shutting it all down,' he'd said before leaving a week earlier. Leaving me to sell the house and start the process of packing.

But I'd been putting it off.

Once home, just after lunch, I stood for a moment at the glass doors, my threshold to the ocean, and tried to imprint a memory of the mood of the water and the waves. Tried to capture a portion of my life here, to create coherence in my imagination's memory of the house, the beach, the sky, the mountains, the land, even the strange shrubbish plants. Fynbos. I went to the bedroom, threw my clothes on the bed, changed into my swimsuit, wrapped a robe around myself and walked the twenty-five careful, bracing steps to the end of the point of granite upon which my house had been built.

My point. My days of being able to casually fling myself into the sea whenever I felt like it were coming to an end. I was starting to behave like a tourist in my own home, swimming every afternoon no matter what, because soon I'd be back in New York, and this would all be ten thousand miles away. I knew I'd only be able to paint this from pictures and memory and feeling. Of course, I couldn't have known how that afternoon's events would affect me, my work and my life.

I only saw the man then. I was used to having this patch of water to myself, and I felt a surge of proprietary irritation. What was he doing here? Casual swimmers in this area were few and far between. It was the beginning of winter in the southern hemisphere, the winter swell of June. Jack and I were members of only a tiny clan of year-round residents. The bungalows that nestled here were some of the most expensive homes in South Africa, perhaps the world, owned by German and Swiss and British visitors who were waiting out the cool African winter, waiting for the holidays six months away. They'd be back in December, would stay until February, basking in the sun. Until then, thousands of square yards of granite and marble countertops sat pristine in kitchens, chrome appliances remained unused, made-up beds lay waiting for occupants and those expensive bottles of wine not safely stored in underground cellars or wine fridges would slowly turn bad.

The sun rose and shone daily into this empty coastal enclave, then set, and the moon looked down impassively.

Yet there he was. Paddling inwards, able to roll with the waves because he was in a wetsuit and on top of what looked like a longboard. *Odd.* This was not a surfing area; the small inlet was used by swimmers and kids – the surfers who did come in here tended to be the children and grandchildren of local homeowners who knew and observed the unspoken rule of keeping a wide berth around the beach houses. You rarely saw tribes of surfer kids in their wetsuits coming down the stairs from the public parking. They parked their battered cars and pickups along the shoulder further down the coastal road before picking their way to the sea. It was wilder there; a stony sea barrier led directly to the waves.

The interloper's arms plunged forward and back in the water and he made his course inward. He was perhaps a hundred feet out; he'd pass me as I swam, I noted.

I dove into the water and the bracing cold woke me, made my blood rise to the top of my skin. I have always felt intensely invigorated in the sea. I paddled underwater before breaking the surface again, bearing for the jut of land just seventy-five yards away. If I missed it, I'd find myself in open water and the ocean would press against me as I tried to make my way back.

I checked the surfer, who was rising up and down in the waves as he neared the point. I swam with the waves, was able to negotiate them with ease in this shortened space, kicking hard and stretching for each stroke, turning for breath. The sea was grey and choppy. The surfer was approaching – I could hear the splash of his paddling hands and even his inhalations. He'd pass behind me as he made for the shore, where he'd be picked up by the break. I pushed myself to swim hard away from him, the bubbles and flow of my own making breaking beneath me before I took a breath and heard the wind and the hollow-shell sound of the ocean in my ears.

The man on the surfboard. Shouting.

I stopped, tread water, turned toward him. He was laying on the board, and what he was shouting sounded like, 'Get out!' and I wasn't about to do that.

He shouted again.

'Shark!'

I looked around me, then back at him. He was pointing toward the rising swell, jabbing the air with his finger.

'I saw a fin. Shark! A big one. It's tracking you.'

I was an experienced sea swimmer. I'd seen sharks from afar. And I knew this piece of water. Perhaps the man had seen a dolphin? This wasn't a hunting ground for sharks – they preferred the seals on Dyer Island, miles away. There were no seals here. No penguins, very few fish. We *never* saw sharks here. These were the assurances I granted myself over a second, and then found myself breaststroking toward him, eliminating the splashing from the strong crawl I'd used to get out here. I nodded at him.

'You're sure?'

'Positive.'

He was tall, clear-eyed, waving me toward him like a man gesturing to a table in a restaurant. It was less likely the shark would follow us into shallower water, although just a few years before a shark had attacked a swimmer close to the beach on the other side of the peninsula, at Fish Hoek. The swimmer had been taken away in a helicopter, one leg gone. If we swam together, toward the shore, we might look big enough that the shark would ignore us. The trick, of course, was not to panic.

But I was already panicking. I could feel myself starting to tremble. His fear was palpable, and he didn't seem the type to be easily frightened.

In Cape Town, I knew that my chances of being hurt by a strange man were far greater than they were of being attacked by a shark. I glanced at him again. Surfers didn't come this far. Certainly not surfers in full wet gear. What was he doing here? I gauged how safe he might be, calculated how fast I could swim away from him (fast), and acknowledged the instinctual level of trust I had in this stranger. I took another quick mental sketch of him. Young; tall; long hair; sharp, tanned face; intelligent eyes that looked sincere. Powerful. Very powerful. He knew what he was doing. An athlete. Not a random bad man floating into my little inlet.

He was already nosing his board toward the strip of beach, which was now further away than either of us would have liked. I followed and then swam beside him, keeping up as the waves began to curl into something resembling surf, but the water behind us was just dark chop, light from the sun obscured by low-hanging winter clouds. Visibility through this water filled with ominous shadows was almost impossible. *Good hunting weather.*

We didn't look at each other; we were two people who knew the water, who knew how to swim, who didn't want to waste breaths. As the surf began to lift he checked the water behind us, turning his head back and forth like a harried driver.

Oh God, I thought. *This is real. This is happening.*

He glanced at me. 'You okay?'

'Keep going. The water gets shallow quickly.' My voice sounded strange. Strangely high-pitched.

'It could be gone.'

'Just paddle in. I can keep up. My house is there but it's too deep off that point. Make for the beach. Two more minutes.'

He nodded. He was pale, with surprisingly delicate features, careful blue eyes. Renaissance Jesus, *Salvator Mundi*. I swam closer, keeping my head up. He was getting tired but he was not losing his form. He knew how to swim low, piloting the board beneath him. He breathed, kicked, rolled into each stroke, his arms like pistons. He pushed the water behind himself, an even swimmer, not giving in to panic. He'd be a good surfer. When he set his lips, I saw they were tinged with blue. *How long has he been out here?*

The sea rose beneath us, just slightly, and I had that sudden queasy feeling of being in an elevator shooting up one floor too fast. Water being displaced.

As we came to the small back line of waves, it happened so quickly. At first I thought this competent man had suddenly rolled off his board next to me. But, no. He'd been dumped off his board, like a man falling out of a bunk. Almost tossed over the water. Had a wave suddenly taken him? No. He'd been pushed up and out of the water, and he exhaled hard, a strange, wheezing *ooooof*, as if he'd been punched in the gut. He went into the water face first. *Ass over teakettle*, my mother would have said.

He came up next to me, spitting water. 'It *rammed* me.'

'Are you hurt?' I was now truly terrified and my voice sounded unnaturally high, something below a shriek. *It tossed this big, strong guy so easily.*

Don't freeze, I told myself. *Breathe and swim.*

He took stock. 'It got the board. It hit the board *hard*. My leash is broken.' He began to gasp. 'Sorry. I can't get a breath.'

His lips looked blue, and he was looking either way, craning his neck. *Surfers don't get scared for no good reason.*

The board had travelled on in front of us into the curling waves. I reached out, urgently touched his shoulder, pointed to the sand up ahead. I could see my neighbour's faded-blue kayak turned turtle on the beach, the one his kids used in the holidays. 'We're so close.'

'Just go!' He was wild-eyed, wading toward me, coughing up water. That pale skin.

This is fear, I thought.

He was floundering. He looked at me, looked around himself, trying to draw a full breath.

Don't panic, strange man, because I'll panic. Then: *You're coughing blood. Sharks know about blood. Blood is the shark's thing.*

'Can you make it in? Do you think you can do this?' I could hear the tremor in my voice.

'Where is it? I can't see it?' He sounded angry. He looked at me. 'It bit through the *leash. Fucker!*'

'It's ripped the leash *off* you.' I took another breath. My heart was pounding, and I tried to relax, to inhale the sea breeze. We were making good distance, bobbing up and down. Below us, kelp fronds waved back and forth. We were just about at the broiling surf. I looked at him, at the sky, at my house, forcing myself to slow my heartbeat.

Out there was a shark. Not here, not yet.

'We can make it back. Easily. You hear me?'

'Go! Go! We need to go!'

But within just a few strokes he began to lag, and I waited, let him catch up, and then swam next to him, took hold of his suit and pulled. We swam like that for perhaps ten feet, and then the fin broke water in front of us.

A flick of a black knife through the brine, a trail of white water behind. A shadow.

Far too close. Slashing the sea, the tail followed perhaps eight feet behind before the fish descended.

The surfer saw it, looked at me, his lips set. Still trying to catch his breath. My legs felt like ice, fear coursing like an electric current, something I would need to shed a little at a time, later.

'It's moved off,' I said. 'Just over there.'

'It's circling.' A confirmation.

We plunged right into the space the shark had just passed through. It was to our left; it would turn, could be upon us in a second, perhaps two. A wave lifted us both, began to hollow, and we plowed on, pushed ourselves down the face of the rising water, foam all around us, the wave breaking apart as we neared the oncoming strip of beach, the shoreline rising reassuringly quickly.

I turned to my left, took a ragged gulp of air, and the huge shark was right there beside me in the bulge of the wave.

Its eye, the one facing me, was black. The snout was a dark, misshapen shadow.

The animal would bank quickly into me, turn itself to starboard and slam its jaws into my body. I closed my eyes, hoping that when it did strike, I would be obliterated.

I could hear the break sighing on the beach. I prayed, or tried to, but the only thing I could come up with was 'Our Father'. Then lines from a childhood poem.

But do not distress yourself with dark imaginings.

I felt myself unable to breathe. I was weeping in the water, inhaling it, no longer swimming. Floundering.

You are a child of the universe,
no less than the trees and the stars;
you have a right to be here.

The fear erupted like a lightning bolt through me. *My legs,* I thought. *My legs are so exposed.* As I swam, I found myself almost slowing down. I was slapping the water. The shark had been so close I'd seen the discoloration between its dark dorsal side and the freckles down its flanks. I'd seen the easy way it moved in the water, how it had registered but not *seen* me, simply tunnelled toward me, vulnerable, on its radar.

The panic was so extreme I thought I might drown from it. The man beside me was no better off. We were pushing toward a shore that looked maddeningly close, and yet we seemed to make no headway. A wave lifted me, dropped me. I lost buoyancy, my legs dangled. I shut my eyes, waiting for the feeling of my muscles being sheared, my torso being ripped, a shark ramming into me like a car barreling down Hudson Street, its mouth full of tearing death. There was no way to escape except to swim, more and more childlike, wanting to scream and vomit at the same time. I wanted one thing only: to not die.

The man moved away from me, stronger, and the two of us were pushed into slightly different trajectories by the waves. I opened my eyes, looked to my side and saw nothing, but there was still enough water for the shark to slip under me, drive upwards.

It didn't. Instead, it bisected my path, its fin stirring the water right in front of me, its tail a scythe. As the wave lifted me toward it, I saw it again. The enormity of it. And when the sun caught the rippled water as it cascaded toward the shore, I saw its gill slits as it slipped effortlessly to my right. I looked to the man who was barreling toward the beach. He looked back, paused, waved me forward, pushed himself on.

That eye.

My mind kept returning to that unfeeling moment when the shark was so close I could see the tiny bubbles of water along its flanks. And that dark eye. An eye that reflected nothing, that might have seen me and might not have. Not the eye of a terrestrial animal, not the eye of a kindred soul, but an eye that might be placed on a reptile or a machine. An eye of a thing that did not know pity or fear or introspection and had no memory or emotion or warmth or family. A dark portal that simply saw and did not blink and would not look away. An eye that piloted the creature through water with pitiless grace, an eye that would not avert its gaze when it closed its jaws around another living thing but would roll into its orbital socket through the dying and the bleeding and the feeding and then roll back to confront the endless sea.

In that gasping moment of soundless terror, I imagined seeing myself from a safe distance far above the waves and the water. I would look like a struggling creature flailing toward a small beach with another struggling creature, the much larger shape of the hunting shark cruising in front of me, behind him, sliding far to starboard before sharply banking, homing into the smaller, hapless, sluggardly prey, violently attaching itself and pulling it downwards in a billowing cloud of red.

I swam onwards. I expected to be ripped apart.

That eye. I would never be able to unsee it.

The man pushed himself back to me, grabbed my arm, yanked my body into the surf. We were jettisoned toward the sand. The scrape of rock sand on my feet felt like a revelation as I threw back the sheets of water enveloping me and splashed toward the beach. The shark that had eyed my soul was gone. I half swam, half bounded through the break until I found myself turning, falling, standing and then turning again to look out into the water, opaque, unrevealing. The man was beside me, on his hands and knees. We were scrambling to dry sand like two castaways thrown from a violent wreckage, and he looked at me, gasping, choking for breath. He reached out his hand as if to assure himself he was seeing something real, and I was nodding: 'Yes, I'm alive, we're alive.' *It is finished.*

He collapsed onto his back, and I sat in the foam – held there by the stunning, sure gravity of the land – looking out over the water, then up at the grey sky, the cormorants circling and diving and screaming.

And the terrible shark was nowhere to be seen. It might have headed back out to sea, it might have been right there, a few yards away, behind the curtain of breakers. Even as I lay gasping on the sand, I was sure it would rise out of the shallows and sink its teeth into my legs as I crabbed away from the water's edge. But then I knew I'd returned to a regular afternoon and that *this* was the land, *that* was the sea and I had not been touched. There was the sun. There was the sky. *Here I am.*

The line of houses seemed impassive. Had the shark killed us it would have happened without witnesses. The board might have washed up, been discovered after a few days, just another piece of flotsam. My house, right there on the point, would have remained with its doors open to the surging wind, the curtains billowing inwards, the appliances humming.

He was sitting up now, his hands hanging over his knees like a boxer felled in the corner, trying to find the strength to stand. His long, wet hair had fallen over his face, *Spartan Warrior at Rest*. The wind was cold, my teeth were beginning to chatter. *I'm going into mild shock.* I tried to stand, felt my knees buckle.

He bowed his head. 'It was right there. Right next to us.'

'I know.' A stage whisper at church. The air felt full of crystals that caught in my lungs. I then did stand, unsteady. I identify it now as the vertiginous sensation of stepping into 14th Street and a truck rumbling by so close I could smell its metal sides in the backdraft.

How would I paint the two of us, at that exact moment? The man sitting, the woman standing, hands to her sides, in the pale light. The perspective from behind, from afar, low. The two figures aware of one another but not facing, each looking out to an ominous inlet, the viewer left to contemplate what was hidden therein.

Title this *Hunted/Haunted*.

Eye

Sharks have an almost 360-degree field of vision and see ten times better than humans.
Contrary to popular belief, the eye of a great white shark is not black.
It is a very dark blue.

Conté Sketch (One of Many on this Subject), from Stella Wright's Private Collection, Cape Town

When he stood, he towered over me. He looked down at his ankle. 'You were right. The board's leash broke off. Ripped right off the cuff and I didn't feel it.'

'It's over there in the surf,' I said. Averting my eyes from the waves I began walking shakily, taking care to only step on dry sand. He had pulled the board away from the shoreline. He was breathing hard and his lips were cyan.

I found myself running my hands over my torso, hugging myself, looking down at my legs, turning my calves, searching for any sign of blood, any proof of what I had been through. For all the world knew, I had just come in from an uneventful swim. Somewhere far up on the main road, a motorcycle buzzed toward Camps Bay. My hands were shaking. I was alone on a beach with a strange man. I was very cold. The feeling travelled right down my back, into my stomach. It occurred to me that I might vomit. Walking, just putting one foot in front of the other, was an effort. I had the weird feeling of pretending to be sober when I was actually on the verge of collapse.

But not this man. No. He was concerned about his surfboard.

Later I would identify his trauma in the manic way he had hopped to his feet to attend to the board and gather his ruined leash. Things he could control. *This* beach. *This* broken leash. *This* surfboard.

The board had settled into the sand and we approached it with trepidation, as if it too was something that would strike. He knelt next to it, pushed it to its side.

'Look at this.'

The shark had come from below to where the board curved and thickened, under where the surfer's knee might have rested. Jagged tears perforated the bottom in a crescent where the shark had jawed it. Evidence that this had happened. This was real.

The surfboard – and it was a strange one – was wooden. A longboard that looked as if it had been formed by hand. What did I know about surfboards? Nothing, really. I believed longboards were from fifties movies. The tears in the wood looked visceral but embedded under the skin of the surfboard two deeper protrusions dug into the board's flesh. I found myself bending over it, and then there were tears in my eyes.

I probed my fingers into one hole, gripped what was inside, pulled. It gave, but only slightly. That annoyed him.

'I can deal with it back at my place. You don't have to …' He looked at me sharply. It wasn't my surfboard to touch. He was still out of breath. The smell of the sea rose off him, and a warmer, male smell.

'Wait.' My fingers, cold now in the wet, slippery wood, found purchase, and I twisted the thing, and it gave with a slight rasp.

I held it up between us. An almost perfect tooth. Fresh. Glazed with seawater and possibly the catarrh of the animal itself. Almost as long as my pinky, and heavy to hold. He squatted next to me, held out his hand like a child asking for something on the playground. *Give it to me.* He held it up to the light, turned it.

'That was a few millimetres from my *leg*.' He slipped it into a small zipper pocket in his wetsuit.

'There's another one. In the crevice near the fin. I can't reach it.' My voice didn't sound like my own. It was the shrill voice of a woman on a beach in the wind, a woman who might shortly need sedation. But I could not stop looking. This board with its wounds, the massive bruise that would be forming on his body, the torn leash, my grinding heart. The tooth was one of hundreds in the shark's mouth. What would hundreds of these teeth have done to me? To my legs? To my body?

I found myself trying to limit that thought. Let only the reality seep into my consciousness. But the truth was inescapable. I would not have simply died. I would have been consumed in jagged chunks. My blood would now be in the sea foam.

'I'm freezing,' I said. 'Are you okay to walk?'

He stood and in one easy movement unzipped the wetsuit, slipped his hand over his ribs. He winced. 'I don't think anything's broken but it's pretty sore.'

'I have towels and clothes ... my husband's clothes ... They might fit you.'

They wouldn't fit. This man was a size forty-four shirt, easily, to Jack's thirty-six.

He looked at me with the palest blue eyes I had ever seen, so pale they were lupine. He was a fallen saviour from an El Greco. High cheekbones, translucent skin, angular face drawn in deep strokes. I noted this like I was simply making an account of the living. My heart was still pounding.

'I'll bring the board up to the house. I need to walk it over to the car park anyway.'

'You can leave it where it is. It's safe here – nothing will happen to it. You can take it later.'

He glanced dubiously at where it lay in the sand, then followed as I led him up the small path to the point and along the rocks that formed natural stairs to my property, right up beside the pool. Jack and I had considered creating an actual staircase, but council rules disallowed it. And there, beside the pool, were my sandals; there, inside the sliding-glass door were my towel and glasses and robe. It felt as if I'd left these things days ago, as if I'd just returned from a long trip. I put on my robe. He walked up to me slowly, looked around, blinking.

'I'll get you a towel.'

'I've seen this house so many times from out there ...' He indicated the waves, the sea further out. 'That shark ... It came in *that* close to the shore. I can't believe it.'

I passed him one of the rolled towels from the shelf by the door and he pushed it over his hair, his chest.

Sunlight tried to break through the clouds.

'I was out there for a while. I only saw it as I was heading in. I thought it was a seal at first.'

'They're never on this side.' I said this as if conferring with him, as if suddenly sharing a secret.

'This one was.'

He pressed his fingers into his side. He was very bruised. An angry red welt stretched from below his ribs around his back, as if he'd been whipped.

'Are you sure you haven't broken anything?' I asked.

He breathed, gingerly touched the inflamed skin. 'Nah. Maybe bruised some ribs. I've had worse being thrown onto coral.'

'Let me at least get you some aspirin. Dry off – I'll get you a change of clothes.'

'Don't bother. Really. I don't need your stuff. There's a fleece in my car.'

'Just stay here.'

Upstairs, I fumbled for the aspirin in the bathroom cabinet. *Stop trembling*, I told myself. *You're shaking like a leaf on a tree*, my mother's bemused voice. I stopped, took a deep breath, closed my eyes, counted. I rummaged in Jack's closet, extracted a T-shirt, a pair of sweatpants and one of his ironed New York Yacht Club sweatshirts. My hands were uncontrollable. I brought it all downstairs, then paused, stopped by the kitchen and drew a paring knife out of the block by the sink.

I handed the clothes to him and he took the aspirin, put them in his mouth, chewed, tossed back his head. He forced the sweatshirt over his shoulders but left the other things in a pile on the floor. He was looking back out to the water, the wetsuit still stripped to his waist, hanging off him like a discarded skin. The wind gusted across us and I felt myself between control and crying. He was squinting at the water, looking at me, then looking back at the water.

'You saw it. It was close, hey?'

'I saw it. Yes. Right next to me.'

'I should have pulled you in, but you're a very strong swimmer.'

'It wouldn't have helped. You were alongside me. It happened very fast.'

'Seconds. I didn't want you to–'

'We were in the waves. It was right there.'

'I could really use a cigarette.'

There was half a pack in my purse, for emergencies only. This counted. He lit one, pinched it, inhaled. He walked right to the water's edge, where the point sloped into the sea, stood there, close enough his toes would be wet. He paced back and forth, holding the cigarette, taking short, angry drags. Stomped up to the pool, paced around it, glaring out at the sea. Stalked the few steps back to the water, then took careful steps along the wet lichen. *Surfer Affronted by the Transitory Notion of Life.*

The shark could come back, I thought irrationally. *It could tear him from that ledge, kill him in front of me.*

Stop it. It's over.

He shaded his eyes, trying to see under the twinkling sea's reflection, but finally shook his head and flicked the cigarette into the shark's territory. And came back to me. Away from the water.

'It's long gone. Long gone.' He laughed.

I pointed to his surfboard down on the beach. 'The other tooth is still lodged in there.'

'It is.'

'I want to see it.'

'You want to *see* it?'

'I do. I need to get it out. I don't know why.' I indicted the knife I was holding.

We descended the beach steps again, and I knelt beside the torn board and tried to insert the kitchen knife deep into the gash, felt the strange, scraping roughness of the tooth. Like a stone. Or something else. A fossil. I tried to pry it out, wriggled the knife in there until I was afraid it would break.

'Look, just stop,' he said. 'You're going to cut yourself.'

I twisted the knife harder and its steel began to bend. His hand darted out over mine.

'Seriously, just stop. It's not going to work. Just ... hang on ... let me.' He bent over the wood, pushed the knife downwards. I let him slide the knife from my fingers, watched as he worked it into his palm, his eyes on the tear where the tooth was embedded. He gently set the blade against the wood, slipped it in, turning it as he did so, and then pulled. The tooth birthed and lay glistening on the wood. He handed me the knife handle first, a solemn look on his face, *Richard I at Fontevraud*, and picked up the tooth.

'That's perfect.' He withdrew the first tooth from his wetsuit, set it down next to this one. We regarded them in silence for a moment. He picked one off the board, held it out to me, a votive offering. 'Keep it.'

A treacherous, deadly instrument. I took it from his fingers.

And now we each had one.

I have only a little recollection of what happened next. I was in shock.

It was as if my heart was suddenly pounding out of the depths of my chest. I found myself standing in front of this man – this stranger – and tears were running down my face. Me, the most reserved person in the world. *One cool Cat*, Demetrius had often said. My husband, calling me *The Ice Queen of Manhattan*. Not crying, not taking those shuddering, gasping breaths you take after an accident, just tears falling silently down my face and my neck, looking helplessly at the man, who muttered something like, 'It's okay, we're okay,' but he was also nodding, as if saying, *Yes, I agree, I understand*.

Suddenly desperate, I said, 'I need to get the seawater off me,' and he nodded again, that was logical, that was fine.

I took the towel from him, peeled away my robe and towelled my body, roughly, up and down my legs, my arms, my torso, scraping it through my hair, and he said, 'Wait.'

But once again I was frantically searching across the expanse of my skin for tooth marks, for any evidence of what had been bequeathed to me that afternoon. But there was nothing. My skin was covered in the goose bumps anyone has after a swim, but I could still feel the salt upon me and under that, the living secretion of what had been next to me, the viscosity of the ocean and its animals and its kelp and its beach, and I wanted it off me, completely. Baudelaire: *I touch my body in vain to find the wound.*

How must I have looked to him? Like a banshee? He regarded me not with curiosity or horror or even disdain, but with a kind of affirmation: *Yes, this is what people do after experiencing what we have experienced.* It was as if we were sharing a joke or confirming something worldly. He was nodding.

I pulled at my swimsuit. Pulled the stretchy fabric over my shoulder, mopped the towel over it, and he looked away, then did not look away. I attempted to scrape the suit down across my legs and this must have startled him, although he did not move to stop me, and I was still weeping and off balance – exposing myself to the wind, to the sea, to him – and I felt as if this was happening very, very quickly, this humiliating moment, but I had to be utterly sure. It was the terrible feeling of not being able to see an awful wound. Of having something on my body, like when you walk through an invisible spider strand or think there's a leech on you, or an insect. I felt like a woman tearing at a burning garment and it had to come off, there was no time for niceties like privacy or modesty.

He was the one who finally stopped me. Not by what he said. He simply stood up, took the towel and wrapped it around me. I might have resisted him, but he wouldn't have it. He walked me back up the steps and lowered me into the soft outdoor chair at the head of the pool and wrapped the towel closer and held it there just for the time it took me to catch my breath. And then we sat beside each other, and I felt whatever had left me – whatever self or spirit had briefly slipped out of me – slowly return, like warm liquid filling a bottle.

'We're going to be all right.'

He did not touch me again and the sea was suddenly steel-grey and distant and I finally, after what seemed like an hour or more, felt the tears stop, as if they'd been dammed. He looked at the surfboard still below us on the beach.

'I'm Ben, by the way.'

'I'm Stella Wright.' Then: 'I'm an artist.' It came out as if I was identifying as something bigger than this man. Demetrius reminding me to tell strangers who I was. *Say you're an artist. Declare that to the world. This is me. This is what I am. First principles.*

'Stella Wright. Artist.' The surfer called Ben found that briefly amusing.

'And you're Ben. Ben who? What's your surname?'

'Hume. It's weird, I know.'

'Like the philosopher?'

He grinned. 'I come from a long family line of people who don't trust logic. Or right and wrong. Or knowing things without experiencing them. You're the first person in years to make the link.'

'Empiricism and surfing don't go together well.'

'Except when you get tracked by sharks. Then it works just fine.' That fierce gaze again. He faced the water and the sky, the birds careening in the wind, the waves rolling into the point, the rhythmic silence. Almost absent-mindedly he yanked off Jack's sweatshirt, stood there with the husk of the black water suit hanging behind him. *A man in rude health*, I thought. He again walked past the pool, down along the point, sure-footed on the spray-wet rock, to where the water was lapping and pulling, grey and cold. Stood alone with his toes gripping the stone. The late sun dazzled the sea, impenetrable.

He regarded the surfboard in the sand below like some delicate, fallen thing, something inanimate that still needed pity.

'Look. I can't strap it onto my car right now. It'll break if I don't do it properly – I don't want my board blowing off in pieces on Victoria Road. I can bring a bakkie from work. I work at the Waterfront. Can I just leave it out there?'

I found myself agreeing. I was willing to agree to anything.

'What's your number?'

'I'll write it down for you.'

'No, just tell me. I'll remember,' I told him.

'Are you going to be all right?' He indicated the water, the wind, the sun, the sharks beneath.

He waited. I didn't answer. Then he nodded once and waved – a wide arc, like the statue of Augustus waving away an empire. He turned, was gone and I was alone.

Even though I was freezing, I couldn't bring myself to move and I remained outside for some time. My body felt leaden. My brain felt numb. The salt air settled on my skin. I was clearly still in shock. *I should probably call someone*, I thought. Like my husband, who was in Midtown Manhattan. Or a colleague. But that would require explaining, and I couldn't summon the energy. I did not yet have the words to describe, even to myself, what had transpired in the water that afternoon.

My chattering teeth finally broke through my fugue state. I needed to get warm, but could not bear the thought of a hot bath or shower. I didn't want water anywhere near my body. I ran up to my room and began putting on layers of clothes. Two black sweaters over a long-sleeved T-shirt. Thermals. Sweats. Socks. More socks. I averted my eyes from the windows overlooking the Atlantic. I still had the tooth and I held it in my hand like a totem while I padded downstairs. Still shivering. The tooth was ungainly, surprisingly heavy, and it smelt slightly of salt water and something else. I went into the kitchen and made myself a scalding hot cup of tea.

My wristwatch.

I was certain I'd left it on the counter, but it was nowhere to be seen. Maybe I dropped it, I told myself, when I walked out to the point to take my fateful swim? For a moment, tears welled. The wristwatch was a gift from Jack. It counted as another thing I'd lost that year, another thing jettisoned from my life, like the house would be after it was sold. But I had also begun to lose things. Misplace them. I *lost track*. Even those things I valued. Dr Patel, my cardiac specialist, once told me that some people believe we never really lose things. Rather, we *shed* them because secretly we despise them and want to be rid of them.

I did not despise that watch. Jack had given it to me; it was heavy and real, and I wore it while painting, sculpting, swimming. It was supposedly indestructible, and I needed something indestructible right now.

I searched all around the deck, the counters of the flow-through kitchen, in the long living room. I checked the smooth tiled floors, looked under the sparse furniture, even out back toward the garage as well as in my studio and Jack's office. It was gone.

Could Ben have stolen it? It was valuable, although it was scratched and the ridged bracelet and face were misted with ivory acrylic paint. No. He didn't seem the type to steal a watch. Had I worn it swimming? It could have come off in my panic over the shark. Maybe right now it was ticking fifty feet under the surface of the ocean.

I felt tears sting again. It was a special gift, it was expensive and it was gone. More evidence of the lack of control in my life, encroaching chaos. I sipped my tea and wept in earnest.

Tooth

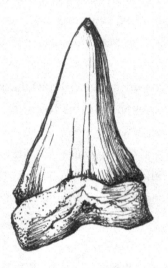

Shark teeth do not have roots and fall out very easily. They are quickly replaced. The great white will use more than 20,000 teeth in its lifetime.

Pen and Ink Drawing from Artist's Private Collection, Cape Town

The impulse to simply crawl into bed and sleep was almost overwhelming. But there were things that had to be done. A line of calls to be answered from the agent who was selling the house, university emails to be replied to and marking, marking, ever-present marking. I could bury myself in work this evening if I so desired. I could erect a wall of work between myself and the afternoon. After all, I was *fine*. My body was untouched. The entire nightmarish episode had taken only time from me. But I found myself unable to focus. To reassure myself, I glanced constantly at my legs and arms.

The impending sale of the house gnawed at me. Although *we* were selling, as Jack told everyone repeatedly, it had fallen to *me* to actually do the work because Jack was too busy. Jack would not see the house again until it was packed up and ready, and he might never see it again because, ultimately, he didn't care about it. It was an asset that had to be 'dumped', he'd told me, and I had imagined the house unceremoniously tipped into the sea. My husband was back and forth between London, New York and South Africa while he 'wrapped up' his investment fund here.

We'd meant to rent this place for only six months. That had turned into two years. Jack had bought it after the owner had been divorced and needed to 'unload' it, as Jack put it. Why did these terms sound so negative, I once asked him? People in his world did not 'let go' of their homes – they 'dropped them' or 'threw them on the market' or just 'got rid of them'. But now house prices were stagnating, the fund was almost successfully deleted from his many computer screens. It was our turn to leave, and the house was not going to sell itself.

I met Jack while I was setting up paintings for a showing in Coral Gables, Florida. The gallery was not due to open until that evening, but he'd walked in anyway and inspected my art with interest, oblivious to the fact that we were still measuring wall space, setting out tables and glasses, adjusting the track lighting and music. He looked at my work for a long while, and finally approached me.

'Do all of your paintings involve water?'

'Many, yes. And animals.'

I appreciated the way *he* appreciated what I was doing, this businessman in his khakis and white shirt, gazing intently but not taking off his sunglasses so the colours would be lost to him, the shimmer of the sea would look brown and subdued.

'You're Stella Wright. I've heard of you. I mean, I've read about you. Actually, somebody showed me your work, and I was impressed. I have a beach house in Martha's Vineyard and I'd like paintings of the ocean for it.'

I had nodded at this businessman who very possibly knew nothing about art, but who was paying attention. Confronting me in his boat shoes and open shirt and the safety cord hanging off his sunglasses, which he finally removed. He'd arrived in Coral Gables on a chartered motorboat – Jack liked boats, I would come to learn, but could barely tie a knot.

I also discovered, as the evening's showing progressed, that he had tried to buy every single painting on display. Every single one.

I found him after the drinks were served, standing around with people who seemed to know him or know of him. Included in the throng were the crew of his chartered boat and some sunburnt associate from London. I tapped him on the shoulder and told him that his interest in my work was very flattering, but it was hardly likely he'd enjoy *twenty* canvases.

'In fact, I really would. I'd like all of it. What I don't hang, I'll keep. As an investment.'

'I'm not comfortable with the idea of these paintings going into a warehouse, Mr Barlow.'

'Call me Jack. Please? Nobody calls me "Mr Barlow". I'm just Jack.'

I waited.

'I won't warehouse any of your paintings, then. I promise.' He grinned, then realised his grin wasn't winning me over.

'You can have *some* of the pieces,' I said, 'but there are other people here who would like to acquire my work. Do you understand? I'd like you to take your buy sticker off at least ten paintings, and at least one sculpture.'

He set his shoulders the way I've seen him do many times since, like he was preparing for some kind of physical combat. 'Then *you* can choose the pieces.'

I shook my head. 'Keep the things you *truly* like. But you can't just take everything in the show.'

'But I *truly* like it all.'

'I'm sorry, it doesn't work that way.'

'Not in my experience, but I don't mean to insult you.'

'I'll have to remove the ten stickers myself if you refuse.'

'On one condition. Please.'

'What's that?'

'You take this. We go out to dinner some time.' And, in a display of matchless hubris, this man handed me a business card. *Jackson Barlow. International Banking and Fund Allocation. Offices: New York/Cape Town/London.* A number, an email address. The name highly embossed in sea blue against a cloud-white background on linen paper, velvet to the touch. The boating crew had politely begun to drift off.

I accepted the card, but I had no plans to ever dine with this Fund Allocator. I went to ten paintings and removed his stickers. Mario, my agent, followed me, berating me. I had no idea who Jack Barlow *was*, he intoned. Mr Barlow was a *highflyer*, a *collector*, he was exactly the *target market*. 'And, Stella, why do we have these shows if not to attract the

Jackson Barlows of the world? You just need to google the man to find out who he is and know he really is *our kind of people*. He would like to be a *patron* of the arts, a *friend* of the art world.'

But I slid the buy stickers in the dark jacket I was wearing, bought just for the occasion, alongside his business card. I wasn't about to have all my work swept up by one short rich man with a smile.

'He's basically pulled himself up by his Louboutins. God, you should offer him *more* paintings! Offer to paint a rendition of one of his homes – he'll be *overjoyed!*'

'This isn't funny, Mario.'

'Stella, just *read* about him. Pick up your phone you never answer and *google his name*. He started this fabulous boutique investment firm when he was younger than you are now! He likes William Kentridge, owns stacks of his drawings, and by all reports Kentridge thinks Mr Barlow's just *grand*, really a *hoot*. He's not knowledgeable but he is *completely avid*.'

When I was back in New York, Mario breathlessly phoned to confess that he had shared my private number with Jack and begged me (he assured me he was actually on his knees in his apartment in SoHo while speaking to me on the phone) not to be rude.

'Be rude to anyone but him,' Mario admonished. 'Yell at me all you like. Berate the gallery owner, send hate mail to the critics, mock my other artists to my face, refer to other buyers as pretentious fools, be rude to *them*. I give you permission. You can be your usual cold and impossible self to all of them and I will *not* complain, I will argue you are truly a *warm person* on the inside. Be rude to *me* – I can take it. But do *not* be rude to Mr Barlow.'

And Jack did indeed call. And I certainly was rude. I informed him after his second call to my studio that some artists don't just take business cards, or do business directly with clients, or let themselves become utter commodities. I told him that his attitude was offensive, in fact, and no amount of flattery or dinner requests or invitations to his house on Martha's Vineyard would change my mind. I slammed my paint-smeared phone down on its ancient cradle after I was finished, did it again when he called back. And three more times, because Jack is faultlessly polite and annoyingly persistent.

Mario was horrified when I told him. He threatened to let me go as a client. Over a testy dinner at a new place in Greenwich Village, the two of us glaring at each other over plates of what he had solemnly declared to be the 'next evolution of Italian-American cuisine', he vowed to take my paintings off his Instagram feed.

'Darling,' Mario hissed, 'the man is *besotted*. Perhaps try to be flattered?'

'Flattered? *Flattered?*' I had to laugh, but Mario always made me laugh. 'He must be at least ten years older than me.'

'A little more vintage, actually. He's an *extremely* well-preserved forty-one. I doubt he has any problem finding women. Women *younger* than you, I hasten to add. Men, too. Essentially, *all* of us want him.'

He knew he'd scored a point. I was approaching thirty. *Une femme âgée* in this merciless, decadent scene. Soon I would no longer be an artist 'to watch' as an online magazine had proclaimed only a year before. I would simply be 'an artist'.

Yes, I still told Jack Barlow of Barlow International Banking and Fund Allocation not to call me quite a few times.

But I also married him.

As the afternoon minutes ticked by, I sat on a kitchen stool drinking another cup of hot tea. The shark tooth glinted on the counter, a grotesque arrowhead. As I began to thaw, I once again became aware of my heart, a cold, fluttering feeling I knew would pass. I closed my eyes. Calm. *Find a space to be.* I avoided glancing at the tooth.

People. Who needs 'em? That was Demetrius's favourite saying, a lifetime ago. He had sublet the studio I'd lived in just after Yale, when I was trying to break into the gallery scene. I shared the space with Demetrius and his friend Lance, who wasn't an artist, he claimed, but a 'Performative Being' who only slept in the space in the mornings. Demetrius painting, Lance occasionally making ceramic tiles with intricate designs, using a communal kiln at the 10th Street Art Co-Op. He performed in a cabaret show most nights. Demetrius cooking vegetarian pasta on one of our two burners, shaking his bald head over the food. *People will always let you down.* That winter in the studio we called The WorkHead, the hard smell of paint and pottery glaze and canvas and dust. Living off a gas card from my sister. *Money, Cat. Ruins it all.*

The things we did for money.

As my body warmed up a kind of heaviness descended, a feeling of what I might only describe as a tired hysteria. It was time to close up the windows from the ocean air, which now rolled toward me like an accusation. I flicked on my phone, searched for Ben's name and location across social media. He had an Instagram account, perhaps two dozen pictures, the last one posted a few weeks before. In it he was walking out of the water with a surfboard under his arm, not looking at the camera. In an earlier one he was sitting at a wooden table on a bar's terrace, wearing a faded pink T-shirt, grinning brilliantly at the camera: 'Bali buds'. Then there was a picture of him in a one-piece jumpsuit, boots, giant rubber gloves, covered in flecks of paint, wearing a full-face gas mask and hood, giving the camera a thumbs-up. The pale-blue side of a boat (a fishing boat? cargo craft?) soared up beside him: 'Another rough day at work'.

Further back, a shot of a beer bottle and a joint. An old man standing on the bow of a surfboard in the waves, wearing a yellow top and board shorts. A picture of a circle of surfers, flowers in the water: 'Paddle out for Shep, Plettenberg Bay'. A dark picture of a cavernous workspace. A battered yellow Beetle, surfboards strapped together on the roof racks, the back of the car filled with duffel bags and a case of wine, the blue sky above, the car parked with a view of the ocean and an endless stripe of beach. He was in the driver's seat, grinning madly at the camera, his skin sunburnt, his hair bleached and even longer than how I'd seen it. A younger version of the man I'd just met. Where was that, I wondered? Knysna, up the Garden Route coast? Namibia? It simply read, 'Paradise found, again'.

Most of the photos had apparently not been taken by him. His profile showed him looking solidly into the camera wearing sunglasses, his hair in his face. Ben Hume. Toronto. Indonesia. Hawaii. Cape Town. The Ocean. He was twenty-four years old, according to one drunken picture of him posted celebrating his birthday on a beach a few months ago, a column of good wishes under the picture, mostly from women.

Twenty-four. The age I was when I moved to New York over a decade ago. My God.

Jack had two social media accounts: Facebook and Instagram. His page featured a picture of the two of us, and the outer doors of his New York office as his background. His feed was limited to pictures of me, his houses and company get-togethers. He still kept pictures of his ex-wife on his feed. He was still friends with her. He always threatened to remove all traces of himself on the Internet, and he wouldn't dream of posting a picture of himself smoking a joint on a beach, next to an obviously drunk girl wearing only a white T-shirt and a plum damask robe, 'High AF'. The girl might have been in her early twenties. Or younger. She was wearing Ben's sunglasses.

Jack's latest picture of me was taken in Cape Town, me wearing my rarely used black suit. Jack was standing straight next to me, smiling broadly at the camera, 'Global Growth, Celebration at V&A Waterfront, Cape Town, South Africa'. Above that was a painting of mine, the ocean off Martha's Vineyard, captioned, 'Auction success for lovely wife. Talent!' These were old. The Cape Town office was already gone. Since Jack had been in New York, he'd posted a picture of himself in an empty open-plan office space with wooden floors. His arms spread wide next to one of his partners, 'Expansion in F French Building'.

I glanced outside, something niggling. I could see that the patio furniture was in place. The pool with its slight ripples looked as it always did, the house as I would have expected. I stepped outside and stood by the water, thought, *I'm fine. I'm alive.* I was just jittery.

But, no.

The surfboard was missing.

I slipped around the side of the house and over the rocks to the beach, looked around for the board, but it was definitely gone. After I'd told Ben it would be fine. Even a chewed-up old surfboard left in the sand could be stolen in this country. I refused to believe it. Could it have been claimed by the sea? Of course not. The tide was thirty yards away. It had been claimed either by some kid or some scavenger.

I went back into the house, grabbed my purse and keys, ran out to the Land Rover. I rolled down the windows, drove out of the garage and by the time I was on the ocean road I had to stop the car in the shoulder and hug myself, knowing this was partly from shock. I sat behind the wheel and collected myself, made sure I was still able to drive, breathed in the salt air through the open windows. I rubbed my palms against the steering wheel, ground my teeth. I needed a glass of wine. Or something stronger.

The afternoon mist coming off the water was ominous. As I was about to shift the car into gear, I braked before a hallucination. Clattering around the bend came a horse cart driven by two men, both wearing T-shirts bearing the name of English football clubs and sporting heavy woollen caps despite the unexpected warmth of the early evening. Men and horse and cart appeared like an illusion conjured out of the diffused ocean haze, directly toward me on the wrong side of the road. Junk collectors who frequented all the suburbs of Cape Town, men who salvaged just about anything they could find and carry; broken electrical goods were especially prized. It was not unusual to see them with their cart piled high with the remains of flat-screen TVs, stereo equipment, toys, plastic sheeting, pipes, gutters, pieces of iron or a washing machine.

They specialised in carting off the remnants of prosperity, somehow eking out a living off flotsam and jetsam. This cart was laden with what looked like bits from a building site: pieces of flooring, skirting board, smashed tiles, broken clay piping and a pile of broken bricks. But they also had found Ben's long surfboard.

I saw it hanging out the side as they clip-clopped by my car. I waved at them out the window, honked. The cart rattled on, the men hunched against the ocean wind, unhearing. I threw the car into reverse, blared the horn again, my blinkers on, followed them – they were moving at quite a pace. Finally, one man glanced back, saw my Land Rover bearing down on them, me still frantically waving, the wind blowing my hair. They brought the cart to a halt.

A motorcycle roared by, then a pickup truck, then a car full of kids, the oppressive gusts of these passing vehicles almost knocking me over as I approached.

They were weathered but ageless. They could have been in their twenties. They might have been in their seventies. I could paint them as seventeenth-century wagon drivers, hunched over into the wind. I could capture their rag clothes, their dark eyes, their misshapen knuckles and hands reminiscent of Van Gogh's peasant work.

'That surfboard you have. Please. I want the surfboard, er … *asseblief*.'

One smiled broadly at my well-meaning Afrikaans and his teeth were a horror. '*Jy koop dit, né, dame?*'

'That's fine. How much?' I went back to the Land Rover, reached in through the open window, found my purse. I came back, held out two notes that flapped in the wind. 'Four hundred rand? *Vier honderd?*' Thirty dollars. Probably a windfall for them.

They glanced at each other, then at me. This was clearly very amusing. The one whose teeth were rotten shrugged and climbed off the cart. '*Nee, dis goed.*'

'No?'

He shrugged, nodded. '*Ja, nee.*'

Yes, no. Here, this meant *conceivably* as well as *probably* as well as *affirmative* as well as *probably not*.

I handed him the cash, which he inspected, folded three times and inserted into his faded shirt pocket beside two loose cigarettes. The horse had bowed its head. It was sweating, wanting a comb. I resisted the urge to touch it. The man shuffled to the back of the cart, muttered something to his friend, who sat examining us, reins curled into his fists. The first man gamely wrenched the surfboard from the back of the cart; it caught the wind and he almost lost it to the road. It was easily three feet taller than him. He helped me drag it back to the Land Rover and together we eased it in. The nose of the board stuck out the back, the fins balanced on the passenger seat and the dashboard.

Satisfied, the man doffed his cap, exposing brown curly hair that was at once wild and greasy and totally unruly, streaked with grey. A surprising, courtly gesture. I gave him a slight bow in return.

'Dankie mevrou.' He smiled, then jogged back to the cart, clambered up, and the two of them waved without turning around. The driver blithely snapped the reins and the cart resumed its creaky way into one of the most sought-after destinations in the world.

It really was the strangest surfboard I had ever seen – not light fibreglass, but a heavy wooden board with rounded sides. It was a natural greyish-white, like a flat piece broken from the hull of a sunken caravel – there were many of these dotting the seabed off the coast here. I had to drive with the Land Rover's right back window down, the nose of the surfboard sticking out the car, its tail against the front passenger seat braced by my free hand. It slid and wobbled as I navigated the bends to my house, and I imagined I was being thrown appraising looks from people in passing cars. When I returned home, the board was so heavy I could barely tug it out of the car.

I dragged it through the rooms of my house, released it onto the deck beside the pool with a clunk. It smelt of seawater and was still sandy, damp. It was formed from a long, knotted piece of what looked like Oregon pine. Battered. Bitten. There were spots where the varnish had been rubbed fine, and then, running my fingertips over this, I realised it was coated with something that had a living sheen. Sap? Resin?

I had to admire the fine, thin sheaves of wood he had used in the tail, fins made of cedar or balsa and waterproofed. It looked like something discovered deep in the ocean or buried under diluvial sands and restored, something not used for pleasure but for aquatic survival. If a surfboard had been used by Halieutican men while spear hunting ancient water creatures, this would have been it. Created by hand, finely worked and roughly used. I left the board beside the pool, carefully turned so the fins were not damaged (how they had not already been torn off I had no idea). I felt as if I was in possession of something of archaeological significance. But its true value, although I did not admit this to myself, lay in the fact that Ben would be coming back for it.

It was almost dark. I was sitting beside the window, hoping the shaking, unearthly feeling of the afternoon would subside, willing my heart to beat rhythmically, trying to imagine it deep within my chest, slowing down, not so erratic. I was afraid to doze off. I was trying to meditate, and the beep of the phone startled me. A text message. Unfamiliar number. I set down the phone. It beeped again.

> hey
> it's me Ben, u there?

I quickly saved the number.

> u OK?
> Yes, I am. Thank you. How are you?
> pretty bruised, I took the train home
> Why? What happened to your car?
> left car in lot. wdn't start (temperamental!) too shaken up to drive anyway

> You could have asked me to drive you.
> is it still there? yellow VW bug?

I glanced out the window toward the public car park, squinted into the rapidly fading dusk.

> Yes, it is still there.
> do me fvr plz? therz box in car. valuable. on back seat. cn you plz get it?
> Box?
> wooden bx. you will see. if not already stolen.
> All right. I will look for it.
> k. thx, will be in touch soon

It could only have been his car and I had no business walking over to investigate it in the half-dark of the evening. It was a VW Beetle, a very old one, a real one. The colour of old mustard, streaked with rust, the windows open to the cold sea breeze. Splayed over the back seat were bungee cords. The seats looked as if they'd been attacked by something with claws. On the front seat there was a dank green rag of a towel. Diving boots on the floor. I reached through the window, pulled the handle and the door groaned open – 1960s security. I lowered myself into the driver's seat, sat contemplating the darkening sea and the slate sky above it through windows coated with salty grime. I cranked closed the windows and the roar of the ocean was diffused. The smell of the car was somehow comforting; rotting horsehair stuffing underpinned by oily engine. Then I saw a wooden box sticking out from under the passenger seat. I teased it out, set it on the sunken passenger seat. It was heavy, the size of a case of table cutlery.

I was aware I shouldn't touch his other things. Like the jumper cables that were also shoved under the seat, or the T-shirt casually lying on the floor beneath my legs. But I did. I clicked open the glove compartment and found a moldy mass of papers. How many VW Beetles were still on the road here in Africa? Would a car like this even be legal in the States anymore? Would a cop *really* allow a person to drive down a highway in this thing? It couldn't even be locked from the inside. I considered bringing everything of any value into the house. There were occasional vagrants from the upper road who might claim the lashing cords, the entwined jumper cables. The car itself was a shelter, a place to sleep.

I gathered up the box and left the car to the wind. I would text him in the morning to confirm that I had it.

As I lugged the box home, I realised I was averting my gaze from the water. I kept to the dry sand, made a wide arc around the spot where we'd climbed out of the sea, miraculously alive. I found myself almost out of breath when I climbed the stairs to my point, ducked back into my home, away from the water and the hissing surf.

The box. Locked with what looked like a simple flip clasp. It wasn't mine to investigate, but I shook it and things rattled inside dully. I poured a glass of wine. I placed the box on the granite counter, regarded its worn sides, its dovetail joints, ran the tips of my fingers over them, feeling nary an imprecision.

Leave that shit alone, Cat.

I drank some of the glass. It would be a collection of mundanities. Car things. There was no point in snooping.

A twist of the hasp. I opened it.

Inside I found a set of the strangest tools I had ever seen, beautiful and odd in equal measure. They looked like knives, or chisels, but were formed in weird angles, the handles made of wood. Unlike the car, the tool set had been carefully looked after. I held one in my hand, noted the smooth contours of the handle. A curled adze, a miniature plow, a flattened hook. I wondered what he worked on with these, tried to imagine what might be formed. My fingers closed around them and I felt powerful, a woman holding a vicious weapon. The tools looked as if they were meant to create things that were obsolete. Antique nautical objects like monkey fists, pulleys, anchor heads, banner staffs.

Or primal surfboards like the one sitting by my pool. An avaricious sense of possession gripped me, the obscene beauty of them in the kitchen's pale light. The inside of the box was lined with dark felt. I shut the lid and thought about the hands that used these strange, sharp pieces of steel.

And then, there was my wristwatch, just where I had left it this morning, beside the coffee maker, resting on its side. How had I missed it? I took it gently in my fingers and looked at the face, the patient sweep of the second hand, the stubborn hour hand and sluggish minute hand. It was about to be night. I put the watch next to my ear. It was running, marking off my time. I put my fingers on my heart, then set the watch face against it. I started at my jugular notch, ran the metal face across my manubrium, over the sternal angle, the body of my scarred sternum. I pressed it against my throat's xiphisternal joint and sensed the miniscule vibrations playing time into me, the answering throbs of my heart.

A helpless fear welled up inside of me. As if I was being observed by that shark's eye, just beyond what I could see through the windows. It saw and waited and did not blink.

I had learnt, quite suddenly, that anything could tear me apart.

Teeth, steel, time.

Just before Jack flew out to New York, I'd been carrying a pile of large canvases into the studio and the world had become watery red. I'd sat down on the floor, unable to catch my breath. My heart had fluttered in my chest, paused like a needle on a vinyl record, missing a groove. I waited to feel it start again, and when it did, and when I was sure I could cross the room, I called the hospital and Jack met me there. As a person recovering from heart surgery, I had to be careful.

Although I was physically fine, I was tired, stressed, anxious about being alone in the house and charged with selling it while finishing up my work. Jack was beside me when Dr Patel told us that communication was essential in such fraught matters. That while selling a home was a 'trifle' for Jack, it might be a challenge for a person like me. These types of 'transactions' were not to be simply assigned to one person, Patel had suggested. They should be mutual decisions and a shared burden.

Dr Patel looked at me. 'Do you feel comfortable selling the house? Are you up to it?'

I replied that I felt that selling the house was certainly within my abilities, but I would prefer that Jack was involved in the final negotiations. The house was expensive. Finances were his specialty.

Jack had agreed readily to this, and then Patel added something that made us both start. 'Professor Wright, do you *want* to sell your home? Do you want to do this as much as your husband does?'

I looked at Jack in the uncomfortable moment that followed. 'I don't think it's really a question of *wanting* to sell the house ... We *have* to sell it.'

Jack nodded intently. 'I understand that it's stressful, but we really do have to move on. We've been in this country far longer than we first thought.'

Dr Patel thought for a moment. 'Is there a pressing financial issue that you are facing? This would be highly stressful.'

Jack looked at me, then at the doctor. 'There's nothing really pressing. I've been involved in an investment fund here for some time and I'm wrapping it up. South Africa is no longer the investment destination I was hoping it would be. Even as a safe haven.'

'You have business interests elsewhere, then?'

'Yes.' Jack was flushing. He didn't like talking about money. More accurately, he didn't like talking about money with people he didn't know. But Patel waited, and Jack added, 'I have interests elsewhere. Other funds. We have a place in New York, one on Martha's Vineyard. Those are our real homes. My business, my core area of interest, is in the United States.' He glanced at me. 'I mean, we're Americans.'

Patel nodded impassively, and Jack took this to mean he was not convinced.

'I like South Africa, I like Cape Town, but the currency is failing, the business prospects are dwindling and doing work here is getting difficult thanks to the, um, tenuous political situation.'

'So, you and your wife are not facing a financial problem?'

Jack bristled. 'No. Not at all. I thought we'd be here a few months, six max, but untying the fund, dealing with the government, tax issues … It's been far more time-consuming than I would have hoped.'

'You've been here for two years. Enough, possibly, for it to start to feel like home?'

'I suppose so, yes. Certainly for Stella. She's been here the whole time. I travel a lot.'

'South Africa, and especially Cape Town, it is an unlikely place. This is how I think of it. I am not from here, of course. I originally come from New Delhi, and I too thought I would only be here for a few months. And yet here I am, some thirty years later.'

Jack nodded patiently. He was trying his best. Jack did not like oblique stories.

'But what if it was an issue of whether or not you *wanted* to leave? To sell your home. To move to a new home. What if you did not think about what you *had* to do, and thought more about what you *wanted* to do. At least in this case?'

'Doctor, the prospects for South Africa have changed. The investments I have in the country are over. I – we, my wife and I – have to go home. There's no logical reason to stay in Cape Town anymore.'

Dr Patel nodded. 'Naturally, there are many reasons to leave the country. I myself am moving on soon. But there are other considerations. One might love a place that is financially unviable. One might simply not be willing to move again. Even back to a place as lovely as New York, Mr Barlow. And this might cause your wife some internal struggle.'

Jack looked at the doctor blankly. It was almost incomprehensible to him that practical matters would not rule all of his decisions. For Jack, selling this house was 'cutting loose an asset made with depreciating currency'. I knew this. But for me it meant losing my fortuitous residency at the university. It meant losing an ocean I loved and was inspired by. And a sky that was bluer and higher than anywhere on the East Coast. A cerulean imagination.

I was quiet in the car the whole way home. Jack prattled on about various nothings in a misguided attempt to cheer me up. The doctor hadn't found anything wrong with me, he pointed out optimistically. I just had to take it easy, and 'do some art'. I could pack when I felt like it. Things would be great.

'Things aren't going to be "great", Jack. Packing up the house is not "great".'

'You can get help. You don't even have to do it yourself, Stella. You can have somebody else do it. Hire a company. They have moving companies here, just like in New York.'

'To move my artwork? My equipment? Your things? Your *computer* things? Jack, how long have we been married?'

Jack thought, then looked at me sheepishly. 'Four years, right?'

'Five years. Five. And even though we've been married for five years, a doctor I hardly know can see that I don't want to leave Cape Town. I've built a home here, for both of us. It's not just a house, another investment.'

He looked at me, then back at the road. 'Stella, look. Are you okay?'

'Try to understand, Jack. There are some places in the world that can't just be replaced like numbers on a spreadsheet.'

'It's a beach house, Stella. You like beaches, correct? They're inspirational for you, I know. We have the Vineyard house. I can buy–'

'It's not just about sand and water and a drafty cottage you can buy anywhere. It's light, it's character, it's a feeling. Jack, do I really need to explain what a *home* is?'

'But we've already *got* a home. In New York! It's not as if I don't *like*

Cape Town ... It's been great, but too long ... Longer than I ever thought this would take.'

'And I'm the one who's here the most. Alone. Weeks at a time, while you're travelling God-knows-where. Switzerland, London. New York ... but you still can't find your way around the City Bowl.'

'Stella, come on. This isn't even our country. I need to be back in New York. This place was never going to be permanent. We've been here, what, two years? That's ridiculous. Tell me you're not a little homesick for a ball game, or Midtown, or skiing?'

'Those are *your* favourite things to do, Jack.'

'Okay, but you get the idea. You like New York. You know what I mean.'

'Jack, when did you decide now was the time to leave? That you wanted to sell up the house and go. Without really even discussing it with me?'

'It's an easy decision, Stella. It's been nice living here but it's really easy to see there's more for us in New York. South Africa's future – I hate to say it – doesn't look bright.'

'So how long did it take you to think about this?'

He pulled up to the house, cut the headlights, looked at me in the washed-out electric-blue glow of the dashboard. 'I thought about it for a minute, Stella. That's how long anyone would take. It's obvious. There's nothing to discuss.'

'That's our problem, Jack.'

I began by standing in the middle of the glass-encased living room – downstairs and outside lights blazing – listening to the Atlantic Ocean pressing its current against the rocks. I pushed open the sliding-glass door and the wind rushed by me, blew papers from the counters. I stepped into the wind and it wrapped itself around me, exhaled salt over my legs. I closed my eyes to the cold and entered the house once again, seized a straight-back chair and tugged it out onto the stones, left it to the wind.

And then another chair.

With effort, I was able to shove most of the heavy furniture outside. I struggled with the long white couch. Alternately pushing and pulling, I wrenched it through the open glass doors. I thought of a meme Mario had sent me a week before: 'No one is more determined than a woman moving furniture by herself'. I thought I'd hurt my back, but kept on until the couch balanced precariously along the side of the natural-looking pool that was not natural at all. It was just a hole that had been blasted into the rocky point the house was built upon. It was meant to look like a forgotten tarn of seawater thrown up by the waves – but it needed chemicals and a pump, and the dark bottom was roughened fibreglass, not the sandstone that crags the Cape coast. I'd been preserving the backwashed water in an underground tank, where it was cleaned and returned, reused – a contained circulatory system. I kicked the couch twice, hard. It teetered on the edge of the pool, lost its purchase, toppled into the black depths. After a moment, the cushions floated to the surface like life vests above a wreck.

Energised, I flung the coffee table through the sliding door with a grunt. I kicked it into the pool and it twirled upside down as it sank to the bottom. Then I ejected from the house two small carved tables, and then the rug beneath them – a snarled ball next to a green canvas-and-steel chaise longue that had blown over in the wind.

My heart thudded in protest against this irresponsibility, but I couldn't stop myself. I took a deep breath, heaved them all into the pool. I stalked back through the large empty living room, a splash of pool water seeping across the white floor. I located my purse, found the hidden package of cigarettes and a lighter. I proceeded to the kitchen, yanked a bottle of champagne out of the racks beside my empty brushed-steel refrigerator and laboriously twisted off the cork. My hands were wet with pool water and they kept slipping until the cork popped merrily. From my glass cupboard I selected a champagne flute, carried this and the bottle outside into the cold air.

I sat in a chair that was never meant to be outside – a soft butterfly chair – and gazed over the wreckage, my heart pounding. I was able to light a cigarette with three flicks of my lighter. I poured myself a glass of champagne. I knew I needed to think about my heart – my *repaired* heart. I had to be careful not to push it too far. If I had another heart attack, I wouldn't be able to explain what I'd just done in a helpless, panic-filled rage. I waited for some emotion to surface, any feeling that might rise through this tantrum. I waited to feel guilty. To feel catharsis. Grief. But nothing came. Whatever I felt about the last few hours would only come later, if at all. In the car. In my office at the university. Possibly in my studio. But here, and in spite of my reckless provocation, nothing could be summoned. Behind me, the house was white and angular. The bottom floor blazed; the now-empty living room like a shining warehouse. It must have been visible far out at sea, a warning to passing sailors, to freight ships heading to Asia, to whales, to anyone who feared being smashed against rocks.

I felt a hollow victory.

I looked at my scattered pieces of furniture. These were things I would not need anymore, that would be meaningless when I left this place. They weren't worth shipping back, Jack had said. They could be sold with the house, lock stock and barrel, *voetstoots* as the locals said. I would leave the house to its new owners soon enough, but I could leave my furniture to the ocean and the wind. These pieces could become home to abalone and barnacles and cuttlefish. They could deconstruct or become coral, they might transform over the years and be all that was left of what was mine here in Cape Town.

For the first time in months I had the urge to draw. I felt it in my fingers, a tingling, a craving to record the absurdity of underwater furniture strewn across the pool's dark floor. I wanted to recreate the shapes underlit by pool lights, blurred within blue/black water, with their playful undulating reflections. From inside I fetched a drawing pad and box of charcoal pencils, sat cross-legged in the wind, and drew, completely absorbed. I sketched a number of versions, the last labelled, *Furniture Tossed from a Sunken Liner Resting on the Seabed*. I carefully piled the drawings on a concrete shelf by the pool, weighted them with a smooth stone. This was how mail was sent from the Cape hundreds of years ago. Travellers left missives under rocks, hoping that future sailors would collect them and take them home.

I was enveloped in that strange, clean feeling I get after creating. I thought, absurdly, that perhaps I would wake up the next day and the drawings would be missing, returned to New York by some ghostly mariner, carried onwards to who knew where.

When I returned into the house, leaving the half-empty bottle outside, I slid shut the doors and in the sudden warmth and quiet I felt the wind just beyond the clouded glass, carrying the momentum of the waves behind it. A rotting kelp wind. I climbed the stairs to the bedroom and strode right past the bed, which sat in the middle of the room like a stone block ready for shaping. I rummaged in the closet and discovered my sleeping bag – a funky thing from the days before Jack – squeezed into a nylon sack.

I carried it downstairs and spread it out before the great glass expanse on the faux-marble floor. I crossed to the windows, flipped open the tiny computer screen on the wall, keyed in a code and the house was instantly encased in invisible laser beams, as was the driveway and even the walkway to the pool. The sensors in the stones leading up to the point were armed. Anyone approaching would set off an alarm that could be heard miles away. Should those lasers be broken, armed men in bulletproof vests and combat helmets would appear carrying loaded guns. I was safe in here – the glass that made up so much of the house's front was almost impenetrable. If it was broken, further alarms would be set off. In Cape Town, any crime was conceivable. The front wall, facing the narrow road leading to my house, was eight-feet high, strung with electrical fencing that would howl in protest if it was touched, summoning the men with their guns. I was like everyone else who owned one of these houses on this exclusive part of coast. Even in the grip of a drunken, fearful collapse, I remembered to key in the security code, wait for the reassuring electronic chirp that said I was safe, I was guarded.

I slept curled up on the floor, burrowed into the musty sleeping bag. I dreamt I was plummeting underwater, endlessly. I yearned to reach the firm sea floor, but the ocean was swallowing me into darkness. I was being ingested. I found myself suspended, looking downwards into a deep black void, and upwards into a vague fading light. I was submerged in miles and miles of dead liquid, water that contained no life at all, not even phytoplankton or bacteria or algae. Mine was an endless, empty ocean that lacked light and tides and animation. And yet something within it stirred, and I found myself before a tremendous black eye, a portal ten times my size, my only company in these lifeless, limitless depths: an eye that regarded me without emotion or recognition or even acknowledgement, just a disk on an amorphous, gigantic body that opened and vacantly devoured what was there. I was frozen with fear and a terrible dread and when I opened my mouth to scream, I inhaled water, floundered, the eye absorbing what warmth I had brought with me. I was filled with an icy horror; the sure knowledge that I would soon be part of this sterile numbness. I would slowly be consumed, alone. My cells began unbinding.

The house shuddered and swayed around me like a heavy, moored ship enwombing its sole crewmember.

Pyjama Shark

The pyjama shark *(Poroderma africanum)* is common and endemic to the coastal waters of South Africa. It is often referred to as the catshark.

The pyjama shark is primarily nocturnal.

Ink Sketch from One of Stella Wright's Many Personal Sketchbooks, Cape Town

Artist Wanted for Special Place/Affordable/Only Serious Artist Wanted

Looking for ARTIST who wants to share a CREATIVE SPACE in West Village. ONLY people who are serious artists need apply as this is primarily a WORK space and living situation (it has been named The WorkHead). Good workroom, industrial windows (former print factory) let in plenty of natural light, deep slop sinks and cleaning area.

The WorkHead features exposed ceiling beams and pipes. Industrial wooden floors add to the general aesthetic of the old manufacturing building (renter notes it has not been gentrified).

Storage available, freight elevator during working hours, kitchenette, steam heating. Often roommates have communal meals.

Bedroom offered comes with desk and bedframe, chair, own sink, small closet and exposed hanging rod. Solid, lockable door. Two electric outlets and use of space heater if needed. One window that opens to fire escape. Guests not preferred but accepted.

A few blocks from the Hudson River and Hudson River Park. Walking distance to NYU, Washington Square Park, SoHo, Nolita.

AFFORDABLE and SUITABLE for ARTIST who wants to work with other ARTISTS. Year lease preferred. Absolutely no pets! See pictures.

Contact Demetrius Wells at listed number,
no text message/IM enquiries.

Demetrius would become my closest friend in New York, perhaps the closest friend I would ever have, although during that time I only really thought of him as a landlord and co-conspirator. My Dutch uncle and my confidant. Also, the only artist I knew who put in the same hours I did. Ours was a quiet competition, a friendship between duelists.

I see him now on Morton Street, waiting for me when I took the taxi from my Yale classmate's apartment in Midtown. I'd looked at a number of places. The West Village was already hopelessly expensive; my friends were telling me to look for art space in Brooklyn, in New Jersey. New York gallery space was now at a premium, lofts were being cannibalised by financial doyens and winners in the roaring bull market. The romance of the meatpacking district, of Tribeca, Little Italy, all of lower Manhattan had already caught the imaginations of the moneyed youth. Glowing coffee shops, vinyl stores, clothing boutiques and fashionable restaurants were taking over the areas once frequented by artists like Demetrius, whose rent-controlled studio was surrounded by chic, ragged opulence. He needed two roommates to make it work.

Demetrius was shorter than I expected. He was wearing a T-shirt and his sunglasses and his clothing were speckled with black paint. He looked at me, amused, as I made my way down the sidewalk from the Christopher Street station clutching a portfolio case, my backpack and my phone. His email had been firm:

Hello Stella

You can come see The WorkHead (my place, the place you have asked about herein) but PLEASE BRING SAMPLES OF YOUR ART and do NOT expect LUXURY because this is not Airbnb.

Please respect our needs as fellow creative souls.

Demetrius

He stuck out his hand to shake mine, formally, that day in the late summer of New York. I had graduated from Yale with my MFA a few months before. Since then, I'd been living in Niccalsetti, NY, with my parents, working on the slender portfolio I had brought to the city a week before. I had sipped one cautious cup of coffee with a gallery owner suggested by my painting and printmaking supervisor. I'd started hunting for a place to live and work. I was impossibly hopeful. This was New York City in the Gold Rush, and I knew only its face, hardly its bones. I cannot believe how naïve I was.

It felt strangely like a first date, and yet, seeing him, I felt two things immediately. He was trustworthy, this man who was only perhaps a year or two older than me. And he was very serious. He turned and waved at the building behind us.

'We have our space on the third floor. The elevator works from eight to five, but we always have access to the stairs. So you can take a look right now and decide if this is for you, because this was a factory until a few years ago. It might not be what you want. People have ideas about what making art should be like down here.'

A real factory, not yet renovated to erase the industrial character of its past, still a place where people had worked on actual jobs. A loading ramp further down Greenwich Street. The door we used, I realised, had been a staff entrance. It was heavy, metal, pockmarked as if it had been repeatedly kicked. I looked over the building, curious more than anything. Demetrius was more like a person working on some construction effort inside the building than an artist auditing roommates.

I had looked him up. I'd googled him. There was not much. An article from *Ohio Art Voice* that described him as 'A New Talent', whose work was raw and fresh and 'someone to watch'. He led me up the wide factory stairs, lit by what looked like filthy windows at the landings, past industrial doors shut to the raw cement hallways. The entrance to his loft was a treated, grooved sliding door with iron studs. He pointed at it.

'Reclaimed wood. From some barn upstate. But it locks.'

The WorkHead itself. A cavernous room, swathed in daylight from the open casement windows all around us, the walls painted in purple, mauve, white, black. Meticulously clean. A corner section, closer to the door, ready for the new roommate (me), with what looked like drafting tables, a stool, folded tarps, and additional floor lighting. And his space, covered in canvas tarps, three easels with paintings in various stages of completion. The online version of the *Ohio Gazette* had described his work as 'multi-tonal'. The *Gazette* had also noted that, 'Each rectangular work consists of many colors built up from horizontal lines of related tints painstakingly painted by hand.' What I could see were digital prints that had been appended to canvases and then brushed over into different shades. Bloated imagery taken from a computer had then been used as an armature for the paint. I would learn later about his pictures, his wanderings around the city looking for the raw material for these paintings. Buildings. Sunlight. Water. People. And the minutiae of urban life: sewer covers, fire hydrants, windows, headlights. Weeks later I would help him bring prints back from the industrial printer, ease them up the stairs when the elevator was closed and lay them out with him, then pin them to the canvas so he could meld them into the canvas fibres.

But on that day, I was not there to gauge or judge his art.

I was shown the kitchenette, functional, surrounded on two sides by a stainless-steel counter from what had once been the employee cafeteria. Two microwaves, a stove with a careful line of Paul Revere pots. A table in one corner with a row of mismatched chairs piled with drawings and brushes. In another corner a pile of stage boxes, lights, suitcases and a smaller easel. A door that seemed merely decorative, covered in what looked like postcards. But inside I heard music softly playing.

'That's Lance. He's sleeping. He sleeps mostly during the day, is in a cabaret at night. Sometimes he makes ceramics, when he's feeling energetic. Also, he's *very* neat. Neatness counts, okay?'

'Can I meet him?'

'I'll introduce you soon enough. Dude is usually up already.'

And a strange golden sculpture, knee high, of a head with a crown upon it, arms stretched in the air above.

A refreshingly modern bathroom, with some touches from the old factory (the toilet's cistern was above my head, operated by pulling a chain). A bathtub and shower space, tiled, and a long metal sink.

'We don't wash brushes and stuff in here.'

Crushingly, I imagined sharing a bathroom with two men for a year. Or longer.

And then my proposed room: tiny. Cell-like. As advertised.

'There's no mattress on the bedframe. I can help you with that. We had to get rid of the old one.'

The desk was taken from the old factory, too big for the room, but useful. Closet as advertised, electrical outlets, and, unexpectedly, a hat stand. But then, the impossible: a sliding door into a windowless cubicle bathroom with wall-hung toilet, stainless-steel shelving, a tiny sink, a corner shower, a wooden locker for my things.

'This is why the rent for your room is more. I didn't advertise the extra bathroom. My bad.'

Sold.

His room was across the space. He didn't show me. But it held only a narrow bed and some of his paintings and a wall of books. And his camera equipment.

I was given coffee that I would later learn he'd bought from Dave's Super Deli on Hudson, around the corner, which would become our lifeline. Hot sandwiches and vegan options, 'Standard New York fare', free delivery. We chatted. Demetrius knew I had gone to Yale, was curious about it, but skeptical. He'd learnt at the Cleveland School of the Arts, had assisted another Ohio painter in Youngstown. Done digital work there. He didn't mention The People's Art Show, where he'd first shown his work at CSU. I'd also found that on Google, during the taxi ride over.

I nodded. I wasn't sure what else to do. I liked the space. The equivalent would be three times as much just a street away. Four times as much in Tribeca. Even in Brooklyn I wouldn't find a space this huge. Even in Washington Heights. I might only find a similar space in Jersey City. I kept waiting for the catch, for the other shoe to drop.

'I've lived here for a year now,' Demetrius confided. 'We had to get rid of the other roommate. He was serious but then he wasn't. And he wasn't considerate of other people. This is a hard business.'

I concurred.

'You do drugs?'

Negative.

'Drink?'

Yes, wine, rarely to excess (a partial lie).

'You want to have lots of friends over?'

Not really. I had few friends in New York.

'You like Hispanic food?'

Not bad.

He told me there was a good place close by. Lots of good places with different foods, in fact. 'Do you mind if I play music at times when I work?'

Possibly.

'You allergic to spray paint, even in ventilated spaces?'

No. But ventilation, we agreed, was important. The chemicals he used to adhere the prints to canvas were quite strong but not unsafe.

He asked me to show him some of the work I'd brought with me. I have no idea why I allowed this, but he wasn't confrontational about it. I showed him only a few drawings, thinking, I suppose, that he merely wanted to assure himself that I would move in and actually work. It occurred to me that I could have sent him JPEGs of my art. But he wanted to see the real thing. I laid out two colour sketches in different sizes for him. One was from Yale, a portrait of my then-boyfriend. One was of the river in Niccalsetti, New York.

At the last minute, I also decided to show him a painting, a piece I thought of as a *concentration*. I had not really wanted to bring it, but it was one of the few I had to hand, and it was in what looked like a more serious medium (I can't say why I thought that). I still remember Demetrius bowing his head over it, then holding it to the sunlight streaming in through the windows. It was simply a heavy-body acrylic ruby slash across the canvas, pushed in with the brush and the palette knife, a plane that had a strange depth that I liked. He examined it and then set it down on the table, looked at me and nodded.

'I need to speak to Lance, and then we can get back to you.'

'How long do you need?'

He smiled. 'Not long.'

We shook hands formally once again after he'd helped me pack up. He slid open the great doors for me, and as I made my way down the stairs (he had switched on the orange light above for my descent into evening), he called down.

'That last painting just sees right *into* me. What do you call it?'

I pushed open the door at the bottom, and the evening wind rushed in. I looked up at him and smiled. 'I call it *Myself*.'

He smiled even more broadly.

Cape Town had been in a drought for two years. Cleaning was accomplished judiciously with as little water as possible. We lived with sticky floors, dirty windows, filthy cars. We drank bottled water. Gardens lay lank around even the most luxurious homes. By the summer of that year, lawns and patches of greenery had long ago turned brown and been swept away, exposing the dark sand that covered most of the city, sand that was once the floor of the ocean. People pulling up their gardens might turn up half a billion-year-old Ordovician fossils and fossil tracks; their leaf blowers might uncover imprints of ancient fish scales beside their modern teak decks. The city rationed the water, trying to avoid the complete shutdown of water services. We showered for ninety seconds; public spaces smelt of rank bodies and dirty hair.

I saved water obsessively. A giant tank beside our home collected rainwater from the roof and filtered it. Jack had resisted its installation until he realised that these ugly plastic tanks were de rigueur for the financial set. People bragged about their water saving at parties. The cost of bottled water had doubled and it was always sold out in the larger sizes. I bought water whenever I could find it. And every week I went to the spring near the university and filled up my twenty-five-litre can, subsisted on this fresh water that had not been treated, that came directly out of the earth. The water from the spring had been flowing out of the mountain beside it for eons. The beer brewed in Cape Town was made from it, the original vineyards were fed from it, and now I and countless others lived off it. It was far superior to what was piped into my home.

A miracle.

The morning after the shark encounter I woke up in my bedroom again, and opened the blinds to the strange phenomenon of seeing all of my indoor furniture lined up beside the pool, drying in the sun; my entire living-room setup recreated on stone under the screaming gulls. Everything in its place, even the modular couch, ready to be moved back into the house once I keyed out the alarm pad. I looked out through the glass in wonder, for a moment believing I must have hauled everything out of the water in my sleep. But of course I hadn't. Mandla had made it happen. He was out there, waiting for me to make him breakfast, standing just outside the reach of the alarm beams. He stood with his back to me, contemplating the drying furniture, then the ocean, as if this was the most natural part of his job as a gardener, arriving early to a house with a living room's worth of furniture in the pool.

I was never sure if Mandla would show up on his allotted days. He usually did, but sometimes he surprised me on another day instead. He was impossible to get hold of, did not own a mobile phone, would not accept one from me even though I wanted him to have it, if only so I could reach him. The man did not own a watch. He always arrived ready for work wearing his usual loose pants, a T-shirt, rope sandals and an utterly shapeless hat. I had bought him other clothes but had never seen him wear them. Other men who worked in the neighbouring houses wore standard blue coveralls, perhaps a white hat, always rubber boots, but Mandla was selective in these things. And I was utterly dependent on him.

I opened up the house, made him tea, which he accepted with a nod.

'Mandla, how did you get the furniture out of the pool?'

He smiled. Nothing fazed him. He worked for a woman who lived in a glass house blanketed with laser beams, who owned a pool that looked like a natural depression in the rocks, who painted and sculpted the sea he could see in front of him.

He pointed at the furniture. 'This must not go into the water again, Miss Stella.'

'I didn't mean for you to have to take it all out.'

He shrugged. 'It was not so difficult.'

'How did you do it, though? It's so heavy?'

He smiled, shrugged, sipped his tea. And that was the best I would get from him.

'Thank you. I would have helped you. If I could.' We both knew I couldn't.

He was taller than I, willow thin, and he wore a beard tinged with grey. He was coming almost daily now, helping me to pack up the house and repair the surprising number of things that needed attention before the place could be sold. He had a list of tasks he attended to when he arrived, a never-ending circuit of work. The small garden around the house needed his constant attention; the grass went wild within a week. Natural fynbos and mosses grew from erratic spots of earth that clung in turn to fissures in the rock.

That day I had another job for him. Near the pool I'd put aside a box containing nails, sandpaper and varnish. There was paint in the garage – he knew where it all was. I pointed to the box. 'I need you to paint today.

Is this all right?'

He looked at the box, then at me, nodded, noncommittal. English was not his first language. It might have only been his third language. I knew he spoke Xhosa but I was not sure of his others. Could he speak Shona – a language spoken in Zimbabwe? Was he comfortable speaking Zulu? I did not know. I did know that he'd preferred to speak to my housekeeper, Rosy – let go now – in Afrikaans. Rosy had once told me he was from Malawi, but I could not be sure. I'd never heard him speak Chichewa.

'What is the language you speak, Mandla?' I had once asked.

'I speak many.'

'No, I mean, what did you speak growing up? With your family?'

'Oh! Always, many.' He had an inscrutable politeness about him, and this kind of obtuse questioning, for him might be considered rude. I was sensitive to his privacy. His space. This country was still healing from its oppressive past – would always be healing – so we spoke to each other with exaggerated friendliness, an ever-present formality.

I took up the box of nails and led him to the windows overlooking the water. I pointed at one, closed against the elements, the paint peeling.

'I need you to scrape off the paint. Scrape it all off with this.' I lifted the metal scraper. 'And can you please sand the windows before you apply the primer and then the paint?' He looked at me thoughtfully and I added, 'Okay, Mandla?'

He held the sandpaper as if sampling cloth in a tailor shop, nodded.

'If you can prepare both these windows and paint them, I would appreciate it.'

He ran his palms over the windowsill. He pressed the wood with his calloused fingers, scraped his nails across it. The paint flew off in clumps; his yellow, tough nails dug deep into the wood, leaving furrows. He pressed his thumb into the wood, twisted it, and the wood crumbled.

'This is very weak, Miss. It won't stay.'

I could not bear him calling me 'Miss'. It was a generic term here. I was married, I was called 'Professor' at work, but I would always be 'Miss' to him, or, even worse, 'Madam'. Terminology left over from the bad old days. 'Please call me Stella,' I had asked several times, but he wouldn't. The best I could get was 'Miss Stella'. I pushed my fingers into the wood, and he was right – it was spongy to the touch. The first inch could easily be raked off with a small garden trowel.

The wood parts of the house were being eaten by sea. They were sodden; the wooden backing desiccated. The bolts holding the joints of the windows together outside were black with rust, the wood around them pitted and stained. Indeed, it would not stay.

And all the windows were like this. The constant wind, the spray from the sea, the incessant salt, were sinking into the house. Mandla would start with the windows, and then he would do the decking, which was also almost never dry. By the time he was done patching up the deck, the windows would need attention again. All Cape Town homeowners who lived this close to the sea needed to think about these constant cycles of repair. Homes built on this steep shore, so close to the water, faced a relentless corrosive blast. But of all the places where I had lived, I loved this house the most, would miss it the most. I'd list it with the real estate agent thus: *Slight water damage. Salt damage. Wind damage.*

Jack had been philosophical about it all. When I had asked that we bring in builders to repair the damage, he had shrugged.

'The next owner will probably just rebuild, Stella. Look at Camps Bay. Cranes, construction everywhere. I know you love the place but it's old. It was developed in the eighties, I think. Maybe even the seventies. Look at it – the living area looks like one of those conversation pits they used to have when people smoked weed and had key parties.'

'Will people buy a house with this kind of wear and tear?'

'Of course they will. This is one of the best locations in the world.' Jack was puzzled that I had no idea about these things. My studio alone, he claimed, could be made into an outbuilding. The value of the house had gone up *considerably* since we'd bought it two years before. Even by *American standards* it was expensive, he said.

We'd made an *excellent investment* when we'd purchased it from my predecessor at the university who had left for a UK residency, an academic who'd suddenly found a foothold in London after her divorce. Recent political events overseas had meant that women who'd written books about South African injustice were being recruited by American and UK African Studies departments enjoying newly swollen budgets. Injustice was in vogue once again. Jack had been pleased when she'd suddenly needed to *unload* the house when it became clear she would not be back: he hated renting, knew a good deal when he saw it.

Most of the furniture was my colleague's; the house had come to her in the divorce settlement. It's how many homes were sold in Cape Town – people emigrated and left most of their possessions behind because shipping furniture 8,000 miles wasn't worth the expense. Many of our appliances were hers. We used her battered steel microwave, we toasted our bread in her red ceramic-and-brushed-steel toaster and made coffee in her matching faux-Italian coffee and espresso maker. She'd left her washer-dryer combo, and piles of things she would never need in a London flat: garden tools, pool cleaners, the living-room furniture I had unceremoniously dumped into the pool, the ominous flat-screen TV mounted on the wall in the master bedroom, and the shells that gathered dust and curious mites on the windowsills in the sleek en suite bathroom. I had found an elaborate metal wind chime set in one of the downstairs closets, tonal tubes hopelessly tangled together, defeated by howling sea gusts. Yet sometime in the last two years I had started to see these inherited things as mine. My stuff. I'd made the studio entirely my own. Built beside the house and entered from the living area, its refracted sea light was otherworldly.

And something else. The sun was higher in the sky in South Africa. Even Jack had noticed it.

'When I go back to New York after a few weeks in this house,' he said, 'the clouds feel like they are right here,' and he'd held his hand at the level of his nose.

When we left – when we sold out to the next owner – we would leave all these things behind. A full container of furniture sent to New York from Cape Town was a waste of time and effort, according to Jack. The electrical appliances wouldn't work in the United States, and besides, we had *way* too much furniture in New York already. It was *a poor return on investment* and a *time-intensive process with not much backend*. But I would send back my art supplies. And my work.

Mandla had started here when we'd bought the house, soon after my appointment at the university. As I watched him select the brushes and equipment he would need, I realised he was still a mystery. I assumed he lived in one of the informal settlements in the neighbouring suburb. I'd simply never asked, fearful he would take offense, or be unwilling to share that bit of personal information. He was vague about everything. At the end of every day, he walked solidly up the path to the main road, turned and disappeared toward the taxi rank a mile or so away. He never asked me to drive him, never accepted when I offered.

I hurried back into the kitchen while he began his careful scraping and sanding, and I made him a breakfast of eggs, bacon, coffee, toast, fruit. I fixed nothing for myself except coffee. As I cooked, I glanced a few times at my mobile phone. Ben's car was still out on the public lot. It had been there when I woke up, the first thing I'd looked for when I pulled up the blinds. His was the only car there in the morning. It might have been there forever.

The scent of eggs and bacon filled the kitchen, making me slightly nauseous. I hadn't slept well. Unsurprisingly, I had not lasted long on the cold, hard floor and had moved back to the bedroom after a few uncomfortable hours. I kept waking up thinking I was being drawn into a void. I imagined shapes swimming around me in the dark. I tried to sleep in the beam of light from the closet, in Jack's pyjamas. At some point in the early hours I'd got out of bed and lit a *verboten* cigarette, smoked kneeling by the bedroom window and looking over the beach to check on the car. Seeing it there, alone in the little parking lot, was somehow reassuring.

I put the food on a tray and carried it out. Mandla saw me, stood, brushed himself off. He took the tray and walked to the end of the point, to where it was possible to jump into the sea. Instead, he folded his length, sat down, meditated upon the ocean. The birds tossed and cried overhead, and he ate slowly, the tray resting on his crossed legs. I wished he would eat inside, but an unspoken code lingered – eating at the kitchen counter would make him uncomfortable. We lived in the shadow of a time when simply having him eat in my kitchen or stay past a certain time was, for all practical purposes, illegal. When I could be turned in for being too friendly, and he could be jailed. How many times had I asked Mandla to eat inside? Insisted on it? But each time he politely refused, the way he had refused a uniform, or my entreaties to drive him to the taxi ranks.

I watched him for a moment, considered another cigarette, then gave up and snatched up the mobile phone, swiped it to life, closed my eyes, and mashed my fingertip against Ben's name.

Hi. I found the box. And your car is still here(?)

But there was no reply.

I waited, and then was startled when the screen suddenly swiped downwards. A video call was coming in. Jack.

I was seized by equal measures of guilt and fear. Did he somehow know I'd just texted Ben? *Ridiculous.*

But my students talked about data being swirled around in 'the cloud'. Whatever that meant. The phone melody echoed through the house, ghostly and frightening. *The day has caught up with me*, I thought blearily, a quote of my mother's. I looked at my watch – it was late in New York. I considered not answering, but the thought of another human was comforting. I had yet to figure out how I would tell Jack about what had happened the day before. I wasn't under any obligation to share it, but we usually talked about everything. It felt like I was keeping a secret.

There he was, on the screen. Jack was standing in some cavernous apartment in New York. He'd turned on all the lights and was holding a Scotch in one hand, grinning at me from across the Atlantic. He was wearing his blue Hickey Freeman suit. His laptop was open on a coffee table behind him. Jack squinted at his iPad, waved at me, and his voice, slightly discombobulated, entered this lonely ocean room.

'London has been emailing me nonstop, and I mean nonstop. How are *you*, baby?' He was expansive, buzzed. I wanted to reach into the screen, loosen his tie for him.

'Where are you? What time is it there? It must be the middle of the night!'

He ignored my questions, irritatingly. 'Have you been packing, Stells? I had an email from the estate agent, and they want to know when they can start showing the house.'

'No. Yes. I mean, I was going to start some things. I was rearranging,' I said, somewhat truthfully. 'There are a few repairs to be finished before ...'

He nodded, his eyes drifting away, probably to the television or his mobile phone. 'There's a mess in London. The Bastard is at it again. He's taken a seat on one of our companies.'

The Bastard was Jack's arch nemesis, a hedge fund investor based on the Isle of Man named Bertie Queensouth.

'I've been on the phone with the lawyers for hours trying to get him and his friend removed from the board. Not that anything helped. The Bastard has bought enough shares so he can instigate the dissolution of the board if he wants to. This time he and his cronies are not going away.'

I do not feel guilty, I told myself. I was, in fact, pleased Jack had called. His voice in the house sounded familiar, comforting; it took up the entire room. I also knew he was checking up on me. To ensure I was packing for our next chapter. He interrupted me as I told him about the outside repairs, how we were going to need specialist movers to send my art works back to New York.

'So, guess where I'm standing?' He squinted cheerfully into the screen. 'Guess, Stella.'

I hated guessing. Jack knew this. I just looked at the screen, half shrugged.

'This is a studio your friend Mario has discovered. We had drinks earlier. And he had the key. So here we are.' I saw Mario peek over his shoulder. Jack had taken a liking to him. 'You can be here from our apartment in fifteen minutes. It's bigger than what you have now, Stella. Much bigger. Nicer. It's available. Look.' He moved his iPad so I could see the high windows. Grey walls. Natural light. He was walking around the room. The iPad was shaking because he was holding it in one hand, the other holding a drink. He showed me sinks, a kitchenette, and someone else's plates, lines of cups and equipment that would have to be moved out of there. I thought I could hear cars and trucks outside. How had Jack got a drink up there? Mario would have brought it, of course. Or Mario was offering him the current owner's whiskey. Seeing it made me feel New York in the summer, at night. Even the sound of his footsteps reminded me of the city, and of him.

I suddenly wished Mario wasn't there. I suddenly *did* want to tell Jack what had happened to me, this experience with its meaning I didn't understand. It was comforting just looking at him on the screen – so enthusiastic about moving from South Africa and its downgrades and slashed credit and the financial travails that drove Jack to distraction and that I tried to ignore.

'That studio must cost a fortune, Jack,' I said.

He frowned in concentration. 'It would be a great investment. And it's beautiful. It's unique. I can see you working here, Stella. It needs your touch.' He had sold himself on the place, obviously liked the idea of owning it.

'Jack, tell Mario to stop serving you alcohol this late in the evening,' I warned.

Mario's face filled the screen. He waved, his fingers flashed in a pixelated blur. 'Too late. We think you'll love this.'

I heard Jack laugh. The two of them had become friendly over the last few years, a friendship I hadn't thought would work. What common ground could there be between Jack the banker, the skier and golfer, the lover of gambling and classic monster movies, and Mario the art dealer and agent whose idea of outdoor exercise was walking to a restaurant or riding the subway? As it turned out, Mario was the consummate salesman, the best listener in the world. And Jack liked an audience.

'When are you coming back?' Mario sounded petulant.

'At least a few more weeks. The house won't be a sold in a day.'

Jack poked his face into the screen again. I heard the Scotch tinkle in his glass. 'Hurry up and finish everything. Sell the house.'

Mario's face again. 'He's been plying me with booze, trying to get hints about what you're working on next. Don't you two share this kind of thing? I told him he's dealing with a samurai. Secrecy is my middle name.'

But a suspicion was forming in my mind. 'What's the address of this studio? Where is it, exactly? Whose space is it?'

'It's in the West Village. It's a thousand square feet with natural light and all the stuff you need. Owned by some hipster art collective or something. And partly by a curator and his partner.'

Mario poked his face into the screen. 'Friends of mine. You might know them?' He mentioned two well-known names.

Jack looked impatient. 'I can have it set up by the time you get back. Just say the word. This is easy, Stella – a great find.'

His exuberance was now annoying. 'It's not easy to set up a studio, Jack. All my things are with me here.'

Jack moved from the screen, then pulled Mario into focus. 'Mario can tell me what you need, right? I'll get him to make me a list.'

Mario nodded, helpfully drunk, into the screen. 'I would do this for you, Stella.'

'I really do need to see it before I can say all right. I need to walk around in it.' I didn't bother to say, *I need to smell it, I need to stand in it and listen, I need to be alone in it. I need to choose it.*

'Stella, trust me, this place is marvellous. Perfect.'

Then I had a very cold feeling again. 'Jack? What's the address?'

Jack grinned into the screen. 'You need to come back.'

'Tell me. It's important.'

Greenwich Street and Horatio. I felt myself blanch, looked away, felt the tears welling up, unexpectedly, a sudden wave of fear and revulsion.

No place on earth like this, Cat.

'I'll see it when I get back to New York, all right, guys?'

Jack's voice: 'It'll be *sold* by then, Stella! It's already online. I'll send you a link.'

I claimed our signal was breaking up, blamed the blameless Wi-Fi, and switched them off. I considered the device for a moment. *Should I call Jack back? Tell him something has happened ...?* I decided against it.

And now they had found a place in the West Village.

Not just any place. I had been there. Partied there. Been drunk there.

Demetrius standing in the small kitchenette – the 'entertainer's kitchen', not the real kitchen – a glass of wine in hand, taking in the studio space beyond. The tiny garden up top, the trellis, the wooden chairs, the view to New Jersey. It had been owned by a curator we all wanted to know. *This is where you go when you make it, right?* Half of it a studio made for an artist in the 1830s. Graffiti on the wall. Hundreds of square feet of gorgeous artistic workspace carefully converted to a chic apartment. *That place? That's like a museum to creativity, man. That's like what people imagine creativity to be, but it's not it. The life? The life you and I lead, Cat? Messy. You don't create in that. You ... pay homage to creation itself.*

Demetrius always serious, the two of us walking down 14th.

Gentrifying that place to its natural-born death.

The WorkHead, a few blocks away on Morton Street, would by now be owned by some other group of artists. Or it would be a tech startup. Or just another huge loft. And Demetrius was gone.

Long gone, Cat.

Jack sent me the link. I swiped through the rooms. Not a trace of the place where a cat sitter had flooded out the stairs. Not a trace of the other two studios – now bedrooms and, incongruously, a screening area. I scanned through the pictures. I took a street view. The building was exactly as I remembered, minus the graffiti and the smashed windows on Greenwich Street. The stores, what you could see, looked nicer. The pictures had been posted in the summer. No mention of what was just a little further down the street.

It was a renovation job. It was genteel. The cost was outrageous, but Jack was endlessly generous. He had only the vaguest idea about The WorkHead, or Demetrius, or what the space he was probably still standing in used to look like. And he had only the vaguest idea of how, while Demetrius and I were creating, the end of our kind of life was encroaching. 'Adaptive reuse': these studios – these factories and store houses and mills and warehouses – were being turned into upscale living spaces. A tidal wave of gentility was rushing toward us. Demetrius and I worked furiously against the tide.

The phone rang again. Caller ID said it was Ian Woodruff, head of my department at the university, pulling me from the West Village to life in Cape Town.

His voice was booming, encouraging. 'The final projects and essays are coming up, Stella. I was hoping we could have you come in for some extra workshops? There are three students especially whose creative projects ought to be of interest for showings ...'

Graduate student projects. My three students – the gifted ones, the rebels.

'Yes, Ian. I've already set up appointments for them.'

'That's wonderful. Do you have the names of their essays for us?'

'I emailed them.'

A pause while he checked his computer. 'Ah, yes. These ones? "Seafaring Feminism: A Complication of Cis-Figures for Oceanic Art"? Is that one?'

'Yes ...'

'Then there's, "Identity and Uniqueness: The Patriarchal Oppression of the Galley Slave in Ancient Vase Etchings".'

'That sounds correct, Ian, but ...'

'You're also down for, "Masochistic Sexuality in Handmade Representation".'

'Those are the three.'

'The students may ask for extensions, but we cannot grant them. They need to go out to the external examiner. So please do not give them extensions. Mark the essays and bring them back, okay?'

'I'll email them about this now. But extension requests will be coming, Ian. They've already started sending me WhatsApps.'

'You might be tempted to give them a few more days but the final board meeting is very tight this year. So, under no circumstances are you to be generous,' he said brightly.

'I'm never generous, Ian.'

'Good! Good! Then we'll see you up here for the final meetings.'

He rang off and I went upstairs to change into my UCT clothes, then relented and greedily checked my iPhone. Nothing from Ben, no reply to my last text. I glanced out the windows toward the sea, which was moody today. A container ship fifty miles out steamed slowly toward Asia as I ventured downstairs to the kitchen again. I'd read once that you should bake bread and make coffee before opening your house to prospective buyers. But I was not the type of woman who baked bread. I was the type who threw her furniture into the pool and needed help setting it all back up again, apparently.

The phone buzzed. *Ben?* But it was not. A message from Katie, one of my graduate students.

> Hey Stella!!!! Mtg today? Am printing draft Leather paper 4 u to look at.

I sighed, replied.

> Please email your draft. I cannot receive a paper and have an immediate meeting. Prof. Wright

Katie absorbed this.

> K kewl! Will email now, meeting L8Tr?

I took a breath.

> Katie, I simply cannot meet today. I need to read your paper first, which should be 10,000 words at least! I can see you tomorrow at 1 p.m. Prof. Wright

The phone vibrated in vigorous assent.

> ahsum! CU 2mor. K

Heart

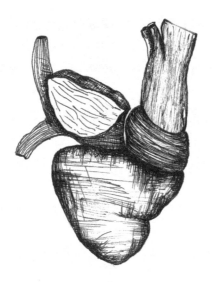

A shark depends upon a single-circuit circulatory system driven by a two-chambered, S-shaped heart. Because of their low blood pressure, most sharks must continually swim in order to keep blood circulating through their bodies, whereas a human heart functions through the involuntary, highly coordinated contractions of four chambers.

Pencil on Parchment from Stella Wright's Private Collection, Cape Town

Email to: All Staff, Fine Arts Dept.
Rat in Lecture Hall A01

Dear All
It has come to my attention that there is a dead rat in Lecture Hall A01. Our UltraCare service providers have been made aware of the problem and will endeavour to remove it as soon as possible. Apologies for the inconvenience. Please do warn students to stay out of the lecture theatre until it has been removed.
Thank You,
Mandy
Fine Arts Secretary
Arts Room 211

To: All Staff, Fine Arts Dept.
Re: Rat in Lecture Hall A01

Dear All
Surely we must call for the evacuation of the building! This is a clear health hazard, Mandy(?). Is UltraCare going to fumigate the learning venue? Do we know how long the rat has been dead for? I have a class in there in fifteen minutes (Post-Postmodern Bodies and Modern Aesthetic: The Corporeal and the Unreal).
Where shall I direct my students? Is the venue closed for the rest of the week? Surely it is?
Concerned, To Say The Least(!)
Prof. Johan Simpson

To: All Staff, Fine Arts Dept.
Re: Re: Rat in Lecture Hall A01

Johan and Dept.
Once the rat has been removed and proper care taken to clean the affected area where it was found, the venue will be usable once again. Please ask your students to wait five minutes while the rat's body is removed by UltraCare, who now should be on the way to the venue.
Thank you kindly for your patience, Prof. Simpson.
Mandy

To: All Staff, Fine Arts Dept.
Re: Re: Re: Rat in Lecture Hall A01

Mandy, Johan, Colleagues:
This doesn't seem right at all. I have a personal horror of rats and to this end agree with Johan: the venue should be treated before we allow students in it. We have a pastoral responsibility regarding the health of these students. What does it say about the efficacy of our efforts toward campus hygiene? I cannot allow my students to use this venue again in good conscience until it has been properly fumigated and aired out.
Prof. Thandi Semanyani

To: All Staff, Fine Arts Dept.
Re: Re: Re: Re: Rat in Lecture Hall A01

Dear Johan, Mandy, Thandi and Colleagues
Have we not forgotten the fact that the UltraCare staff member who is charged with removing the corpse of this rat is now (surely)

acting outside of his or her assigned duties and might well be exposed to any number of (possibly fatal) diseases and the like? Why is it, in this department, the first concern is for ourselves and our phobias and not the well-being of those working on the campus?

And that suggestion that the UltraCare folks do not keep the place hygienic smells of classism, Johan!

Dr. Allan Venter

To: All Staff, Fine Arts Dept.
Re: Re: Re: Re: Re: Rat in Lecture Hall A01

Dear All

Pursuant to my last email, UltraCare have sent me a message saying that removal of dead rodents from teaching venues does not fall within their current contract. I have been advised to call an exterminator and will unfortunately have to use departmental funds for this by paying on my P-Card.

The exterminators will be here within the hour to remove the rat from Lecture Hall A01. They have assured me it will be disposed of properly (via incineration).

I have asked that they confirm the hygienic safety of the venue before leaving. They think fumigation will not be necessary as there was no report of a dead rat in Lecture Hall A01 yesterday, when it was used all afternoon and into the evening for the student showing of 'Broken Bodies and Broken Societies, Englishes and The Impact of Neocolonialism in Societal/Personal Thought'.

Your patience is appreciated this morning.

Mandy

To: All Staff, Fine Arts Dept.
Re: Re: Re: Re: Re: Re: Rat in Lecture Hall A01

Where shall I bring my class now? Perhaps I will cancel.
Johan

To: All Staff, Fine Arts Dept.
Re: Re: Re: Re: Re: Re: Re: Rat in Lecture Hall A01

Dear Prof. Simpson
Please do not cancel your class. You may use Seminar Room 26. It is free this morning as Feminist Poetic Weaponry has been postponed until next week.
Mandy

To: All Staff, Fine Arts Dept.
Re: Re: Re: Re: Re: Re: Re: Re: Rat in Lecture Hall A01

Seminar Room 26 has no microphone, Mandy! Can classroom facilities please install one for the day? Thank you!
And please do confirm to all when the rat has been properly removed and the lecture venue is safe and usable?
Johan

To: All Staff, Fine Arts Dept.
Problem Solved

Dear All
I removed the rat a minute ago.

My loft in New York had rats; I killed and removed many. Rats hold no fear for me. The ones in the West Village were much worse before the place was gentrified.
Please cancel the exterminator, Mandy.
The venue is usable and plague free. I sprayed the affected area with Dettol from the staff room.
Your (slightly grossed out) students are waiting for you in there, Johan.
Stella

To: All Staff, Fine Arts Dept.
Re: Problem Solved

Thank you, Prof. Wright!
Mandy

To: All Staff, Fine Arts Dept.
Re: Re: Problem Solved

Prof. Wright
Have you disposed of the rat properly????
Johan

To: All Staff, Fine Arts Dept.
Re: Re: Re: Problem Solved

I held a small funeral for it. It is buried in one of the gardens.
Don't ask where, Johan.
Stella

After this email thread had been deleted, I went in search of the university coffee cart. The cart and its keeper roamed around my part of the campus and sold the only coffee strong enough to be worthy of the name.

I had not been sleeping well, had stayed awake waiting for Ben to call. I'd started to conclude that he was gone. This was not good for me; no one else knew about our meeting in the ocean with the shark. The previous night I'd slept with my closet light on, the sound of the ocean a gentle whir outside. I'd dozed fitfully and found myself awake at odd hours, wandered around upstairs, listening to the wind pressing against the windows, the house feeling as if it was moving – the same almost imperceptible sense of speed I felt travelling through clouds on a jet liner. All was calm inside; outside was a fury of wind and ocean and night and creatures in the sea. Now I was drifting through the day.

There was a time when staying up all night had invigorated me. Now it was frightening. In the back of my mind a voice gently warned: *Think of your heart, your heart, your heart*. A heart needs deep sleep. It doesn't function well in stressful environments, when faced with death-by-being-eaten, when its owner is guiltily thinking about a stranger. These are heart-unfriendly activities. I also drank, occasionally smoked and regularly took sleeping pills; more bad habits.

And I drank a lot of coffee from the campus cart. Large cups with dollops of sugar – I didn't need Google to tell me my heart didn't like this either.

When I did, finally, find the cart and its owner atop one of this excruciating campus's many flights of outdoor stairs, I was out of breath. The kid who operated it took my money and switched on the cheap espresso machine after deftly banging out the fine coffee powder into the pressure cup. He grinned, showing off in the sudden burst of steam and foam. Was that friendly recognition or pity? Perhaps it was obvious that I needed sleep and decent food.

While I sipped my coffee, I breathed *with focus* – in through my nose, out through my mouth, actually counting as I did – taking in the southern part of the city, my heart slowing its cadence, my brain absorbing the caffeine like a hungry undersea sponge. I then inspected the ruffled concrete on the wall beside us. Some of it was rotted, and a pile of it had fallen into a corner. I could see the rebar inside the wall, already oxidized and rusted. I pointed. 'They need to fix this. It's going to cause a leak. The water damage here is extensive.'

The coffee kid shrugged noncommittally. There were many places around the university where concrete or wood or stone had started to crumble against the elements; for some reason it seemed inconceivable that a pile of rubble that large could be left unattended and ignored. Perhaps I was the only person who noticed these things, these ancient faux-Oxfordian buildings, built of shale and brick and concrete and tile, faced off against the drought and the wind and slowly eroding. I fished my phone out of my bag, snapped a picture of the damage, vowed to send it to the buildings and grounds department, who would assure me, as before, that they were aware of the issue, did I realise how many problems they had to take care of on a daily basis?

I knew this was probably true – I only had to think of my own corroding house. I'd taken dozens of photos of different eroded places on campus. Photos of spilled rubbish bags with burst guts. Of grass growing through staircases. Snaps of stairs falling apart, a women's toilet pulled from the floor, gutters that had popped out from the eaves, poles that had mysteriously crashed into the parking areas. The buildings were quietly, unexpectedly deteriorating, like everything else. Why was I attracted to this evidence of decay? I was aware of the mountain claiming back its space. The wind rushing between the structures. The coolness of the outside steps. Nature continually trying to take over. One evening, walking back to my car, I came across a huge male baboon sitting impassively in the grass by the road. The two of us shared that moment, each considering who had the greater right to be there. I would draw his solemn face later, in my studio by the sea.

I finished my coffee and left the cup on the stand. The phone began to vibrate and I looked at it hoping to see a number I did not know, thinking it might be Ben. It was Ian.

'Stella?' He sounded concerned. Perhaps he could hear my shortened breath. 'Do you want to stop by and pick up the third-year essays? I've had a look. They're all right, I just want you to follow up.'

'I have a doctor's appointment, Ian.' I said this with a bit of irritation. I walked over to the heap of concrete, noted the moss already forming within it. Some kind of scrappy Cape weed had taken hold.

'I see. Well then, can you come to the office right afterwards, please?'

'Okay. Give me just over an hour. I'm only going for a check-up. It'll be quick.'

'I doubt that. Doctors are never quick.' And he rang off.

There was nobody in the waiting room save for a harried-looking mother with a toddler who was passively playing with some grubby blocks. I sat opposite the woman and wondered if she was bringing the child to see Dr Patel or if the problem was with her own heart. I couldn't tell. The receptionist nodded at me when I arrived, and then picked up the phone, intoned my name to the best heart surgeon in Cape Town. As I sat in the antiseptic silence, I was aware of my heart slowing. The child had turned his attention to a doll's house and was unselfconsciously singing while his mother looked on. I tried to tell myself that this child was not dying, this mother was not praying to avoid heart surgery. I smiled and my smile was meant to say, 'I'm a survivor. Dr Patel helped me and he'll help you, too, or he'll help your baby. There's nothing to worry about.' But the woman merely looked away.

And I could not, in truth, offer any such assurances. It was through sheer luck that I was sitting here smiling at a stranger.

On that fateful morning soon after our arrival in Cape Town, I was dragging a grinder across the floor in its beat-up plastic crate when suddenly I felt as if I had a trapped bird in my chest, fluttering against my sternum. I was awash with a dreadful fear and helplessness. I began to wheeze and my lungs felt heavy. Jack glanced at me from his computer and immediately stood up, a beam of sunlight streaming around him, my banker-saviour. I stood in the corner, trying to draw enough breath to speak, then lay down on the couch. Somewhere I'd read you are meant to elevate your feet when this type of thing happened, that I possibly only had half an hour, max, before things really went south. Jack was standing over me.

'Stella, what's happening?'

'Something's wrong ... You need to get me to a hospital ... I think I'm having a heart attack.' I could barely breathe. *Breathe consciously*, I told myself.

Jack absorbed this calmly, considered his options and then reached into his jacket for his phone.

'Give me one moment, Stella.'

He looked up at the ceiling as if he was doing a calculation, and spoke into the phone, explaining to whoever he'd dialled that he needed a heart guy.

Heart guy, a term they'd never use in South Africa.

There was an affirmative sound on the other end of the line. Jack's face grew dark, and I felt that flutter rise up in my thorax again.

He listened, nodded. 'I want him there now. Make sure this is understood. This is an emergency.' Jack looked at me. 'Can you walk to the car, Stella?'

'No. Call an ambulance.'

He simply bent over and picked me up, a bride being carried over the threshold of death.

'The hospital's ten minutes away. Hang in there.'

Jack meant to sweep me into the car but he was not quite that big and strong. He staggered to the garage with me, banged my legs as he struggled to open the door to his Mercedes, almost banged my head as he all but threw me onto the back seat. While I felt my breath come shorter and shorter and my heart begin to petrify, Jack navigated the morning traffic, drove over the shoulder bursting through throngs of beach-going tourists and honked the entire way. I thought about yoga class on Bleecker Street in New York, of deep relaxation, and I looked out at the landscape. I tried to imprint myself upon the sea, the birds, the houses clustered against the beach. *These could be the last things I see on earth.* They were not bad things: my husband and the sea.

I swear that above the noise of the car and the blaring of the horn and Jack's low, swearing mantra, I heard the birds one last time – screeching gulls, petrels and gannets, crying me out to whatever was next.

Dr Patel saved my life.

Twenty-four hours later I awoke in a private room, alone and torn at the chest. I spent almost a full day by myself, groggy and exhausted. The phone on the nightstand beside me was hard to reach; I could barely negotiate it. I felt drunk. I was visited by nurses who informed me that my recovery was going, 'Nicely, very nicely' and that I would be fine.

I was fed a steady supply of drugs through a PICC line, but it wasn't until Dr Patel showed up that I had any idea that my heart had been a time bomb. I had a 'ventricular septal defect' that had been gnawing at the upper chambers. Dr Patel informed me that he had used a 'biopolymer' to close a hole that had developed. When I asked what that was, exactly, he said it was an 'elastic clotting agent that acted as a natural tissue sealant'.

I thought about that. 'Do you mean you glued my heart together?'

And he had smiled. 'No,' he carefully replied, 'I believe it is more that I helped you glue your own heart together.'

Hours later Jack showed up, walked into the room on his phone and winked at me while he spoke in broken German to whoever was on the other end of the line. When he finally did hang up, I simply stared at him.

'Doctor will see you now,' the receptionist said, politely.

I stood and went into Dr Patel's small, nondescript office. He was on the verge of emigrating to New Zealand with his family, to be near his children. This man who had saved my life, who spoke with a light South African drawl atop a lilting Gujarati accent, was leaving for good. As I undressed and laid out my clothes on the chair in the tiny changing area, I realised I was not looking forward to a life without this one man who knew my heart so well. I pulled on the modesty gown and then slid onto the table, and he pressed the cold stethoscope against the scar on my sternum, gently pushing aside the cloth. He listened intently, non-committally, and I wanted to listen as well, hear my heartbeat without any murmur or echo. I'd calculated I needed another 250 million perfect beats in this lifetime. The next five paintings would cost me eleven million beats, perhaps only nine million. I'd done these calculations a few times; the numbers were staggering. Millions more beats required from a heart that was literally glued together.

He deftly wrapped the blood-pressure cuff around my upper arm, checked the falling needle against his gold watch (no automatic BP reader for him), a satisfied look on his face. It wasn't simply his professionalism – it was his *bedside manner*, as my mother would have said, the way he matched the beats of my heart to his ticking wristwatch. Soon he'd be gone, as would the degrees hanging in a neat line on the wall beside me: University of Cape Town Medical School, KJ Somaiya Medical College in Mumbai. We'd spoken about India on his frequent visits to check up on me in the hospital. We'd discovered a shared affection for the Pattadakal and Jyotirlinga temples and the Himalayas. He had not been back in thirty years, save once to spread his father's ashes in the Ganges.

'How have you been feeling?'

'This has been a good year, overall.'

'You have given up smoking, I hope.'

'Mostly, yes.'

'You must not "mostly" give up this habit, Professor Wright. You must *totally* give it up.'

Dr Patel was, I knew, almost impossible to get an appointment with. Jack had had him 'checked out' by one of his minions in New York, who'd sent back a bibliography of all Dr Patel's papers. We had notes about his presentations at the United States Medical Congress and at Harvard Med, where he held a visiting fellowship. Jack had even ordered a copy of his monograph: Ventricular Valve Replacement, a Study.

Despite his formidable reputation, the doctor always had time for me, and I appreciated this. I knew this was partly due to Jack twisting arms. I'd told myself I needed to be worthy of this consideration. I needed to take better care of myself.

'You must also meditate and eat well.' His voice was soothing, and I found myself agreeing to everything.

'This I do, Dr Patel. I really do.'

'Have you stopped drinking alcohol?'

'The drinking is still happening, I must admit.'

'Only wine? Perhaps one glass a day at most? This is important, Professor.'

'I am trying. I eat well and I exercise. I know I can cut down on the wine.'

'Your heart is functioning at about an optimal level and you must keep it this way. You must stick to the diet we worked out and avoid stress.'

'There's been a great deal of stress lately.'

'It must be controlled then.'

The gown flopped over my back. I felt totally unselfconscious around him. He had a strange way of touching me, a non-intimate but very exact touch, the formality of a pianist playing at a keyboard. He looked up at me expectantly.

'Something very stressful happened to me recently.'

'Have you been hurt?' He glanced at the rest of me, his voice edged with concern.

'No, but–' I wasn't sure if I could express how frightening the shark had been.

'If you have had psychological trauma you must try to see somebody about this. It is not good for you to suppress these feelings.'

'I know. It *was* a traumatic experience. I was in the ocean next to a large shark. It attacked a man and I helped to save him. Well, we saved each other.'

'Oh my! This *is* a different experience than you are used to.'

'Yes. Of course.'

'Do you fear the ocean now?'

'No, I do not.' *Liar.*

'That is good.'

'But ... I fear my heart *more*, now.'

He nodded. 'Perhaps you have been reminded about the fact that you need to take care of yourself. Perhaps the shark has only told you what I have been telling you for some time.'

'I know. I was not physically hurt, but it was close. I was very frightened.'

'This is physical activity *combined* with a stressful event. I do not advise you to radically raise your heart rate. Light exercise, your art, this is different. But fear and excitement? I cannot recommend these.'

'They are part of living though.'

He thought for a moment. 'Have you heard of this thing young people do? It is called "bungee jumping"?'

'Yes.'

'This stunt accelerates the heart. It gives you a jolt of adrenaline. My son calls it a "rush". Maybe this is what people do to scare themselves. But it is a false excitement.'

'Like a roller coaster?'

'No. The brain knows a roller coaster is just a carnival ride. This bungee thing is different. The brain and heart do not want you to jump off bridges tied to a cord. It places stress on the heart. For most people this is fine; for young people who can afford to be careless, it is like experiencing almost crashing your car. But this is not for you, Stella.'

'I've swum in the sea my whole life.'

'I know. You are something of an expert on the ocean, in the manner an artist becomes intimate with her subject. I have been told this many times.'

'By my husband?'

'Yes. He has told me a lot about you and called me often at my home to discuss your case. And my colleagues who learnt you were under my care have also been in communication with him. Remember that I retain a lectureship at UCT as well, where you are highly regarded.'

'What about *emotional* stress?'

'It is not to be advised. You have enough stress.'

'It is hard to imagine a life where I don't have any kind of excitement.'

He smiled. 'I know. And stress is hard to avoid. My wife tells me this all the time. But I, like you, do not listen. I put myself in stressful predicaments at work. But I try to control it. And I do not drink or smoke anymore.'

'Am I going to die, Doctor?' My eyes were suddenly full of tears.

He seemed confused as to what to do, and I composed myself.

'We are all going to die, Professor Wright.'

'But am I going to die *soon*?'

'I would like to tell you that you will live a very long time. I would like to. I have seen patients, and read about patients, who have lived very long with exactly the challenges you face. But I must emphasise that nothing is ever guaranteed.'

'But right now, today, you can say I'm fine?'

'Yes. You are as well as one might reasonably expect given what you have experienced.'

'That could mean absolutely anything I want it to.' I was trying not to weep.

He thought for moment. 'You have always been in and out of the sea. You know of its dangers, I am sure. For most people, the sea is a place to relax, despite these dangers. I have never felt you were the type to take the risks that would affect your heart. If you do not mind me saying.'

'I know. I *am* careful. The sea is my ... oh, I don't know ... It's my happy place. At least it was.'

'It is good exercise if you swim moderately, if you are careful. It is good to have a patient who is active. The heart wants to be active, you know.'

I slipped off the examination table. 'That is not very comforting, Doctor.'

'I think it is. I do. Telling you to be careful is one thing. How you feel about having to be careful, that is another.'

'As I said, I wasn't alone out there with the shark. There was a man who was also swimming that day. Well, he was surfing. He experienced this with me. He was a stranger but we ... survived it. Together.'

'Have you spoken to him? How has he been?'

'I assume he's fine. He's younger. He's a surfer – he spends his life in the ocean. I don't think he's taken it as badly.'

'He feels more indestructible. Immortal.'

'Yes. But we went through it together so at least he understands.'

'There can be a strong connection between survivors. It can be a good thing, and it can be a bad thing.'

'The truth is I haven't been able to get back into the ocean or even swim in the pool. I can't even look at it. I've been having bad dreams and panic attacks. I haven't even told Jack what happened.'

'You should tell him. This has obviously had a great effect on you.'

'I feel as if I can't tell him. As if I've done something that would disappoint him. Like I've let him down.'

'I don't understand.'

'I'm supposed to be packing up our lives and selling the house, and instead I almost get killed by a shark. I meet a strange man ...'

'Excuse me, please. I do not think you can say you were *almost killed* by a shark. It did not attack you.' He sighed. 'And you must also think of your other emotions now, when you are in a vulnerable state. I am not trained to deal with every matter of the heart. Nor do I wish to be.'

'I was close enough to a shark to be killed, Doctor. And it *did* try to attack Ben, the man on the surfboard, and then it swam next to us. It was terrifying.'

'I think it is important to note that the sharks are always in the ocean. I have read that you are always close to a shark when you get into the water. Whether you see it or not. Whether it swims beside you or not. You are always close enough to be killed. If the shark chooses. Yet people come from all around the world to swim here.'

'I'm still in quite a state.'

'You've experienced a bad shock. It will be some time until you feel yourself again.'

That did not make me feel any better.

> Jack, I need to tell you that I had an experience in the ocean right in front of our house. I was swimming away from our point and a shark tracked me, it swam so close to me I could see its eye. I wasn't hurt, but something has changed. I feel like I don't have the time I thought I had. I feel like my heart is running out of beats. I feel like I'm living a life I never planned on living. I'm very, very aware that I'm fragile, Jack. And the strangest part: I didn't want to tell you. Maybe I didn't want to bother you. I didn't want to have you flying in to rescue me from a shark that is long gone. And I didn't want to hear your voice. I feel that I should have wanted to hear your voice, Jack.

I wrote this text in the dark garage, sitting in my parked car. I read it a few times, and my finger hovered over the send button. But I deleted it.

I tried again.

> Jack, something really frightening has happened.

Deleted it.

   Jack

Delete.

Hound Shark

The hound shark can be found along the entire Cape coast of Southern Africa. It has notably low growth and reproduction rates, and this has contributed to its vulnerable status.

India Ink Sketch from Stella Wright's Private Collection, Later Works, New York

Doctors' appointments have a way of draining my energy. Leaving the quiet sanctuary of Dr Patel's rooms, I felt utterly depleted. The finality of it. Everything I was, everything I might be, was dependent upon a bored receptionist, drab medical records, the smell of rubbing alcohol, the small examination room and Patel's office, which was not much different from any other academic's office. A bureau for managing aging bodies.

I wanted to paint, I wanted to walk on the beach, to embrace my life. I wanted to radiate energy to prove to myself, if not to him, that my life, despite its obvious fragility, was enough to be counted on. My story of age, fault and deterioration, would not drain into the files and the florescent overhead lights and the readouts on his computer. What was happening to my heart was nothing special, really. Dr Patel, for all his wisdom, knew many others like me, met with them daily, people who came to his office full of hope and expectations and fear and were met by measured words and careful phrasing.

After the appointment, I wanted to make art, I wanted my life, but I also wanted to sleep. Nap in the car, restoration. Instead I found myself doing what I often did on these late afternoons …

In the ancient duty of the world's women, it was time to fetch the water. Only my hydria was not a painted, earthen jug but a twenty-five-litre plastic container.

The natural spring was close by the university. By avoiding using the taps in my house, I was mitigating the drought problem, in a small way. It was my acknowledgement that being sick and isolated didn't absolve me from dealing with the country's severe water shortage. Growing up in upstate New York, my father had taught my sister and I to *dig out*, be a *good neighbour*, take care of others and *pitch in*. Good values. *American values*.

If the rains didn't come, I told Jack, Cape Town would die of thirst. It was that simple. But Jack did not know what it was to live with imminent catastrophe. He complained when the pool wasn't topped up, drank directly from the faucet, switched on the irrigation system around the house to feed our tiny patch of grass and tinier garden. Cities don't run out of water, he assured me. It was unheard of. Cities located in the *desert* had plenty of water, and here we were located next to *rivers*, springs, the *ocean*. Cape Town has subterranean water everywhere – *lakes* of it underground, or so Jack had read. He repeatedly exhorted me not to get the water from the spring – it was a great way to sprain a back muscle, or punch another hole in my heart.

'Anyway, they'll still sell water in the shops,' he insisted. 'In the *liquor stores*. If things get dire, I'll buy us a *desalination machine*, make fresh water straight from the sea right out in front of the house.'

'It doesn't work that way, Jack. You can't always just buy your way out of every difficulty. You need to think about this. We need to conserve water. We're supposed to be using only *fifty liters a day per person*. Thirteen gallons; that's not much. You go through that in a single shower. Why should you be exempt from doing your bit?'

It was a useless argument.

There was a bitter, Yankee part of me that actually embraced the water shortage. *Let it come*, I thought. It would get rid of the people who drifted down here but didn't really try to understand the country, people who thought they wanted to live here but knew *nothing* about the ocean. The nomadic rich.

So I fetched the water every few days and the extra chore made me feel as if I'd pushed back the inevitable.

Sitting in the medical suite's parking lot, I texted Ian to inform him I'd have to see him tomorrow after all. I then headed toward Newlands until I found myself in the narrow street lined with cars ramped up on the curb. Nearby, a natural spring sprouted water from the depths of the mountain. Prior to the drought, the spring was an occasional tourist attraction, a place where hikers might fill their bottles with the subterranean, bitterly cold water.

The small suburban lane now saw hundreds of people arriving daily to collect their free water, and the police had set up a trailer at the end of the access lane. As the drought had worsened and water-panic had set in, arguments and scuffles had broken out over parking spots and how many containers could be filled at a time.

I parked, walked down the sidewalk toward the cops, who nodded at me over their Styrofoam cups of tea. Within seconds an angelic kid named Vusi had sprinted toward me in his large floppy neon yellow hat, his T-shirt hanging off the wings of his shoulders. He was always here, and he always helped me.

'Hello, Professor, hello! And how are you?'

'I am exhausted, Vusi. Is it crowded?'

'Not too bad today.'

In front of the pipes which flowed with artisanal spring water, an orderly line of supplicants held all manner of vessels – plastic jugs, paint cans, used Coke bottles, buckets, canteens, casks and flasks. Within moments, Vusi had deftly set my container under a vacated stream.

Next to me, a man wearing a long brown gown and sunglasses looked me up and down, making no attempt to hide his interest.

'You are a teacher. I can tell.'

I nodded, unsure as always how to answer the friendliness of strangers.

'I know this from your bearing. You are used to being in front of people.' He tapped his forehead. 'I know this, you see. This is how I see the world.' He glanced down at his ceramic jug, which had started to overflow. He lifted it with some difficulty.

'You also see the world differently. You're seeing more now. Your eyes have been opened even wider.'

Vusi looked up at the man. 'She's a professor. She's an important lady, this one.'

The man tapped his forehead again, looked around the men in their yellow vests who helped move the water down the lane. 'I need a Water Uber!'

Laughter from the crowd.

'Bring me a Water Uber!'

A vested man – his 'Water Uber' – pulled over a battered shopping cart, helped him load his ceramic bottle and horsed it away with an almighty rattle.

'Goodbye, Lady Professor. See you next time!'

Vusi slid out my water container and yanked it onto his worn-out trolley, immediately replaced at the pipe by a woman in high heels, tight pants and expensive sunglasses.

I followed Vusi to my car, his broken flip-flops crazily slapping the pavement.

'Where have you been? We missed you yesterday, my prof.'

'Busy. I've been working.'

'Is your husband back from the USA? Are you going to New York to see the *zama zama* Yankees for me?'

'I need to go soon, Vusi.'

'You must send me a picture of the New York Yankees. And a new baseball cap from New York.'

'I tell you every time I come, I'll do this. I promise.'

He thinks. 'Send it to the policemen back there. They all know Vusi. Send it to the police station at the spring.'

'I will.'

'Don't forget like you forget to come this week.'

'Vusi, I was almost eaten by a shark.'

He stops, sets down the water. '*Wat?*'

'I was swimming in the ocean and I saw a huge shark.'

'*Tjoe!* Then you must not swim in this ocean. Too much shark. Too much.'

'You're right. Too much.'

He hoisted the heavy container into the Land Rover with ease, though he could not have weighed much more than I did. He accepted the proffered bill with a wide smile, folded it and slipped it into his poor shorts. I noticed, for the first time, a deep scar next to his left eye, like a divot.

'How are you, Vusi? Are you all right?'

'Prof, I can't complain.' *He could.* 'You must remember my Yankees. The greatest American team of baseball.'

He pushed away the trolley, smiling at newcomers, cheerfully offering to carry half his weight in water all day long, in the sun.

I drove along the ocean road. The rusting Land Rover smelt of paint and turpentine. I listened to the hollow, sloshing sound of the water in the container in the back. I'd have to leave this car behind, too. I might be able to sell it to a student. Or somebody off the Internet. *Throw it in with the sale of the house,* Jack had suggested. *Just make sure to take your name off the registration and insurance.* Thinking about selling the car made me feel, acutely, the urge to smoke, but I'd decided to stop smoking.

The road along the touristy section of Cape Town was carnivalesque. Tourists walked and filled the cafés overlooking the beaches. In a few hours the partying would start, young visitors from the UK and Germany and the USA would mingle with locals. I pushed the car through the herds of garishly swim-suited people carrying surfboards and towels and beach umbrellas and baskets. When I got into my garage, I sat in the driver's seat while the electric door creaked closed behind me. I was briefly illuminated by the automatic light and then I sat in the darkness. The roar of the ocean through the garage walls. The frigid surf that hid the sharks. I touched my chest and my heart thudded hopefully within.

The water container was impossibly heavy. I pushed it across the garage floor, took a deep breath and lifted it through the door into the hallway. The shifting water within had its own resistance and inertia, and I pushed and pulled it to the counter in the scullery. The effort felt Herculean. A stupid stunt. I could have waited for Mandla's help, but he had already left, walked away toward the taxis having stowed his tools in the tiny shed near the garage. The foliage outside was trimmed, the leaves raked. He had sanded the windows perfectly.

I stood by the pool and looked into the dark water. Wind rippled across the surface and for a moment I was struck by the notion that something carnivorous could be living there, unseen.

Then a dog appeared – a brown Staffy, short, squat, strong, that I'd seen before – and regarded me with bright, intelligent eyes. In his mouth was a smooth, oblong stone. He dropped it at my feet and looked at me hopefully. I picked it up, wet from the dog's slobber.

'Where's your ball, boy?'

I knelt beside him, stroked his neck and he permitted me to run my hands along his ruff, rustle his piggish ears. His strong jaws were formidable, but he sat placidly while I stroked him, and he felt warm and alive.

I wished he would stay. I imagined what it would be like to have a dog like this sleeping at the foot of the bed.

'Did you have your dinner?'

The dog sniffed the air, seemed to smile. Then he nosed the stone, took it in his mouth, looked toward my house. And there was Ben, standing beside the sliding doors.

'Oh.'

I started. The dog looked at me expectantly for a moment before trotting away across the rocks, taking his stone with him.

Wordlessly, Ben followed me into the house. He was much bigger in the room with me, and when I slid the glass door shut, I was aware of how he smelt like the outdoors, like sand and sweat. He might have walked here.

'Hi. I have your tools, and your surfboard is around the back of the house.'

'I was hoping you'd be here. How are you doing?'

'I'm not sure, to be honest. Actually, not great. I haven't been sleeping well. What about you? How are you feeling?'

'Still pretty sore, but otherwise okay.' He glanced round the room, took it in, his eyes lingering on the kitchen.

I pointed to the box. 'Those tools. I took a peek. They're beautiful.'

'Thanks.' Downright unfriendly.

'May I ask what they are used for? They seem ... unique.'

'They are. I made them.'

'You *made* them? How?'

'Out of garden shears and things. Old gear. Things I no longer needed. Useless things. I reshaped them. I had access to a machine and grinders and all that.'

'That's impressive. What are they for?'

'You won't understand.'

'Try me.'

'I use them for shaping things. Carving wood and also fibreglass. To make surfboards, and for my work. I build boats down here. For now, anyway.' He was looking around the house again, as if memorising it. He glanced at a painting. 'This one's amazing.' He said it as a matter of fact. It was a waterscape from New York entitled *Dawn off Governors Island*. Mario regularly received emails from collectors asking for it, but I didn't want to let it go quite yet. Ben reached out as if to touch it, stopped himself. He was barefoot and had the tanned feet of a Greek peasant.

'I'm going to have to leave the board here. If that's okay. My roof racks have been stolen and it won't fit in the car. I guess I'm lucky the car's still there.'

'It's fine.' I said it too fast; he noted this. 'I'm really sorry about your roof racks.'

'It's happened before,' he said. 'I'm going to have to buy the expensive kind that can't be removed. They cost a fortune.'

I thought of the men literally carting his surfboard away and decided not to tell him about it. To change the subject, I asked the first thing that came to mind. 'Have you told your parents about what happened?'

'My *parents?*' He smirked. 'How old do you think I am exactly? I guess I'll call them soon enough. They're not in the country. They moved back to Canada a few years ago. Via Hawaii. I'm supposed to be following them over sometime.'

'When?'

He shrugged. 'The surfing in Toronto is not great. They keep telling me to be reasonable. I am being reasonable.'

'Will you tell them about the ...'

'The huge shark that hung with us? And give them even more reason to demand I leave? I don't think so.' He laughed. Changed the subject. 'So, you're an American.' He said this as if there was something incongruous about me, something that didn't fit. In New York people think I have an upstate accent, and in Niccalsetti I have a rich accent. My mother would laugh: *I spent a lifetime trying to make sure you and your sister don't sound like you're from Niccalsetti, for nothing.* She with her antique Beacon Hill inflection.

'Yes, I'm American. My husband and I both are. He's working here for his company, and I teach at the university.' The mention of my husband felt wrong.

'At least you have somebody to be with you after ...' He waved his hand at the water, the sharks within, perhaps the transitory nature of life on a beach.

'Do you?'

'Do I what?'

'Have a person to look after you. Perhaps treat that bruise on your chest?'

'It doesn't matter. I've been banged up much worse. Where is he?'

'Jack?'

He nodded.

'He'll be back soon.' That could mean hours, days, weeks – whenever New York didn't need him anymore, or he didn't need New York anymore.

I thought I saw a flicker of disappointment. But I might have imagined it. Or hoped.

'Sorry for asking. None of my business. I was just thinking this would be hard to explain. The two of us here, I mean.'

For a moment I wondered what Jack would think if he saw us. The truth is it wouldn't occur to him to be jealous of this much younger man. Jack would find this entire meeting amusing: 'That hippy kid came back to see you.'

Ben's gaze lingered on the white chairs, the severe cocktail table, the glass doors open to the sea, and the paintings, most of them mine, some hung, some leaning against the wall. I'd been stacking them, thinking about how they would be crated back to New York.

I tried one last time. 'So, you're Canadian?'

Another temporary visitor. Like me.

'Not really. Not anymore. I guess I don't know what I am.' He approached another painting, examined it. 'Wait ... is this Kommetjie beach? It is!'

'It's called *Sunrise*.' He didn't reply, so I found myself adding, 'It's been sold. To an expatriate South African in England. It's about to be shipped.'

'You got the light just right. Like, *perfect*.'

I wasn't sure what to say. The light on the beach was everything, a bright swipe of it, the sky somehow higher, paler than in the northern hemisphere, the sand a crisp white. Even beaches in Florida are not that white – there's something about the minerals in the Cape sand, the quartz and the calcite from the stones. He reached out again as if to touch it, but perhaps he felt me about to protest.

Still looking at the painting, he said, 'I'm a painter, too.'

'You are? What do you paint?'

'The sides of sailboats. The hulls of yachts and fishing boats. That's my regular job.'

'That's great. Sounds like hard work.'

'It is.' He looked at me directly and something passed between us. A flicker of recognition. 'What we went through the other day was pretty intense, hey? I wanted to thank you. For being out there with me.'

I never knew how to answer this kind of directness, this naked politeness. In New York, our experience would be called a *shared trauma*.

'You don't need to thank me. I'm glad we could help each other. It was terrifying. I've been having nightmares.'

He ran his hand over his side. 'I've seen plenty of sharks. But they've never had a go at me. Never.' He gazed evenly out the window to almost the exact spot where I first saw him, a placid, rippled stretch of water. 'The worst was thinking I was going to get you killed. That you were going to die with me.' He glanced at me, furtively. 'I keep thinking about how many times I've almost died out there. Waves have pulled me under. Rocks. Pilings. I nearly drowned when I was twelve years old, when I first started surfing in Durban. Before we moved to Canada. But this was different.'

'You were never going to "get me killed", as you put it. It was my choice to swim out there. I swim every day.'

We stood in the room in a kind of uncomfortable peace. The silence of two supplicants meeting in a chapel.

'I'll never come that close to dying again. Not until I actually peg,' he said.

'How do you know? You can't know that.'

'I know.'

You don't know.

'Why were you surfing here anyway? You guys usually surf further up the coast.'

'I was trying out those fins. On the board. I shape them. You know? Like, I make them.'

'I know what "shaping" means. I'm not *that* old.'

'I didn't want to be in the way of other surfers. I was out there for a while.' He grinned. 'I didn't think you were *old*. You don't look old.'

I willed away my blush. *Blushing is the colour of virtue.* I wanted, suddenly, to be alone. I wanted to change clothes. I could feel the emotion of the day rising, overwhelming me. The panic returning.

'I think you should call before you pick up the surfboard. I'm not always here.' I looked around for my briefcase. It was where I'd left it, beside the counter, full of student papers, pens, brushes covered in specks of paint. There was a fistful of unpaid bills in there, things from daily life, life without sharks and strangers. Was that briefcase even mine? I dug inside, past the detritus (mints, a hairbrush, receipts, a crumpled envelope, a note to myself, a grocery list), fished out one of my cards and handed it to him.

'Professor Stella Wright,' he read out loud. Then frowned. 'I thought you were an artist?'

'I am. I'm also a professor.'

'You're a professor-artist?'

'I suppose. Or an artist-professor.'

'It looks like you do a lot of painting. Not just teach it. Or write about it.'

'I paint. And I teach. And it's never *just* teaching.' I was surprised by the venom in my voice.

He took up a pen from the table next to the couch. He turned over the card, scribbled down a phone number, handed it back to me. I already had his number.

'You can call me when you're ready for me to come for the board.' He shielded his eyes, looked out to where we had met, further. Searching, I thought, for some sign of the shark.

'I grew up next to water. The sea has been a major part of my art,' I told him. 'I live next to it. I swim in it every day. And now I don't think I want to be in it ever again.'

He nodded. 'So do you want to offer me another one of your emergency cigarettes?'

We stepped outside and he lit the cigarette, inhaled, jabbed it at the sea. 'You know what they call them in Hawaii?'

'What? The great white sharks? No.'

'Surfers, guys out on the line, call a shark "the man in the grey suit". You get the point?'

I nodded and took the cigarette he held out to me, pinched it, inhaled. The wind whipped the ash off the end.

'Cigarettes at the beach taste different from cigarettes in a bar or a club or whatever. I never smoke in bars. Out here it feels like it doesn't count.'

'Cigarettes taste like art studios to me.'

'Yeah?'

'Long nights painting. Drinking coffee. Wine.'

'How many packs does one of those paintings put you through?'

'I don't smoke anymore.'

'Yeah, but you have cigarettes.'

'For emergencies only.'

'The watermen in Hawaii don't call the shark by its name. They have another name. They call it "the landlord".'

'Don't mention its name lest it call disaster upon you? The Greeks did this.'

'You give it a name, you give it a reality.'

'*Death and life are in the power of the tongue: and they that love it shall eat the fruit thereof.*'

'What, is that from a poem?'

'The Bible. King Solomon said it.'

'Oh, right, I'm a godless heathen. Are you?'

'Maybe. Once. Long ago.'

He took the cigarette from my fingers, jabbed it at the sea. 'That ocean? It was once a Norse god called Ægir, who had nine daughters in charge of the waves.'

'He was their Poseidon?'

'He didn't just rule it. He was … the ocean itself.' He thought for a second. 'That's a forgotten god, but if you're out there long enough you start to think about him.' He stood at the end of the rocks, shaded his eyes. 'The Zulu people call the shark *ushaka*. Some Hawaiians call the shark Manō, but he's also sometimes an *'aumakua* ... an ancestor that's come back to remind you of something. Like a friend who's still looking after you.'

'What? What would a shark be wanting to remind me of?'

'That's between you and the *'aumakua*.'

'There's nothing to learn from that shark. I don't think he thought about me at all.'

Ben carefully stubbed out the cigarette. 'Our Manō – the one who visited us out there – is long gone.' He handed me the pinched butt of the cigarette, placed it in my palm, warm and gritty against my skin. I had a sudden thought of Ash Wednesday in boarding school. 'I'm not trying to tell you that what we experienced was easy,' he said.

'It was terrifying.'

'That landlord, Manō, was thinking maybe you owed him something. Do you owe any debts to anyone?'

'Actually, *you* brought the shark in.'

He grinned again. 'Nah. I'm good with Ægir. As far as I know.'

'So this is what you do? Surf and tell stories to frightened women?'

'Do you feel frightened right now? Is that what you're feeling? I feel something else. I feel alive. Do you know what time it is?'

I told him; it made sense that he didn't have a watch.

'I need to get to a pharmacy before it closes. To get real painkillers so I can sleep. My ribs are killing me.' He looked like he had something else to say, then decided not to say it. 'Can I borrow some cash? I'm sorry to ask. I don't have my cash card with me and I don't have time to drive back into town to get it. I can leave the tools here. As, like ...'

'Collateral.'

'Yeah.'

'Take your tools. I have a lifetime's supply of painkillers. I can give you some.'

'I'll still have to leave the board though.'

'Sure. But sooner or later you'll need to remove it.'

We went back inside and I found my purse on the floor by the studio, the accrual of my life inside it, including my blood-red leather Gucci wallet (from Jack) that was falling apart. There was something revealing about opening it in front of him. He stood looking at *me* instead of the purse and I felt self-conscious. Did he find it odd that I happened to have strips of prescription-strength painkillers in my handbag? I found myself holding out the pills like an offering to some kind of scruffy, savage god.

He looked at me curiously, cocked his head, as if seeing something he hadn't noticed before. Then he took a step toward me, and I could smell him, and he smelt like the beach. He'd certainly walked here, along the road from town, alongside the ocean. I was looking up to him and holding my breath. And then ... wanting him.

When I was actually in his arms, my face gently pressed against the tender frame of his chest it felt perfectly natural, so reassuring and powerful that tears welled in my eyes. When he kissed me, first a friendly kiss and then more insistent, my fingers scrabbled up to his perfect, unscarred clavicle and my nails dug into his shoulders. He smiled and then he was not smiling. And we stood like dancers waiting for the music, until he seemed to come to a decision. He opened his palm in front of my face, gently placed it between my breasts and held it over my surgical scar, surely felt my heart beating. Demanding. Air surged in my lungs.

He turned, walked away from me, slid open the door to the ocean wind and disappeared. He didn't take his tools or his surfboard – he'd left them like an explorer staking out his territory. The cough of the VW motor and then the engine choking to life, a beast surfacing from the water, roaring away.

That night I dreamt of the eye again.

I was suspended, unbreathing in the water as the shark passed, impossibly huge. The gargantuan animal was endless and inevitable; I had drawn out a leviathan, far bigger than an actual shark. It swam past me like something somehow both industrial and living. The shark trained along its tired course with its mouth closed, as if frowning, as if it had seen something terrible. The monster offered no warmth, no recognition, no hope; it was utterly ageless, something from before history, an eternal, distraught giant. It was patient and brutal and methodical and totally undisputable. I had dreamt up an immense creature that would outlive the land and consume everything in its path until the end of time.

It swam past my tiny, vulnerable body.

It took a very, very long time to disappear.

Hammerhead Shark

Hammerhead sharks are found in all temperate and tropical waters worldwide. In South Africa, adult hammerheads are found off the shores of the entire country, with juveniles often swimming just under the water's surface.

Ink Sketch from One of Stella Wright's Many Personal Sketchbooks, Cape Town

'Professor Wright?'

I was in my office at the university, on the ground floor of the Fine Arts Building. I had one of the few 'real' offices, one with its own door and a small display area and a modern desk bolted to the wall. It was right next door to my seminar room but, annoyingly, two floors from the student studios. To get there I had to use the stairs since the freight elevator was at the far back of the building, and the elevator for handicapped people and those with glued hearts was three corridors away and was usually out of order.

To get to the studios, one passed bronze casting and ceramic kilns; metal and wood workshops; etching, lithography, relief and screen-printing workshops; photographic studios, darkrooms and digital-processing laboratories. On the very top of the building were the video-editing suites, iMac-based computer labs and a new digital-fabrication workshop with a computer-aided laser cutter and router. I had a terror of being locked in one of the studios, as one custodian had been when I'd first arrived. He'd spent the night in this ancient building before being freed by the guards in the morning.

I was trying to focus on a paper entitled 'The Polysemantic Vices of Disruptive Public Art'. I had a pile of these to mark, and some were tough chewing.

'Prof. Hey.'

Katie was in the doorway wearing men's trousers and a tight tube top. It was 20 degrees Celsius out, and she was dressed for summer. Her fingernails, black, were wrapped around her iPhone. Her hair was swept in a messy bun. She was carrying a black hobo bag ... or a travel bag. It was hard to tell. I was sure I'd told her I wouldn't be here. Her paper remained unread in my briefcase. She was one of my favourites, but she was also infuriating.

'So, do you mind if we chat?'

I nodded. I should have said, *I'm nodding because yes, I do mind.* Chatting with Katie was a minefield.

'Okay, great. Thanks. So, my final piece? This is what I'm thinking? This is the idea I have.' She took a breath. I waited. 'I want it to be leather. Right? Like a woman made of black leather. A woman who is life size, possibly *two* women. I've been studying leatherwork? And I think this is possible. And so, okay, I know it's not *totes* original. It's derivative in some respects, I get that, but I want to see what it will look like.'

I was unsure of what I was meant to say. It was very hard for me to imagine a leather woman/women. This was the part of the job I did not relish.

Katie continued, as if she'd practised this pitch. 'Here's my idea. I want to build her around a real skeleton. I mean, okay, not a *real* skeleton, but an accurate *plastic* skeleton I can source from the medical school. I'll build the body around the skeleton.'

'Or a department-store dummy,' I offered.

'No, I want it to look, you know, real. Authentic. Or, at least organic?'

I nodded. I simply could not imagine this. Medical knowledge might be necessary. It sounded vaguely carnal.

'I can source the leather. I found a shoemaker-guy who has *swatches* of it.

'Shoe leather?'

'Yes, but I can also make it, you know, like rubbery and shiny. Like S&M leather.'

'Around a skeleton?'

'Yes. But it will be stylised, you know?'

'Will these be *bodies* of women in leather? Will they have *faces*? Nails? Hair?'

'Yes. I plan on painting these on. It'll look cool.'

'Will they be, um, wearing anything or … will they be nude?'

'Like, nude leather women?'

'Or a single nude leather woman?'

'Like a statement on, I dunno, bondage? Pain? Containment and sado-masochistic identity? The confinement of the gaze?'

I wasn't sure, but I nodded.

Katie grimaced. I'd let her down.

'No. I don't do ... fetish. It's not about that. It's not about women clothed in leather garments. It's an actual leather-skinned woman. Or women. So I guess in that sense they *will be* nude?'

I tried again. 'Do you think you can teach yourself to mould leather into such sophisticated shapes? It'll be challenging, and if you do master that skill, that in itself would be impressive, Katie. Do you understand? Simply by doing that, creating a form that shows you have learnt how to work with leather and plastic and wood and whatever else, that has value. I would really love that.'

'But I'm not sure if it will get me the grade I want, Professor, you know? Like, now you've made me think it could be mistaken for fetish. As if I'm *pandering*.'

I sighed inwardly. 'Then pander. Feel free not to get the best mark in the class. If this is what you want to create, then you need to create it. I'm not going to stop you. I can't visualise your creation, Katie. Neither, perhaps, can you. You can only do it ... once you've done it. Once you've sourced the leather and, I don't know, soaked it, looked at it, dried it, torn it apart, sewn it. I can't give you a license to make art. Does that seem right?'

She nodded. But what she wanted to hear was, *I think the idea is brilliant.* She wanted me to reassure her that if she came to me with a line of female leather mannequins, I'd give her a first-class pass, and so would the external examiner, and she'd have a gallery show within six months. But it doesn't work like that, and I could not tell her so bluntly because she'd find that discouraging.

I tried again. 'Katie, perhaps do some research. Revise your paper.

Look into the artists who work in the medium, show me that you are conversant with what they've done. It might be the best first step for you, okay?'

'Okay. Thanks.'

'Just try that and then maybe work with the leather a bit, bring in a sample of what you're thinking of doing? It *sounds* interesting.' I wanted to add something else. I wanted her to feel invincible, not fragile. I wanted her to feel reckless and flamboyant.

She stood up and gathered her colossal bag. 'Thanks, Prof. I'll see you in the seminar this afternoon.'

'Katie? *Email* me with any new ideas, okay? Try not to text me unless you *really* need to?'

She nodded and she was off. My concentration broken, I couldn't return to the paper I'd been marking. Instead, I started wading through email. We'd been sent five reminders about a departmental meeting. Five. And there was a faculty meeting on the other campus I needed to go to. I needed to RSVP for a presentation that I did not plan on attending: 'Why Privilege and Art Cannot Co-Exist in the Postmodern University Sphere: A Brief Examination'.

My phone pinged. *Ben.*

I swiped the dark screen and felt an instant flush of irritation. It was Katie. After I'd just told her, barely two minutes before, not to text me. She must have been standing right outside the building.

> Yeah, I wanted to talk to you about something else re the paper bt forgot.

I waited. Then I texted,

> Yes?

Regretted it. I should not have answered.

> K, so I'm only going to be able to handwrite paper
> Katie, I cannot accept a handwritten paper! Against dept policy. As you well know.
> I know bt I'm asking cuz I dyed my hair on Thurs and computer screen light really hurts my eyes, cannot see properly. Unless I cn get extension (??)
> The paper is not due for three more days!
> Yes but eyes v sensitive, cannot write notes on paper and then finish academic work on screen
> You cannot type your paper due to hair product stinging your eyes? No, Katie, I am sorry. This is not a reasonable excuse.

I almost flung the phone across the room. It pinged and vibrated. I swiped it again.

> OK, I will try to write paper on computer
> Good!
> Will still not do fetish
> Please don't.
> K thx prof

Later, I could hear chatter as students began congregating next door in the seminar room. This was my one seminar a week, a laughable amount of teaching, part of my being 'phased out' of my role as visiting lecturer since I'd already handed in my resignation. When the students came back after their mid-year break, I'd be in New York with Jack. It did not seem possible.

I only had the end of this term to worry about, but I still had to oversee student work, which was time consuming. I had eight advisees in my seminar, and they were all talented. They needed to be – students around the world wanted to study art in Cape Town. If I'd known about UCT when I was a student, I would have been tempted: there was enough eclectic culture, natural beauty and social grittiness for any artist. I would have been able to create at UCT and would have left without debt.

I was attired for the class in a severe suit, one of three that I'd brought from New York, all from the same online shop, and none of which fit the way I liked. I was shrinking into my clothes. And Cape Town was not a pant-suit place. When I gave workshops, I taught in overalls or jeans, but when we did the research component, I opted for a more formal look since dressing like a fellow artist took away from my academic gravitas, I thought.

As I waited, I went over more of the papers that had been emailed over the weekend. Most of the students had done their analyses on art installations that were, to be honest, a bit out of my sphere. I would have preferred to lead a class on art history, or Grecian urns or Japanese wood blocks or classical sculpture. These papers were mostly interpretive pieces, and, annoyingly, the students were referencing artwork they'd not seen *in situ*. They were writing about showings in Paris and even Norway that they'd found online, and referenced articles from magazines the university didn't subscribe to. Some references were from blogs; some, unbelievably, from Instagram. We'd been encouraged by our head of department to think laterally about these kinds of papers, to accept that space and our relation to art could be interpreted broadly in the McLuhanesque sense. A visit to an Instagrammed art show had value now.

I had assigned topics I truly felt could not be personalised. But for this group, everything was personal. The topic of the paper was, 'Provide a critical perspective of a South African contemporary artist, illustrated with representative examples of their work'. This was straightforward enough, but several papers spewed outrage and vitriol. Two of them were about the work of a local artist, Stephen Mpho, whose work had gained some acclaim and who happened to have been a student here. He'd graduated only a year before and some of the students knew him. One paper railed against the Anglo name appended to an African artist, and another was a rant about how the male gaze permeates Mpho's long, straight-backed figures of women at attention, with skulls that were disturbingly elongated.

The students in the seminar room spoke freely to each other in the mistaken belief that I couldn't hear them. They were arguing about the final dates for the projects. I tuned them out and tried to get rid of some of the emails clogging my university inbox.

The first was easy. Ian wanted to call a quick meeting on upper campus for all staff overseeing creative work that very afternoon. I wrote to say I couldn't make it and opened the next mail. It was from Jack, who said that he knew he shouldn't email me at the university, 'but you never check your fucking Gmail'. He wanted to tell me he had a possible buyer for the house and we had to 'make the call' soon.

I was not ready for new gawkers to come by, to look at my things. From his New York office, Jack had just managed to add more chaos to my life. I forwarded the mail to myself, moved on.

Ian emailed me back.

To: Stella Wright
Re: Crucial Meeting

We really need you at the meeting, Stella. Your institutional knowledge is required! Please come!

I thought about ignoring him, but I could possibly make it if I left right after the seminar and the traffic was not too bad. I replied in the affirmative, appending a smiley face to the email. I hated emojis. I knew he did as well.

I stood, looked up at the rafters of the building, caught my breath. I sat back down, checked my watch, double-checked the mail. Updates from the university, notices about not putting readings online ('Please could staff print readings when possible, as students have paid a hefty printing levy'). But students had no stomach for the printed word anymore; they read everything on their phones anyway.

It was time. I stood, gathered up the papers, put on my glasses and opened the adjoining door to the seminar room. There they all were; young, ambitious, earnest, passionate. Johan van Staden had a cigarette behind his ear and was conferring with Zondi Ramphele, a tall woman with an afro. Seventies style was back, but it was different on this generation, more cultivated. Van Staden's beard was auspiciously trimmed; he angled it at me, a silent greeting. He looked like royalty in exile, Prince Albert in a Can. Katie immediately sidled up to me, asked if we could meet after class. I told her I could spare two minutes max after class; I had a meeting to attend.

The others were Prince Zulu, Johnathan Winter, Nathan Hendricks. We sat in soft chairs in an informal semicircle; the students preferred the casual discussion format. They had, in fact, petitioned for me to remove the long table that had been there – they felt that 'stratified power relations' were not 'conducive to creative processes' in the 'learning space'. Now, paging through their notes, which were balanced on my knees, I suddenly had the feeling of being seated in an airplane that was lifting too quickly. I found myself gripping the arms of my seat. I sucked in the stale seminar-room air, held it, pushed it out.

Zondi glanced at me and a look of concern crossed her face. Johnathan noticed this, then me.

'Everything cool, Prof?'

I nodded. *Everything's cool. Nothing's cool.* 'How are your projects going?'

General murmurs of assent. This was a moot question as I could easily walk through the student workshop upstairs and see what they were doing. Van Staden had been using the plasma cutter for his ironwork – I knew because he had to sign in for it online, and I'd been copied in to that. I knew that Zondi was painting the exquisite figurines she'd been crafting all year, set in even more exquisite pottery, because she'd posted pictures of them to me.

The students had a certain louche rivalry, but outright competitiveness was not cool. The actual coursework – the written component of the class – was part of the requirement for their degrees. The students themselves would have preferred to simply work on their projects, hoping to display them in the university gallery during Cape Town Art Week or in other galleries. I privately agreed with them. Research into art was good, but making art was better. I was not suited to being a disciplinarian and the students regarded me, I think, with curiosity. My own work had been shown around the world, why was I teaching *them*? There was a latent sense of jealousy, I felt, and also ... the feeling that they saw my work as less than *avant-garde*. None of the students painted seascapes.

'Your papers were good,' I answered the unasked question. The tension in the room slackened. 'Everyone has passed.'

Van Staden rolled his eyes, slow clapped. Zondi grinned at him and he winked at her. A flash of attraction shimmered between them. I scented it like a waft of cinnamon. *Why do bulls and horses turn up their nostrils when excited by love?* Darwin.

'However. All of you need to work on your referencing' – communal eye roll – 'and I've marked where this needs to be corrected. You cannot only use contemporary sources. You need to use academic sources as well. You know this.'

There was a collective grunt.

Prince looked bemused, unfailingly polite. His work was the boldest: collages of found objects, bunches of wild paint strokes. Prince designed heavy murals with explosions of vibrant, earthen colours; his first mural towered fifteen feet high. He welded, glued and burnt onto each piece objects that would be familiar to anyone living in any city, but which were also somehow eminently South African: taxi windows with garish sayings ('Luva-luva Boi'; 'Stone Kold'), discarded street signs from the ganglands, café notices, local cigarette wrappers, old cans of Koo Samp and Beans, gutted radios, even half a Weber barbeque welded into a frame, all of this sold and shipped thanks to the miracle of social media.

Katie had told me he was already a sensation on Instagram – he'd sold some of his paintings to foreign collectors. They'd been interested in the evident rage in his work, their provenance the fact that he was the son of a prominent politician, a distant relative of the Zulu king. Prince Zulu was dressed, as usual, in a three-piece suit, a beautiful fedora, leather shoes. Was that a real diamond-studded watch? And, to top it off, he carried a cane with what looked like an ivory head. He drove an actual Cadillac, one of the few American cars one might see down here. The Cadillac was painted neon blue; the windows were smoked. It sat in the student parking lot like an interpretation of the vehicles of the wealthy. Something Elvis would have owned.

Zulu raised his hand. 'We'd like to know when final projects are due for the university showing?'

'You already know this. It's clearly stated in your course outline, and we've discussed it several times. Final pieces need to be submitted before exams start. No exceptions. We'll probably stagger the exhibition – at least that's what's planned – but regardless, all final work must be in before exams.'

Prince flicked his eyes toward the other students, already considering whether his brand could handle association with the neophytes.

Van Staden popped up a finger. He glanced at Zondi as if they'd rehearsed something. 'Okay, so, about Cape Town Art Week. It's, like, two months away and I know only a few of us will get in ...'

'They're still deciding what work to take.'

He nodded understandingly. 'Yeah, well, some of us' – he meant himself and Zondi – 'are uncomfortable that this is yet another art showing that has been colonised by minority capital.'

I tried not to sigh. 'Yes, it is sponsored by a bank. That's practically the only way to get funding so people can come. Renting the art space is difficult, and costly. There are two artists flying in from Nigeria and Ghana. This is expensive.'

'So that's the problem. I mean, both of them work in traditional mediums, right?'

'If you're referring to El Anatsui and Igshaan Adams, you might say they have provided an *interpretation* of traditional mediums and found objects.'

Van Staden glanced at Prince, who looked back impassively. Prince had never voiced much of an opinion against capitalism, for obvious reasons, but he listened attentively. And because he was not objecting, he seemed to be in agreement.

In a sense, I was too. So was Zondi, who was glaring at me now. I was a gatekeeper, in their eyes, not a fellow artist guiding the way. I was a captured creative working for Big Money, or the nefarious Colonialist Project, or White Minority Capital, me with my own studio at the university, another in Bakoven on the sea, my husband being who he was. Me and my seascapes and landscapes and occasional sculptures. They'd followed up on all of this. I wanted to tell them I *was once them*. I too would have felt uncomfortable being part of an investment bank's rebranding as a friend of culture. But when I was starving with Demetrius in New York, I would have shown my work and taken the cash. That's life.

I heard myself say: 'The bank's support means that locals from around Cape Town, and the thousands of tourists here, get to see real African art.'

Van Staden looked defiant. 'So, like, maybe we should boycott it, you know? Like, make it clear that our work isn't available? We're not for sale.'

Prince looked at me expectantly.

'You could do that. But the university *wants* you to show your work. It's an opportunity to be seen, written about, perhaps bought, that isn't likely to come again soon. Remember, you're not always going to like the people who support your work.'

Demetrius's voice: *Sooner or later, Cat, we're all for sale. It's the system, not a choice.*

Katie put up a hand. 'Like, some of Van Gogh's paintings are in some bank, right?'

'Yes. And at least they're on display. Much of the work that gets bought is put into storage. In a temperature-controlled warehouse by some millionaire art collector who's been told by an art appraiser to buy it as an investment.'

Like some of mine. At least five of my paintings were in a vault outside St Petersburg, held by a Russian who'd bought them over the phone during an auction the previous year. Jack had two paintings in a warehouse in New Jersey. The only people who saw many of my beach paintings were those who came to his parties or his private office in Bermuda. I thought about this for a moment. I felt like sharing it but I could *not*. It would only underline to them how far I'd sold out to the patriarchy.

Katie raised her hand. She had a new French manicure, I noticed. I couldn't remember the last time I had a manicure. Or wanted one.

'Prof, we brought this up last week. The diamond grinder isn't working properly. I'm not sure, I think it needs another blade?'

Relief at the change of subject. 'It's fine, Katie. We tested it.'

'I think the cut is skew? I'm not sure ...'

This was my chance to make good. The offending tool happened to be sitting in the wide windowsill near my desk. I stood, crossed the room, opened the adjoining door to my office and snatched it up. It was surprisingly heavy, heavier than I remembered. I strode back into the seminar room.

'We tested it over the weekend, Stephen Brodrick and I, and established that it is working perfectly. The blade had been screwed back incorrectly – you guys were forcing the threads. But it's okay now.' I pulled the trigger to show that the spinning cutter wasn't wobbling like a child's broken tricycle wheel. The screaming sound, the cracking, the grinding (all so familiar to me), brought on a wave of nausea. The smell like burning chalk.

I looked up with some satisfaction at Katie, who looked stricken, and I eased off the trigger. Only then, when the whine of the cutter stopped and silence was resuming in the room, did I *really* feel the weight of the machine in my hands. I found there was no way to hold it – even though I'd spent hours with this very tool in this very building. It crashed to the floor and for a moment I had the terrible feeling of my knees buckling. Then Prince was by my side, easing me onto the floor, and the students were standing, confused as I slumped over, gasping for breath. *Oh God, don't let me throw up in front of them.*

Prince cradled my head, kept me from toppling over. 'Are you okay, Prof?'

Van Staden was kneeling next to me. Tears had sprung to my eyes. The diamond cutter had spun across the floor away from me. In pieces.

Katie had her iPhone out. 'I'm calling Emergency Services, hey?'

I shook my head, gasped, 'No, Katie, don't call them. I'm sorry. It's just been a long day.'

Then I thought perhaps I *should* have the students call emergency services, I had no idea what was wrong with me, the saliva in my throat tasted like copper and the room was blurring in and out of focus. I could have been having another heart attack. *Heart attack is the leading cause of death for women over thirty, despite being thought of as a 'man's disease'.*

Just as suddenly, the world slipped back into focus, as if I'd emerged from water. I waved away the students huddled around me and rose to my feet, steadied myself with the chair. Their looks of concern turned slightly judgemental. Art is an animal business; teaching it requires a leader who charges from the front.

I smiled wanly at the class. 'I think I need to cut this session short, people. I apologise.'

'Do we need to call a doctor? Can we take you anywhere?' Van Staden offered, at the same time quickly gathering his things to leave, shutting off his phone's screen and pocketing it, the universal student signal for departure. He'd probably already posted on social media: *Prof fainted in class, bru. So hectic.*

'Thank you, but no.'

The students filed out and when Prince Zulu had shut the door after one solicitous glance back at me, I collapsed into my chair. A rank feral scent was rising off me. My chest was heavy and suddenly I had a headache; a metallic, stabbing pain reserved for subway rides. I rose unsteadily and walked the few steps into my office, closed the adjoining door. I found my purse and dug around for a bottle of aspirin, swallowed two dry, then dug further, found my painkillers *to be used only as needed*, strong stuff, and swallowed one. I sat in my desk chair for forty minutes waiting for the gentle pharmaceutical gauze, the familiar, comforting warp and weft of reality. I would not be attending the meeting with Ian.

Once I was sure the meds were working, I trod carefully into the winter wind, across the parking lot to my car, and drove home, peering over the wheel in my huge sunglasses. For all the world just another crazy lady in a suit heading into the tony section of Camps Bay.

Grey Nurse Shark

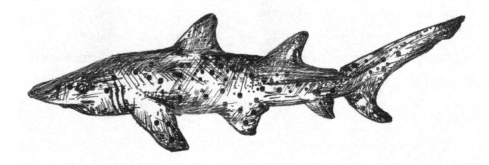

The grey nurse shark is a migratory species of shark that is often solitary. The largest specimens have been found in South Africa, where they are known as ragged-tooth sharks. The grey nurse shark is known to be highly aggressive when provoked but contrary to popular lore it is not considered a man-eater.

Listed as vulnerable.

Pencil Drawing from Artist's Early Private Collection, Cape Town

When I pulled into the garage and walked into the house, Mandla was at the pool waiting for me. His eyes crinkled in a question.

'I'm fine, Mandla.'

He nodded, solemnly.

'It's far too late for you to still be here, Mandla.' I looked at the clock, pointed at it. 'Too late. Time to go home. Have you eaten?'

'But I want to show you something, Miss Stella.'

'Please, maybe next time?' The drive home had been long and I was definitely not feeling myself. I'd taken my time, breathed the way a therapist had taught me: *Breathe it out and focus on anything. Focus on the wall. Focus on me.* Urging my mind to slow down, to *find the energy in my heart.* The tall, furiously beautiful woman had cheerfully offered to explore my 'female tantric energies' in a separate session at her flat. I'd been tempted.

'But I must show you. Please.'

I followed him along the pool, claw marks of dust settled at the bottom – *I need to turn on the Kreepy Krauly* – particles of moss and lichen floating above. Why had I never asked Mandla to clean the pool?

But Mandla had no interest in the pool. He didn't even skim it. Perhaps there was an unspoken contract we observed.

Around the side of the house, a long window led up to under the gutter. Above that, in the slanted roof, was the pyramid of the studio skylight, frosted with salt. He pointed at the windowsill.

'You see?'

I didn't. It looked the same as always. A long white shelf under the bay window looking over the waving kelp fields. Mandla placed a hand on this, gripped. The entire thing shifted.

I reached out and touched the sill. It felt hollow and damp. I yanked downwards and a fistful of mouldy wood broke off in my hand. It looked as if an animal had taken a huge bite out of it. Wood dust floated to the ground. I shook the sill again and realised that even in my condition I could have torn the entire thing off. It was thoroughly rotted through. I peered into the damage, saw two rusted screws buried in what looked like a pelt of rotten pine.

Mandla looked at me. 'All around the house it's like this. I cannot fix it all.'

'But you can patch this? Maybe do something?'

'I do small things. I cannot hold your house to the ground.'

'You can fix this? Paint over it?'

'*Painting*, Miss? *Painting* does not fix.' He pointed at the pitch of the tin roof over the main living room. 'I will go up the ladder, but this roof looks no good. I think the wood has rusted.'

I understood what he meant. The bolts had rusted and the corrosion had carried on into the wood, into the material that bound the roof to the house, the struts and beams that formed the entire structure. Mandla smiled as if there was some vague humour to be found in this. He waved at the sea, at the mountains, the clouds, waved his calloused palm through the air. 'This big wind from the sea. Too much damage.'

'I thought the drought would solve this. I thought the sun would dry all this wood.'

He laughed long and hard and then he bent over and coughed and laughed again. 'I do not think the ocean dries anything? Even when there is sun, the ocean is *wet*. No, this ocean does not dry things.'

I burst into laughter. It was absurd to think that this house had started to crumble. *Because rust never sleeps.* And the cost of it! Damp had worked its way into the roof and the walls and the foundation and we were discovering it all too late.

'I cannot tell Jack.'

'You *must* tell Mr Jack.' Mandla laughed again, hooted. He pointed at the wood, the flaking paint, the joins below the roofline. 'Anyway, he can see this? He will notice?'

'Mr Jack doesn't notice what he doesn't want to see.'

Mandla considered this. 'I must go now.' He pointed at the damaged sill. 'There are many places like this in this house.' He solemnly shook his head.

'Thank you for showing me.'

He beamed merrily, walked down to the back beach and through the public access, disappeared. Perhaps he was laughing as he climbed up to the roadway. I believed I could hear him. I stood, breathing gently, looking at the rotting wood he'd exposed, a pile of soft, hidden feathers under the paint. I willed myself to relax in the wind. Breathe.

A few months after we moved to Cape Town, Jack had left me to go back to New York. I was still finding my way around the city. Jack had made it clear that this trip would only be for a week and then he'd be back. I was nervous about being alone in a new country.

The second day of Jack's trip, at eight o'clock in the morning, I'd woken to the sound of desperate banging on the door. Palm slapping against the wood. I threw on a robe and went downstairs.

I found Mandla collapsed at the front door, his legs splayed out in front of him. His teeth were stained with blood and he was wet with it. He had his hands under his shirt and he grimaced as he tried to get to his feet. He fell back, rose again as I helped him up, panicking now at the blood on his clothes. We staggered inside the house. He could barely walk, was struggling to breathe. I asked him what had happened and he shook his head. Blood and mucus bubbled from his lips.

'They beat me. They say they will kill me like a dog.'

'Who? Who beat you?'

'*Skollies. Skelm.* The men near the taxi.' He collapsed and I screamed, knelt next to him, cradled his head on my lap.

'You must not move, Mandla. Do you hear? You must not move. I'll call the doctor. Why did they do this?'

'They have stolen eighty rands from me. I came here. I have nothing now. I am thinking I was going to die here in the front.'

His eyes were wide. His wet body was ropey and calloused, and he smelt of the street. I found my phone, called the ambulance. I told them a man had been beaten and was lying on my floor and I was told to try to stabilise him if I could. I felt faint. I didn't want him to see me panic. His shirt had been torn to shreds. Underneath, he had ugly welts and cuts in his dark skin.

'They beat me. They had a sjambok. You see? Sjambok.'

A *sjambok*. A cruel leather club stretched into a whip. A device meant to beat animals into submission. I imagined he'd been left for dead. *He was attacked in the street with a sjambok. He lived through it to walk to my house.*

He lay against my leg looking worse than a swimmer attacked by a shark. This gentle man viciously beaten by people who might live near him, who might have shared a taxi with him or passed him on the way to work.

He looked at the ocean and winced. We sat there together, and I thought that if he fell asleep I would slap him awake. But he didn't. He just contemplated the sea and I started talking, saying anything that came to mind. I told him how much I missed Jack. And New York. That being ten thousand miles from it was hard but I would make this work. That the ocean was beautiful and the light was unlike any light I'd ever seen, and the sky went on forever and ever. I believe he heard me and understood. I knew my secrets were safe.

Mandla and I stayed like that until the ambulance came and he was transported into the emergency room of the hospital in town. There, an exhausted-looking doctor told me that the people who had attacked him – street people, possibly locals with a grudge against foreigners – had hit him hard enough to bruise his musculature, which had leaked toxins into his bloodstream. The welts on his body would take weeks to heal but he would be mobile. He was lucky he hadn't been stabbed or shot, I was informed. Mandla was sedated, cleaned up and bandaged. He was given a box of painkillers.

By the time I was presented with the release papers, when it was clear Mandla could not read them, it was late evening. He had slept. The nurses changed his bandages twice before the dinner trays were pushed down the hallway in one of their sad trolleys.

'Surely he needs to spend the night here?' I said.

The doctor, young, tall, possibly Somalian, seemed exasperated. 'I could admit him, but it will serve no purpose. There's nothing more we can really do for him. He needs to rest and heal. He is also not on medical aid.'

'I'm happy to cover his costs.'

Mandla had been listening intently. He was wearing Jack's golf jacket from the Vineyard Golf Club, one of his polo shirts, pants that were slightly too short in the leg and notably too big in the waist, socks and Adidas squash sneakers – things I had grabbed in a hurry after driving back to the house while they worked on him. He simply shook his head and stood up.

'I am going home now.'

I put my hand on his, where he was not wounded. 'Mandla, you should stay. They can look after you here. You're badly injured.'

He smiled but shook his head. 'I am fine, Miss Stella. I am fine. I feel better. I will go home now and see you maybe next week.'

The doctor shrugged. 'I'll discharge him then.'

'Mandla, I'm worried.' I turned to the doctor. 'Can you tell him what he needs to do? I just don't have the right words.'

The doctor was offended. 'I cannot speak his language.'

I turned to Mandla. 'I'll drive you home, Mandla.'

Mandla drew himself to his full height with obvious difficulty. 'I will go home by taxi, Miss Stella.'

'Do you have money?'

He didn't but he was undeterred. I gave him some bills. He slipped them into a pocket, turned and walked carefully out of the discharge room and into the night. I turned to the doctor.

'Will he be all right?'

'You can go to reception now. They have his details. He's a lucky man.'

'He is hardly lucky.'

'Luckier than many.'

'I cannot *believe* he doesn't want to stay here and recover.'

'He's afraid.'

'Of what?'

'He's afraid those who did this will come here for him. To finish him off.'

'What? Why?'

'Because he's not from here. Because this is the country we live in.'

'I'm not from here either.'

The doctor smiled grimly. 'No. You are not.'

How long would it be until this happened again? Until he got stabbed or shot? Mandla could not hide his otherness.

I could not hide mine, either. My accent was different. Had I ever felt unwelcome in this country? Had Jack? Never. We foreigners from the north lived like migrant birds here. Part of the scenery. Thousands of us in these houses that dotted the coastline, flying in and out as we wished, never at home, never *not* at home. But Mandla couldn't fly away.

After we'd inspected the window and Mandla had left to go home, I went up to my room. I kicked my flats into the closet, stripped off the suit jacket and pants, my bra and panties, stood in the shower and damn the water shortage. I contemplated our corroding house while water cascaded over me and I found myself holding my hands in front of me, as if in supplication, as if I was pressing my chest together, healing it with running water. The nausea had disappeared, and while I wanted to lie down and sink into painless unconsciousness, I also had the urge to do something else. I stepped out of the shower, dried myself, buried my face in the towel, wiped my eyes and nose.

I thought of the pills I'd swallowed in my office coursing through my body like fat sharks, eating blobs of pain. Tearing them apart into tiny droplets.

I knew I should call Dr Patel. At least tell him what had happened in the seminar. But not yet.

I could call Jack. See his face on the iPad, hear his voice. But I didn't feel like his immediate call to arms. I didn't fancy a dozen text messages instructing me to call Patel *now*, to get rest, to call another doctor, to check myself into the heart clinic, and then the inevitable callbacks that would follow as Jack garnered his forces and decided to fight my body's battles for me from Midtown.

I possessed a different kind of energy. Lately I lacked *kinetic energy* but was now amassing *potential energy* to transform into *radiation*. A sudden remembrance of an almost perfect hand-coloured facsimile of Blake that Jack had bought me on auction in London, on a whim. A gift of such generosity I dared not touch the book, and then only while wearing absurd white dancing gloves. *Energy is an eternal delight, and he who desires, but acts not, breeds pestilence.* That book now sat in its box within another box in our apartment in New York.

I threw on one of my painting smocks, an old Brooks Brothers shirt of Jack's. I slipped on my cargo pants and sneakers, went back downstairs and stood in front of the ocean, roiling and humming. Normally by now I'd be bobbing up and down between spouts of waves in the sudden sun. I'd float out, like a bottle thrown into the blue.

I walked into my studio and the late afternoon light made it positively incandescent. I breathed in the smell of paint, of oil and canvas and also the pungent sting of granite and dust ('This dust gets all over everything,' Jack had complained, repeatedly). I looked over at the electric tools lined up above my bench. The polishers, pneumatic drills, hammer drills, hand drills, adzes and scrapers. I picked up a five-pound hammer and hefted it, flipped open the steel box of chisels, drew out one as big as a railway spike, shut my eyes, waited for inspiration. Nothing. I waited some more. Then felt beneath me the foundation of the house on the rock, the water smashing against it, the vibrations travelling up through the rock into the house, into me, the wind breathing against the studio windows, the skylights.

I hadn't touched these tools in months. I had a square yard of quarried granite and one natural piece I'd been saving for when I was brave enough to turn my hand to sculpting again. I wasn't sure what I had planned for the natural rock (salvaged from the university, hauled here by willing students in the broken-down studio truck). It was set on a plinth in the back of the studio, within runner boards. It was like the rocks outside, but smoother, seamless. I set the edge of the chisel on it, hefted the hammer. I sucked in a sharp breath, steadied myself, brought down the hammer on the chisel with a satisfying bang. The claw bit into the stone, skidded. I reset it, slammed the hammer into it. One more time, then again.

The metallic ping of hammer on chisel was satisfying. I would not let a student do this – I'd make them wear goggles and gloves. After I'd hit it twenty-seven times (I counted), the chisel clumsily, violently broke off a chunk of stone, which fell open like stone fruit, revealing the jagged, sparkling inside. I dropped the chisel, set down the hammer.

I was breathing hard, sweating. But I was not faint, I was not vomiting; *I was not dying.*

I set everything back where I'd found it and walked back into the living room, pushing the studio door closed behind me.

That was infinitely stupid, but for the first time in a while I felt like me.

When I awoke from my nap it was early evening. I poured myself a glass of wine, sat helplessly in my living room. I called Ben. Of course I did. He was the only person who understood what I was feeling, who could help me process. I needed to see him.

His number rang twice and I rang off.

His box of tools still sat on the kitchen counter like a deformed collection of family silver. I had examined how he must have made the box. The joins of the wood fit perfectly together. The insets had been machined and then covered with felt, then sewn and glued into the leather corners. When the box was closed it looked like any another battered wooden box one might find in a tool shop.

I snatched up the phone and called him again. *If he doesn't pick up I'll ring off and nothing will happen.* But he did answer. He sounded as if he'd been sleeping.

'You left without your stuff.'

'I know. Can you hold on to it? I'll come fetch it soon.'

I paused. It was six o'clock exactly. A boat carrier trundled out toward a floating driller. Gulls were screeching at land birds and the wind was lashing the roof and the sides of the house, blowing hard enough that I could feel slight puffs of air against my ankles.

'No problem. But I was thinking … I could bring them to you … Your tools. You might need them.' *And my heart is weak and I cannot sleep and I'm doing things that might be self-harming and I don't want to be alone.*

'I don't need them right now. Don't stress.'

I rolled my eyes, looked up at the rafters thirty feet above my head and thought this would be a good time to agree with him, but I decided to give him one more chance: 'I feel like a drive. I'll just drop by your place and bring them to you. The truth is, I've had a bad day and I'd like to see you.'

In the few seconds that he made me wait for a reply I recognised my mood as reckless.

'Okay. You can come by. I'll see you soon.' And he hung up. I was about to call back to ask for his address when my phone pinged with a location pin.

Still in my cargo pants and smock covered in rock grit, I carried my bag and my coat and his toolbox heavy under my arm to the car and then steered through congested rush-hour streets toward the old warehouse district where he lived. *This is absurd. What am I doing? I should call him back and say I've changed my mind. I'll hold on to his tools and surfboard until he's ready to collect them himself. I have no business going to his home ...* But I carried on driving, telling myself that common sense would prevail. I would simply drop the toolbox with him at the door and walk away. Deliver it like an Amazon package in turned wood.

Parking in front of the massive, almost derelict warehouse where he lived was nonexistent. I finally ramped up next to a shop that sold everything from fish and chips to SIM cards and also offered bike repairs. When I stepped out of the car, I was accosted by an impossibly skinny man wearing a colourful beanie who assured me he would 'nicely' look after my 'magnificent vehicle'. I tipped him because perhaps he would, and the thought of being stranded here was not a pleasant one. I apparently tipped him enough that he literally stood sentry in front of the car, hands folded in front of him.

I slipped through the rushing people and the noise – vagrants, kids, dogs and endless shouting – to an aluminum sheet set in the wall with a hole where the door knob might have been (stolen, if there ever was one). A doorbell button was duct-taped in the alcove, and I pressed it and waited. Somewhere in the bowels of the building a door banged open and I heard him on the stairs inside. The door vibrated and then he yanked it open.

He was wearing loose-fitting trousers made out of a strange material. Hemp, maybe? Sneakers. A long, flowing black shirt that he might have slept in. I immediately regretted coming to *his* territory. Hippies and students and transients and struggling people lived here in Salt River. Artists and collaborators and drug sellers. I was uncomfortably aware that I was no longer part of this bohemian world.

He looked at me expectantly. 'Hi. Come in?'

When I reflect on this moment, I think about how clear it was to both of us that I could easily have declined to enter that wreck of a building. I could have handed the heavy wooden case to him and I am sure – I know – he would have taken it without comment, perhaps just a muttered thanks, and clanged the wobbly door shut. I could have gone back to my empty home and dramatic ocean, and that would have been the end of that.

Instead I followed him up the narrow stairs. The apartment above held a series of smells I remembered from The WorkHead. Different from my studio at the house. The smell of tint. Oils. Raw varnish, dust and street smells wafting through the dirty windows. Industrial scents. We entered his space and it was bigger than I had imagined. Cans of paint lined the far wall, pieces of wood and fibreglass on the floor. An electric jigsaw lay on top of a pile with its guide light blinking. Three different malformed surfboards stood at the sash windows that were open to the crowded road below. We walked past tables piled with tools, a computer glowing dully, precariously balanced on a board itself balanced on sawhorses, through to his kitchen. Or what passed as a kitchen. This was littered with wine bottles and wrappers. *He's a slob.* He seemed to exist on coffee (there were many dirty mugs) and food eaten out of Styrofoam pods. He turned, looked at me, and I realised he was practically standing in his bathroom: a tiny space with a shower and a small toilet. Across from this was a closet vomiting clothes: towels, shorts, more towels, board shorts, workout gear. And beyond that the bedroom. Or a room he was using to sleep in.

Artists don't need luxury, Cat. You need to remember that if you want to survive this.

He held out his hands, and for a moment I thought he was holding them out for me, but he simply scooped the box out of my arms. Then he read my mind.

'Uh, I would have cleaned up if I had more warning.'

'It would have taken you a week. And I doubt you would have. Cleaned up.'

'It would have taken a while, yeah.' He grinned. 'Do you want a drink or ... you know, something ...?'

'A drink? Yes.'

'Wine? I have wine in the fridge. I think. Hang on.' He yanked the door to the ancient refrigerator, which opened with a screech and then settled on its hinges. The freezer compartment was frosted with three inches of white snow. But he had a full bottle of wine in there. He rummaged in the kitchen drawers, discovered a corkscrew that looked like it had been salvaged from a sunken ship, and deftly twisted it into the bottle after carving off the round of foil. Even in this he was amazingly precise. He carefully drew out the cork, and I thought of Jack struggling with a Laguiole wine key at home, the wine bottle between his legs, and the corks he had destroyed, crumbs of them floating in how many glasses of Rupert & Rothschild.

I sipped the wine from a glass smudged with someone's fingerprint, and I sensed his closeness in this messy kitchen. He flipped open the wooden box I'd brought and checked the tools, adjusted them.

'It took a long time to make these, you know?'

'Did you machine them yourself?'

'Had to. I never know when the next yacht project will come in. Business comes and goes – not like being a pro artist, right?'

Oh, he's teasing me. 'What you do *is* art, Ben. Shaping things. Moulding them. It's not just about galleries and paintings. Many of the art pieces my students are making – pieces that may get them a gallery showing – aren't as impressive as this. One of the professors has a workroom that looks just like this. He works in wood, leather and steel. One showing he had was a collection of everyday electronic objects rendered in wood.'

'What, like toys?'

'No. Representations of things. See that alarm beam you have?' I pointed at the red blinking eye set in plastic in the corner of the room. 'Everyone has seen these things. Capetonians have them in their homes. They're a part of our daily lives. We don't notice them. But when you see them in wood, moulded, polished ... then you perceive them differently.' I glanced at the tools, selected one whose end was round, smooth, orbital. It was cold in my hand, and a grooved blade jutted out from it. It was heavy, utilitarian, somewhat obscene. 'What is this for?'

'It's just a scraper. It's designed so your hand doesn't get tired. I think every scraper and screwdriver should be designed this way.' He reached for it, his hand gripped mine, enveloped it. 'You hold it like this and you have much more power, see?' He turned my hand over, pressed the end of the tool into the counter and I felt an even strength as he helped me turn it. He guided my hand over to the box, I dropped it, looked at him, chose another tool. This one had a wooden handle, ebony. A flat blade ran out of it, and there was a notch at the end. He set my fingers over it, and I pulled it from its place. It too was heavy.

'That's a chisel. Not one I made, though. I just restored it.'

'You did a good job.' I set it back. Selected another one, a small, blunt dagger.

'That's a file.'

'Files are flat.'

'Not if you need to file a bored hole.'

He took it from me, set it back, selected a tiny scythe. A scalpel. He slid it into my palm and I turned it in my hands, held it like a pencil. *Perhaps Dr Patel had used something like this when he opened me up.*

'I saw that one in a dentist's office. I just made a larger one. I have to replace that.' I waited for him to take it, but he didn't.

'Show me how to hold it.'

'That's about right.' He adjusted my fingers, moved them slightly further back. 'That's better.' He didn't let go of my hand.

'Show me how to use it.'

He glanced around, guided me into the workroom. A variety of torn pieces of wood, carbon fibre and fibreglass sat on top of a set of trestles. One piece looked as if it had been ripped from the lining of a pool. Smooth. He guided my fingers and the knife downwards and I made my first incision. The material spread open, but it was hard to control. It would be very easy to cut myself with this odd tool, so unlike the ones I was used to working with. I pressed further downwards and realised I was short of breath. *This is what it feels like to cut into skin.*

'Wait,' he said, and guided me again, the strength of his fingers allowing me to pull open the rubbery material with ease. 'I checked out your artist's page.'

'Oh, yes?' Mario ran my official site, but I knew there were several bios on the Internet attached to auction sites, and I'd done a few interviews over the years. 'What did you find out?'

'You don't only paint. You chisel granite. I would have thought that took a bit of strength.'

'It does. But this is different somehow.' The feeling here was so alien from what I had come to know as my everyday life, and yet so familiar. This space could have been one of any number of the studios I'd worked in before I had my own. There had been shared places, reclaimed spaces or places that were not meant to be studios: warehouses, dead storefronts. I'd once worked for a month in an abandoned paddle-tennis court.

I luxuriated in having Ben so close to me.

'There was a picture of you. You were dressed in overalls. You had a baseball cap on and goggles. You were making a sculpture.'

'Yes. I've made a few.'

'What of?'

'I've tried quite a few animals. It's hard. Some abstract stuff. It's not my core skill but I enjoy it. I sculpt when I'm blocked with my painting. Jack doesn't like me working with the heavy tools though.'

'Why not? And who's Jack?'

'You know who he is. My husband.'

'Does he know you're here?'

'He does not. He's in New York.'

Ben glanced at the clock on the wall, which was cracked and scuffed and spattered with paint. He waited for me to say something.

'I had surgery a few months ago. Well, more than a few months ago. Last year.' I cleared my throat. 'And before that, my gardener was attacked at a taxi rank. Simply because he's a foreigner. He had to go to hospital.' Why was I telling him this?

'Did he die?'

'No. But he was badly beaten. By criminals with a sjambok.'

He shook his head, registered that atrocity without comment. 'What kind of surgery did you have?' He was curious, a kid hoping to hear something disgusting.

'I had to have my heart operated on.'

'Did they fix it?'

'They did their best.'

'So, are you dying?' An abrupt, rude, immature question.

'I don't know. I suppose we're both dying.'

'But you could be dying faster than me.'

'I'm told I'll be fine if I'm careful.'

'Did it hurt?'

'What?'

'Having your heart operated on. Does it hurt now? Do you feel it?'

This had never occurred to me. I tried to feel my heart, feel it pumping in my chest, sweating in the close air of the studio. Perhaps my pulse was up because of the wine. Because I was with him.

'I can't feel any pain. But I know what's been done.'

'That's okay, then, right?'

'They showed me a scan.'

'How did they get to your heart?'

'They cut through my sternum.'

'With a *scalpel*?'

'No, with a tool like a jigsaw.'

'No *fucking* way!'

'They spread my ribs and clamped the arteries and sealed my heart and that's it.'

'So were you in hospital for what? Months?'

'I was back on my feet in less than a week.'

'No big deal?'

'It *was* a big deal.'

'I want to see it.'

'What?' The question made me laugh, the first time I had laughed in a while, the first time ever with him.

'Where they sliced into you. I want to see.'

'Are you kidding? Why?'

'I want to see what heart surgery looks like.'

'I had *laser* surgery. And a silicone sheet over that to shrink the scar.'

'Is it gone?'

'It's nine inches long. Over my sternum. Then lower. It's not gone.'

'It can't be too bad. I would have noticed, you know, when ...'

When I'd ripped off my costume in front of him. So he had been looking.

'A clinical therapist helped me. When I woke up, I was upset.'

'But happy to be alive?'

'Yes. But also angry. I now had a damaged heart that could stop functioning any time. A scar across my chest. Tiny staples, yellow antibiotic goo over it.'

'But it's better now ...'

'It's better. But not perfect.'

'I still want to see it.'

Again, like a kid in the schoolyard. *Show me.* Like a dare.

I glared at him. I could simply have said no. He raised his finger, cautiously pushed open my collar, and still I did nothing. He pulled downwards and stepped closer, and my hands covered my chest. The top of my scar was low down, below my cervical notch, a slight depression above my throat that had been violated by Patel's scalpel, now only a tentative incision thanks to the miracle of plastic surgery. He glimpsed the top, then he unbuttoned my smock, just two buttons, two flicks, and the scar was almost completely exposed. I watched him, his blue eyes taking it in, the line like a meridian between my breasts. He bent closer to examine it, touched it, his fingers gentle against my sternum.

'It's just a line. Like a palm line. Your lifeline.' He looked up at me. 'Does it hurt when I touch it?'

I shook my head. It used to hurt. It throbbed when I woke up and I was aware of it for weeks before they started the cosmetic surgery. Two rounds of it. One here in Cape Town, the other in New York. I wore turtlenecks in the sun for months, mortified someone would see, and now here he was examining it, and my shame and my attraction were overwhelming. He regarded it as it was, with curiosity, almost affection. Not in the clinical way Dr Patel examined it, or the way Jack glanced at it from time to time despite himself, before quickly looking away. Ben looked at it with something like compassion.

I wanted to button up again but I couldn't, didn't, and we stood for a moment like two dancers awaiting the orchestra.

What he did next was unexpected.

He leant down, held my hips, and tasted the scar. It was such an intimate and startling moment that I held my breath so he wouldn't stop. I permitted him to pull my shirt apart so he could taste the entirety of the scar, and he did this on his knees, burying his head into my stomach and forcing the shirt off my shoulders. I half pulled him toward me, then pushed him, testing his body, and when he stood up again and yanked my shirt off my arms I was gripping his chest, looking at him as he grimaced and pushed me against the hard workbench and I realised I didn't want to be undressed in that room with all the dust, but I also didn't care. Half groaning, I found myself looking around the room, pulling him into the bedroom that wasn't even a bedroom, just a room with broken blinds and surf gear and sheets in a ball on a mattress on the floor. I felt stronger than I had in months when I pushed him down.

He smelt like dust and salt and work. He playfully, lazily, yanked off my cargo pants (I was already barefoot). I felt impatient but he kept grinning at me, which irritated me so I pounded him hard in the chest, hard enough to bruise him.

'Hurry, Ben.'

He didn't hurry. He touched the places where I hit him and laughed, snaked out of his shirt and trousers, or whatever they were – cotton pantaloons worn by a castaway on a pirate ship, frayed, unwashed, rolled at the cuffs. He lay on top of me and I pulled him into me and looked out the window and it was agony not to see his eyes. My heart pounding, I silently begged it to hold together for just a while before it spilt in two.

Later, dressing in the miniscule bathroom and looking at my dishevelled face in the water-dappled mirror, I knew that while I did not feel guilt then, I would feel it later, when I was away from this hot room and the smell of him and the desire to stay the night comingled with the need to go back to my own place and wash him off me and pretend this had not happened. Although every cell in my body knew that it had happened and wanted it to continue happening.

I arranged myself, buttoned my work smock, and went to the kitchen where he was standing shirtless by the sink, drinking a glass of water.

'You're going?'

'I need to get back. I have to go to UCT tomorrow.'

'You can stay.' But he didn't insist. He might have known already that if he'd asked me to stay, I would.

He picked up a pack of cigarettes from the raw-wood counter. Benson & Hedges. He shook one out, took up a box of wooden matches, stuck the cigarette in his mouth and lit it, sucked, blew the smoke into a lazy arc above us, where it settled into the furious night.

He offered it to me.

I inhaled the smells of late-night parties I'd been to, the taste of thwarted death, of faulty aortic canals being something that others worried about. The nicotine joyfully tainted my blood. It flooded my lungs, curled into the chambers of my heart like an affable ghost. I was invincible.

Bull (Zambezi) Shark

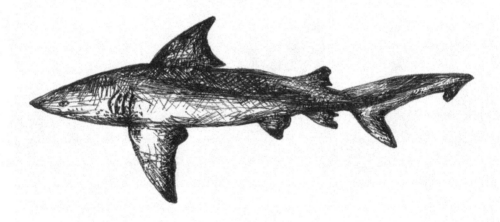

The bull shark is known as the Zambezi shark throughout Africa. It has a bold silhouette with a flat snout. The females are larger than the males. It is the only shark in the world that can thrive in both saltwater and freshwater and often travels far up rivers seeking prey.

Charcoal Drawing from Stella Wright's Private Collection (Later Works), New York

Cocooned in the Land Rover, I drove home along the warehouse district's main road imagining that the people on the street – people walking home in the new darkness from clubs and bars, druggies, street people – were aware of what I'd been doing. I motored past Sea Point and along the giant, dark ocean, past apartment blocks that slowly grew more modern, more forbidding, more orderly, more expensive. Past people with hearts that were just fine, hearts that could withstand drinking and smoking and the rich beach food served in cafés and restaurants that glowed warmly in the sand. Today I was part of it for the first time perhaps in years, part of the crush of living people on Camps Bay, part of the roaring sea that rolled in endlessly.

    I shut off the air conditioning and buzzed down the window, felt the night breeze on my face. The cool sea air filled the car, blew my hair crazily (as if it mattered now). I was driving barefoot. I promised myself many things. I promised I would not see him again. I was a married woman, a person of small celebrity, a university lecturer. I then promised myself I *would* see him again, despite the warning signs. I ignored the deft way he had let me go, barely saying goodbye (I liked this, in fact). I ignored the fact that he was far too young for me, his youth uncovered all the more when he was naked and in his careless, brutal way with me. I, who was older and weaker and much smaller and who had not had a lover like him since I was his age and even then I went for men who were not as athletic, not as strong. I had, long ago, been attracted to artistic, rebellious types, not the kind of guys who drove rusty cars with surfboards tied with clothesline on top.

    And when I thought of that apartment – that disgrace of a place that would take days to clean – where he was probably lying in bed not thinking of me, I thought of the honest grime of The WorkHead. I had slept there and created art there and possibly would have been there still if life hadn't taken the turn it did. Being in Ben's living space felt *familiar*. It was like stepping back in time. How many years ago? I was thirty-five years old. How old was Ben while I was saving to buy my first paints for art school? Primary school?

I was suddenly seized by a deep, homesick longing for cheap food and late nights and the freedom to do whatever I wanted, the rest of my life open like an endless blank canvas of possibility. It occurred to me that I would never meet another man like Ben. Yes, I knew there were men like him … I just wouldn't know them. They had been forsaken. I sighed, poked into the ashtray, teased out my newly finished cigarette butt, stabbed it into the leather seat beside me. A dark tar scar. My symbol of defiance.

I ignored the fact that I wanted to drink more. I ignored the fact that I wanted more of his cigarettes, and then ignored the fact that I was once again glancing at my phone hoping I had a message from him, or missed a call. Hoping he'd call now and ask me to come back and I'd tell him if he wanted to see me again he had to come to *my* house, although if he refused I would maneuver my way back into the city and leave this car in front of his studio and if it was stolen I wouldn't care.

Most of all I made excuses. I told myself this was the only time. I told myself there was no way Jack would find out and this had nothing to do with him anyway, was actually none of his business, even though it was. I knew I shouldn't be waiting for Ben. I knew I shouldn't be hoping he would be so consumed with the embers of our lust that he'd drive over the mountain in that tin can of a car and bang on my door. (To this end I considered leaving the door open, taking my chances with whomever might walk in from the silent streets.)

I returned back to my home. My adult home. And when I walked into the main room, my studio comfortably right there, the clean lights glowing, the perfect lines of wine glasses hanging under the cupboard, I felt myself relax. I'd arrived back from a life I'd had when I was a bohemian (is that word even used anymore?), when men like Ben Hume were not an exotic species.

But still, as I stood in my cool-lit kitchen – beachside perfection – a memory surged of another late evening, standing in The WorkHead in front of a canvas, my fifth attempt at a painting that had challenged and taunted me for weeks. This was another kind of sea, not recognisable unless you saw you could reach out and feel it, feel the oceanic realness of it, the memory of not looking at the water but being in it, a furious cacophony of blue and black and grey that bore no resemblance to the things I was painting now. The blue sea in the gathering night A dark sky above, the strokes there ragged and unworldly, as if they'd been put down by someone else, the paint pushed into the cloth, forced into something that snarled from the surface of the painting itself. Demetrius standing next to me, squinting at it, looking again. Finally he would shake his head, take my hand in his, and we would stand there, cold evening light filtering through the windows, and then he would hug me. Tears glinting in his eyes.

'Damn it. I don't know. This is you. Me. This.' He didn't look at me, but brought my fingers to his mouth, kissed them in admiration, let go. 'What's it called?'

'*Blue, Blue Sea*.'

'This. This is *something*, Cat.'

I smiled in victory. I looked at him and he was gazing at me with the look of a fellow climber in a storm, witnessing the other summit from an impossible distance. I was famished but we had nothing of substance in the sighing fridge. We celebrated by eating Ritz crackers and drinking our last beers before my drying work. Standing there passing the box until they were finished. The most delicious food I have ever eaten.

I now stood at the sink in my perfect Cape Town kitchen with its stocked cupboards and (relatively) full refrigerator and drank three bottles of water. I searched for the Advil in the cupboard, swallowed two, poured myself a glass of wine. I helped myself to a cellophane-wrapped chicken sandwich. I turned on all the outside lights and stood in the wind, a ravenous wine-drinking animal.

At the pool I noticed a network of tiny cracks spread out against the slate brickwork. Small fissures followed the wavy basin all the way around – some deeper than others, some bearing what looked like calcite – and made the pool reptilian. The pool deck, faux and real rock, might need rebuilding. The point's hard sandstone, the dolomite, might not be enough to hold it fast. From one perspective, the pool looked as if it might break off at the point, float away, leave a sheared face in front of the house. I had lived here for two years and not noticed how precarious this was.

Knocking.

I woke in a haze. My body ached. Even my toes were sore. I sat up in bed, listened, stood, stretched. The knocking had stopped. I wrapped a robe around myself and made my way down into the kitchen, feeling as if I might pull a muscle at any moment. I turned to face the ocean in the morning's streaming light and stifled a scream.

There, behind the misted windows, standing wrapped in a long coat and tapping gently on the window, was an apparition of a man. The homeless people of Victoria Road occasionally ventured down here. They rang the bells and asked for old clothes and food or cash, but none of them had ever actually knocked on the sliding doors. I shooed him away, like some errant seabird pecking upon the glass.

But it was not a seabird. It was *him*. Wearing a shapeless coat and boots, cut-off shorts, a T-shirt that looked as if he'd found it on the street. His hair a mess. I slid open the door, and it caught on the salted runners. I didn't slide it all the way, just enough to look out at this bedraggled human. He waved weakly.

'Ben, it's six o'clock in the morning. What are you doing here? Don't tell me you drove here in that state. Do *not* tell me that.'

'Not a big deal. I wanted to see you.'

'What have you been doing?'

'Thinking. I worked most of the night and thought about stuff. Decided to come over.'

'That was stupid.' But I stood back from the door.

Inside, being near him made me want him, despite my anger, despite what he looked like. He smelt of the city and his apartment and himself. He probably, in fact, also smelt of me. He stood in the doorway and his eyes adjusted.

'You look like you need a shower.'

'Ja, well, you know. We're all doing our bit to conserve water.' He stood at the counter, was actively avoiding the light.

'I think you need to go back home and get some sleep. You can't just arrive here with no warning, Ben. I'm not always alone. Do you understand? If anyone else saw you ...' I couldn't actually come out and say the words *my husband*. And seeing Ben here after what we'd done the night before seemed incongruent. Especially given his condition.

He slipped off the ruined coat and focused on me. 'Listen,' he said. 'I don't mean to barge in here or anything ...'

'You have already.'

'Okay, and I can go whenever you want. But I just need to ask if you have any more of those tablets.'

'You're here for *painkillers*? I thought you wanted to see me?'

He shrugged. 'I do. But I'm also in, like, pain.'

'I can give you Advil. But what did you do with the other pills? You haven't taken all of them already? Those are serious opioids.'

He shrugged again.

'Ben. I need you to do something for me.'

'Oh, yes? What's that?' He flashed me that raffish grin and winced. Maybe he really was in pain. And he wanted me, despite the pain and yes, it was flattering. I was dismayed with myself.

'I need you to really understand something, okay? We need to be careful.'

'It's not as if I'm *telling* anyone. I know you're married to some guy.'

Some guy. 'Yes. I'm married. So you can't just show up here and give me the fright of the century.'

'Okay, I'm sorry. You said he wasn't here. I just thought ...' Petulant.

'Just warn me when you're stopping by. Call. Send me a message.'

'So, yeah, my phone ...' He shrugged yet again. Whatever that meant. The phone could have run out of batteries, airtime, or been lost, stolen or sold – it was all possible.

'Look, Ben, I'm sorry about last night. It was wrong of me to come to your house. It shouldn't have happened.'

'Whatever, man. *You* were the one who came to me. I didn't force you to do anything.'

'I know. That's what I'm trying to say. I ...' I was feeling that awful reminder that we were a man and a woman, alone in a room that had a couch. And a floor.

'I'm the one standing here with a thump from a shark to my side, trying to sleep and live my life like a normal person. And I miss you. I didn't want you to leave last night.'

I was reminded of a piece of advice I'd been given about a pride of lions Jack and I saw in a private game reserve up north. We'd flown in that afternoon in a small plane. We'd drunk wine at a fire in the evening and when we stood up to go to bed we realised there were two female lions not ten yards from us, just outside the perimeter of firelight, near the four-by-four that had brought us there. The guide had unshouldered his rifle. The lions, in the darkness, regarded us impassively. And the guide said, casually, *Just stand your ground and don't show your fear, don't move.* We'd stood very still and the lions had peered at us, at the camp, at the guide, and then simply slipped into the grass to attend to the predatory business of the night. And this had felt incredibly natural. I'd been both terrified and exhilarated and I had waited all night for them to come back while Jack snored beside me. But they did not.

With Ben so close to me I looked up at him challengingly. He was upset. He hadn't taken our experience as much in his stride as I'd assumed.

Looking at him, I saw myself. A glimpse into what had been left by the lions, the shark. We were two survivors, nothing less. He reached out, ran his fingers through my hair, kissed me, made a fist of my hair.

'Do you like that?'

But I did not hear a question. I heard a statement.

I like this.

'Please don't just drop by here unannounced again,' I told him later.

Silence.

'Did you hear me?'

'Yeah, I heard you. You've made that very clear.'

'And you look like something the cat dragged in.'

He shrugged on the coat, clumped over to my kitchen, pulled open the stainless-steel door to the fridge.

'Are you living off water and yogurt and salad? Tell me you have bread, at least.'

He discovered a leftover pita, shoved it in his mouth. It was like watching an animal feeding itself. He snatched up one of my bottled waters, consumed it, tossed the bottle on the counter, reached back into the fridge and extracted a bottle of Chardonnay from the interior rack.

'Not so fast.'

He looked at the clock. There were crumbs on his chest. I picked them off.

'Do I need to go?' he said, pushing my fingers away.

I nodded. 'My gardener is probably coming soon. When do you need to be back?'

'Never.'

'Good.'

He kissed me, departed through the sliding doors, skirted the pool, disappeared down the path beside my home. A fallen god.

What could I do in the sudden absence of him?

The pool required constant attention and keeping it going during a drought, I had learnt, was not easy as the pool level kept dropping. Keeping it clean was a constant chore. It was invariably filled with dirt and things that had blown across the rocks: dried moss, dead plants, leaves, sand and other leavings of the sea.

I had made the pool my responsibility, my contribution. I wanted to keep things functioning, though it felt these days like a losing battle; that no matter what I did, Jack would sell it, and the new owner would probably modernise the pool. Or get rid of it, fill it in with concrete, cover it with shale or granite in observance of the drought.

'We can get a service, Stella. Some crew will come by every other day,' Jack had said irritably, as he watched me test the pH. 'They can deal with the chemicals and ... that sucking thing that goes along the bottom.'

'That sucking thing is called a Kreepy Krauly, and it's a proudly South African invention.'

'If somebody sees you working on the pool, I have no idea what they'll think.'

'They'll think that I'm the kind of person who looks after her own pool.'

He shrugged. 'Let it not be said I *wanted* you to be my hot cabana girl. Although now that I think about it ...'

My personal project, the pool required creativity. I'd become proficient at water harvesting. I filled it using water collected around the house, water from the spring, water from the roof that flowed in plastic tubes attached to the downpipes. I'd even managed to get Jack to collect his shower water in buckets. I was an expert on pool maintenance in dry weather.

Now, I changed leaf-catcher bags and tinkered with the chemicals. I checked the pool's temperature, cleaned the filter. A clean pool gave me a sense of satisfaction – I was a woman who could identify when the salinator needed flushing, and how, and when. All because I was trying to let go of a house I loved, leave something behind that was mine.

I carried my plastic pool kit of chemicals to the small outbuilding nestled against my house, where the pool pump whirred and grumbled. I slid open the door to return the box among the neatly ordered garden implements in the sauna-like heat, and as I lifted my arm, something moved and then glistened in the dim light. The way it moved was somehow eerily familiar and I froze. My face was perhaps only two feet away from a rinkhals, a spitting cobra, extremely venomous. It arched almost lazily, scrutinised me with surprised curiosity. I held my breath as it reared backwards and then was still. The pool kit was still heavy in my hand, and I told myself not to move, but the wind blew my hair and the snake's black tongue flickered. I tried not to breathe. I could see the dull sheen of its scales and the jagged white stripe around its hood. I was so close. Another gust of wind and this snake would strike my face or spit burning venom into my eyes, or both.

There was a whistling sound by my ear. The snake moved, but not fast enough – the blade of a shovel caught under its head and slammed it into the side of the shed. Mandla's shoulder pushed me roughly to the stones as he slashed the writhing snake into the wood, and then its body was limply sliding to the ground next to my scattered pool kit, blood exploded all over the shovel. Mandla set it down with a clang, reached out and pulled me to my feet.

'You must be careful, Miss Stella.' He found the episode amusing. 'When I see these snakes I just sweep them. Sweep them over.'

I stammered an apology, but I felt like throwing up.

'This was a small one,' he said, prodding at the oozing body. He rummaged into the shed, palmed something – the snake's head – and cast it far out into the water, for the birds.

A snake head, thrown into the sea. The fangs intact. I took a breath, felt the tears spring to my eyes. *Those fangs in my face.*

'Thank you, Mandla. I don't know what to say. Thank you.' And not for the first time I marvelled at him. The speed with which he had killed the snake, his fearlessness. 'How did you know it was there?'

He looked at me quizzically.

'Did you see it?'

He smiled, pointed to his eyes, then pointed to mine. 'I did not see it. No, I see *you* standing like this.' He stood stock still, frozen, eyes wide. 'I think, now, something is wrong.' He waved at the rocks. 'It is cold here. This snake likes to be on the big stones in the sun, then he sleeps in the warm pool room. Maybe I have seen him before.'

Were there more? Snakes between the stones, in the pool room, under the house? There might have been. They could have been living off insects, small birds and tiny rodents, the teeming life we don't think of when we imagine a beach.

When I reached out to him, an awkward gesture of thanks, he clasped my hand, almost crushing it. We shook formally, as if sealing a deal around the extension of my life. I let go of his hand and hugged him, his body hard and wiry and firm. His hands remained at his sides, and he laughed. *My serpent heart.*

'Thank you, Mandla. You saved my life.'

Hu shrugged. 'This snake? His life is not saved.' He took up the shovel, the snake's body obscenely twisted on the tip of the blade, and walked it back to the garage.

The phone chirped just as I was finishing tidying up the spilt pool kit, still trying to stop shaking. Mandla had cleared out the pool shed – removed the old bottles and plastic jugs that might provide hiding spaces for another deadly snake.

I knew the message was from Ben. I ignored it. I let the phone sit on the chair outside while I fussed with the pool, made lunch, cleared it away again. Until Mandla had gone. Hours later, when I stepped inside the house and pressed a switch, the pool obediently lit up, a cold blue beacon against the night. I took out a bottle of wine, a glass, set my chair far away from the pool pump room. I drank a full glass. Only then did I relent and swipe the phone.

> hey

I hated that. Pressed:

> ?

He immediately answered. As if the phone had been in his hands this entire time.

> what u doing?
> Why don't you just call me and find out?
> wd rather text
> Why????
> no airtime. no batts. who calls ppl?
> OK ...
> how you doing? have you swum lately?

I waited. How did he do this?

> No. Not even in the pool.
> Same
> I found a snake in the pool shed today. Cobra.
> !!!!! GTFO
> The gardener killed it. Took it away.
> hectic! hectic! swim in ocean! no snakes
> Have you swum ... in the ocean?
> we shd talk. maybe I'm not all good with mano
> I'm afraid of the ocean. For the first time in my life.

Pause.

want to see you again
Where?
yr place?
Yes.
now OK?
Now perfect.

Blue Shark

The blue shark inhabits deep water in both temperate and tropical oceans. They are named for the deep-indigo colouring on their backs and vibrant blue shades on the sides of their bodies.

Females are literally thick-skinned to cope with the tendency of the males to bite during mating.

Ballpoint Drawing from Stella Wright's Private Collection, New York

It was almost fully dark when he appeared, almost exactly an hour and a half later. I'd been watching the clock in the kitchen, thinking perhaps he wouldn't come, counting the slow progress of minutes between sips of wine, nervous glances at my phone. He brought along a bag, a towel. He was wearing loose cargo pants and a heavy cotton chemise that hung off him. It looked like something he'd sewn himself, like something out of medieval times. A peasant's shirt. He kicked off his flip-flops and we walked out to the edge of the water. He tested it with his toe.

'I went out to Kommetjie. On a fairly small day. Just wanted to paddle out on my old shortboard.'

'The weather must have been perfect.'

'Yeah, but I just sat there on the beach. You know? Just sat there looking at the birds and the waves coming in. These little kids were doing barrel rolls on body boards. I'm watching them like some sad old man; I didn't even get my feet wet.'

'Maybe you should speak to someone?'

'I'm speaking to you.'

'Someone who's not me.'

'My whole life I've been in the ocean. Almost every day. I've seen tons of sharks. Big ones. Little ones. Loners. In groups. I've never even thought about it.' He rolled up the shirt. Still that cruel bruise down his side. He dropped the shirt back into place. 'I'm not ready to just give up surfing. Even if I go to Australia or something, there are sharks out there, everywhere.'

'I was hoping I would also stop feeling this way. You know, in time.'

'You saw it. It wasn't about being bitten. It was about it being in the water, that close, checking us out. They don't usually do that. That shark, man, he was *right there*. Just *watching* us.'

'You need to get back in the water – it's that simple. The chances of being, you know ...'

'Attacked.'

'Why don't you call one of your surfing friends, paddle out. During the day. Go to one of those easy spots, like Muizenberg.'

'They're there, too.'

'You need to start somewhere.'

'*You* were with me. *You* were the only one. *You* need to go in with me. I need *you* to want to do it. Because in my opinion you need to do this even more. All your work, it's about the sea. And now, you can't even get into a plunge pool. How much are you going to want to paint the ocean now?'

'I might start painting my pool. Like David Hockney.'

'What kind of artist only paints *swimming pools*? Your paintings – you can tell how you feel about the sea. You need to do this with me.'

'Do what?'

'Get in the water. Right here. Now. Just get in.' He pulled off his shirt and stood in the cooling wind from the ocean.

'I need to go in and change. And we do this for two minutes only. I don't want to catch pneumonia.'

I admit there was something I liked about having him here. And he was right. I was surrounded by water, and I feared it. I looked at him waiting poised on the rocks as if he was made of the same substance. In his element.

'I can't.'

'You can. I'm asking you. Just go change.'

'You don't understand.'

'Two minutes. That's it.' He held out his hand. 'We'll do it together. I swear. Come on ...'

I shook my head.

He shrugged, turned, dove effortlessly into the water, like a seal, disappeared under the surface. I waited, holding my breath. *Please come back.*

He surfaced ten yards away, facing away from me, an exhaling figure in the water. He went out deeper, the same route the shark had followed. He swam effortlessly in and out of the waves. His splashing would have carried subsonic vibrations for miles. It wasn't until he was almost at the far away rock that he turned, swam directly back, slipped under the surface and then hauled himself easily out of the water. He squatted, looked back at the sea with satisfaction, then came over to me, dripping wet, the cold rising off him.

'How did it feel?'

'Doesn't matter how it felt.'

'You know it does.'

He took my hand, pulled me gently, then firmly, toward the water. Right to the edge of the point.

'I'll come with you. If we do it together, we win.'

I stepped back, and he tried to yank me toward him.

'I don't want to do this, Ben. I'm just not ready.'

'I'll make you a deal.' He knelt by the water and pulled me gently to his level, close enough so the raw, salty smell of the ocean met my nostrils. Salt and kelp and something else, a living brine. The ocean was inky black, the reflection of the house tenuous in the gentle undulations of the sea. He took his hand, held it over the water, palm down. 'See? Just do this.'

I held out my hand, realised I was holding my breath. He took my wrist and gently began to lower it to the surface of the water.

'Just touch it with your palm.'

I bit my lip. He kept lowering my palm toward the water and I mashed my lips together, pressed myself against him. With my hand an inch above the surface I could feel coolness, the icy comfort. I closed my eyes. I imagined the shark, alerted to our presence, silently rising from the depths, mouth agape, pumping upwards. Ben gently pushed downwards and my palm kissed the water. We stayed there for perhaps a minute, maybe more, until I began to shiver.

He let go of my wrist and grinned in the darkness. 'That wasn't so bad?'

'That was *terrible*.'

'It's a start.'

'I only touched the water and I nearly died from fright.'

'I'll stay with you until you can jump in.'

'Why?'

'Because when you can do it, I can do it without ... feeling what I just felt swimming out there. Because that used to be easy, and now it isn't.'

'I'm not going to be able to jump in, no matter how long you stay with me. I'm just telling you.'

'You might. You could.'

'I won't. But stay anyway.'

Demetrius and I continued to share The WorkHead after Lance left to *gig around California*. We could barely afford it but neither of us could go back to our families and ask for money. My parents wouldn't give it even though they could; they wanted me home. And Demetrius had only a mother in Cleveland who was unable to help. By the end of that winter, eight months after I'd moved in, the large workrooms were cold and we couldn't heat them properly. There were only patches of warmth in the room. I painted wearing a ski hat and the warmest jacket I could find; he worked standing over one of his huge abstractions in a sweater so spattered with paint it was encrusted. We pooled money for food. Many nights we ate only packaged noodles. We had two couches in front of a TV that didn't work, and we stayed up at night planning new paintings, wondering if we could find a gallery out of state. Three gallery owners came to see our work, all of them were encouraging. *But this is a town where they encourage you to death, Cat.* We earned nothing.

A friend from Yale came to visit. The studio was covered with art, so much we hadn't sold. I was working on landscapes, figures, but also from pictures of seascapes. I'd started my first sculptures. I introduced my friend to Demetrius, who was again strangely formal in his greeting, showed her one of his canvases, then went back to work while we walked toward Washington Square Park to the nicest coffee shop I knew. We sat in the warmth and ate cookies; the cost was astronomical. My friend was getting married. I privately thought we were too young. She and her *fiancé*, I was told, were renting on the East Side, upper Midtown. The husband-to-be *supported her work*. He'd *always been supportive*. They were going to figure out a place where she could paint, although the apartment was too small for a real studio. Nothing like The WorkHead. She thought they might take out a shared art space. There was a place in Midtown on Broadway where you got your own key, and an even cheaper place in Brooklyn. This was what she was thinking of doing. She had a new mobile phone and a perfect manicure and needed to go because she was meeting the fiancé for dinner near their apartment. She wanted me to come for drinks sometime and meet him. She admired what I was doing. It was inspiring to her. My production was *off the charts*. And The WorkHead was *so cool*.

It was indeed. It was literally freezing.

She said she would call but she didn't.

I went back to The WorkHead and threw my jacket onto the hanging rack near my futon and sat in my only chair and cried. Demetrius studiously ignored me. I could hear him out there, the boards creaking under his boots while he circled his painting. He was *producing*. He was *in the flow*. I would have really liked to go out to dinner just once, and not face another night of whatever we could scrounge up.

Demetrius saved the day, as usual. When I finally came out to our dingy kitchen, he had set the table and ordered up a vegetarian dinner from the Mongolian restaurant we couldn't afford. They delivered everything to the door in a white plastic bag.

'What we need, Cat, isn't a *job*. What we need is *money*.'

Demetrius and I spoke about it all night, finishing two already opened bottles of wine. There was work, but it had to be work that still let me paint in The WorkHead. That wasn't selling out. It was a brief compromise. A truce with reality. Demetrius would use his savings to keep the place. We'd paint in the afternoons and evenings. If we found a new tenant, that would be extra income, but the tenant had to be a *real* artist, had to be cool and in sync with our common goal, which was *devoting everything to lifting off*. It wasn't *supposed* to be a normal life, we reasoned. The WorkHead was like a rocket ship. We were astronauts, working furiously inside, burning all of our creative energy to get maximum lift, to get our careers off the ground. We were months away from breaking through. Somebody was going to buy our stuff. It was a matter of time. Then we'd go out to dinner. Feast. Just watch us.

I began the hunt for work. It was all just a temporary solution. Soon our art would pay for this life we had chosen. Success meant holding on for just a little while longer. I had never had such belief in myself, my art, another person.

I did it, finally. Ten days after the encounter, I emailed Jack and asked when we could talk on the iPad. I considered writing to him but every time I'd sat down to send him an email it had seemed absurd.

> Dear Jack
>
> A few days ago I went swimming as usual and a huge shark tracked me to the shore. I thought it was going to eat me. It was really a tremendous shark. You have no idea how huge a shark is until you are beside it in the water or you see its dorsal fin cut the surface of the water in front of you, knowing you're just another swimming thing that probably looks like food.
>
> I did not die, however. Hence I can write you!

Oh, and I was with a man who also wanted to get away from the shark. I hugged him afterwards. I was very scared but now I am slightly less scared. And I really do not want to go into the water again.

S xxx

I deleted this. Obviously.

I called him one afternoon when I knew he'd be getting ready to go to the office, and I found myself gripping the phone. I didn't FaceTime him. I didn't want our wonky coastal Wi-Fi to cut off my voice, and I didn't want to see his face when he heard what had happened to me. I'd put this off long enough. I didn't believe in keeping secrets from Jack, and now I had two: the shark, and Ben.

I had started to read fairly deeply about trauma. I'd spoken to Patel and I'd found a website with a kindly looking woman sitting at a desk going over shared slides about trauma; I had a right to the support of those closest to me, they had an obligation to support me. But the advice was maddeningly ambiguous. It went like this: 'Talking with family and friends *may be* good. Support and understanding at a difficult time *can be* very helpful. You don't have to face it alone.' Jack was not supposed to take my irritability to heart and should encourage me to 'practice self-care'.

I called his mobile phone and he picked up almost immediately with a puzzled 'Hello?' I imagined him standing in our kitchen, pouring coffee, the city spread out in front of him, our view of the Hudson. 'What's wrong, Stells? Everything okay?'

'I wanted to tell you something. But I don't want you to get upset or tell me what to do. I'm ... I'm handling it.' I thought of myself trying to handle an unwieldy shark.

'What's going on, Stella? What's happened?'

I told him in one long, very convoluted sentence. *I was swimming ...*

didn't see it at first ... then it came and circled ... then it was beside me in a wave right next to me and I saw its eye, it was looking right at me ... then it was gone ... I made it to the beach ... I thought I was going to die ... I'm fine ... I'm good ... it was terrifying ... but it's all good. Why did this feel like an admission? Why did it feel like I was revealing something embarrassing about myself?

Jack didn't say anything for a bit. I was out of breath and I had to sit down. My heart burned in my chest. Having made my admission, I wanted simply to hang up. Or get a line of priestly penance: *Atone for yourself by packing up an entire house alone and forfeiting sleep.*

'Are you sure you're okay?' he ventured.

'I'm fine. I really am.'

He waited. 'So the shark just ... swam away? It didn't ...'

'No. It didn't try to bite me. But ... I really thought it was going to.'

'That sounds – I don't know – surreal?'

I wanted to tell him I was still thinking about the shark. Having nightmares. I wanted to tell him that I'd dropped the diamond grinder in front of my class. I wanted to tell him about my erratic heart, my newfound fear of the sea. The snake.

'Okay, well, I'm coming back soon. You're lucky, you know? How many people can say they've had an experience like this? You obviously kept your cool, right? You just swam to the beach. I sometimes tell people here what it's like down there in Cape Town and I don't think they believe me.'

'Jack, please don't tell anyone about this. Okay?'

I could almost see him smiling. 'You have to admit, Stells, it's a great story. How many people have swum with a great white shark right in front of their home? Definitely don't tell the real estate agent, though ... Listen, you need anything? You want me to fly back now?'

Yes, please. I wanted him in the house ... and I wanted the house to myself.

'I'll come back now for you, Stella. I will. Just tell me.'

'I know. It isn't necessary.'

He waited. 'I'm glad you weren't hurt. And there are fewer great whites here in the good old US of A.'

I made a sound like laughing. 'That's true.'

'Stells?'

'Yes?'

'You're ... not afraid of the ocean now? Of going swimming? The chances of that ever happening again are ...'

'I'm not. I'm really not.' *I am.*

'So much of your art is about the ocean.'

'Jack, I have to hang up.'

'If you change your mind and you want me back earlier, I can arrange it.'

'I don't.' *I do.*

'Love you, Stells. See you in a week. Maybe less. I'll email the date.'

I hung up, gasping like a woman underwater.

Blue, Blue Sea did not sell.

I was naïve. I knew nothing about self-promotion. The art world was changing, major components were shifting online. Instagram was stealing artists from agents and galleries. Artists could sell direct to buyers. It all seemed very easy: get a phone, set up an Instagram account and you were in business. I read up about it, downloaded the app, told Demetrius about it.

'You think people will buy your paintings because they see pictures of them on their *phone*?'

'Yes. Some artists have thousands of followers.'

'How many "followers" do you have, Cat?'

'A few dozen,' I admitted. 'Just friends. It can take years to grow a following.'

Demetrius was skeptical of the profile picture I'd taken: me in work clothes, gazing challengingly at the camera, trying to look unimpressed and not hopeful. Pressed for time. He was right: I didn't understand the intricacies, had been impatient. In the meantime, I felt encouraged to keep creating. Other artists were doing it. But the blue painting on social media looked dark, like something from outer space, a nebula rather than an ocean.

I would ultimately find Mario's site and his Instagram postings and the arrangements he made for showings. And I now have a list of collectors in Europe and the USA who wait for my agent's uploads. But back then we were all still making this happen.

I made every mistake possible: I filled the screen with the painting, took it in pale morning light, didn't create an atmosphere. I didn't show The WorkHead, Demetrius painting in his dark jacket, examining the canvas in front of him. Bald, wearing a longshoreman's cap, working with paint and spray paints and silkscreens. I didn't post pictures of myself or atmospheric shots of the West Village and SoHo or close-ups of my brushes and brushwork. I didn't use hashtags, I didn't link to local art. I uploaded just a few paintings and my profile to drum up interest that did not come. I got a few follows, a few desultory comments from people I knew, some of whom thought this was pure vanity, I'm sure. I was just another woman in a loft in New York posting pictures of her paintings.

I posted and prayed.

Demetrius looked at the Instagram page and shook his head. 'You came out here to be an *artist*. Artists sell to people who come to stand in a damn gallery and see their work. Nobody buys paintings of pictures from somebody they can't *see*. Off a *phone*.'

I showed him articles I'd read but he waved them away. 'Get your name out there for *real*, Cat. You didn't go to *Yale* to run an *online grift*.'

He was wrong, but he was also right. I needed a showing if I was going to be legitimate. The sad dark photo on my half-finished Instagram page wasn't going to do it. It looked amateurish because it was. I painted. I snapped pictures and painted some more. I didn't frame them correctly, or show them hung in living spaces, or create a world around them, or photograph them at different angles, all things advised on the Internet. I didn't *grow my following*. A few men sent me lecherous messages.

But after a few weeks, someone liked my work. And they hashtagged it.

I doubted anything would come of it.

One evening I dug up Demetrius's email address. I sat in front of my phone and plucked up the courage to write him and say I was in Cape Town. I told him I was married. I told him I was painting. I told him I was selling. My paintings now were nothing like the ones I'd worked on with him, I added. I walked around the house with a wine glass in one hand and the phone in the other, and snapped pictures of my recent paintings to attach to the email.

Then I decided I would paint one for him. I'd capture the Atlantic, send him a photo of it, and he would know I was the same authentic artist he'd worked with and lived with and almost starved with.

Because I had the gnawing feeling that he wouldn't approve of me.

Late-Night Notes for Painting a Sea You Cannot See
Brushes: Medium brush, blending brush, small brush
Acrylics: Titanium White, Cerulean Blue, Ultramarine Blue, Phthalo Green, Cadmium Red, Raw Sienna, Yellow Ochre
Also: Palette knife, jars of water, bright light, coffee, rags, photographs of sea
Begin by spreading ultramarine two thirds of the way across the canvas, with raw sienna blended in one-third of the way up for the shore. Layer in cerulean blue neatly for the sky you also cannot see. Blend. Blend. Mix raw sienna and ultramarine blue to phthalo green. This becomes the horizon. Brush across these, mixing paint as you go, all the way to the sienna shoreline as water shallows, then add small amounts of titanium white, allowing sea to become more green – this creates lines of shallowing water. It looks messy

but keep blending in the paint until it reaches the shore. Do not think of the depth of the water or the reflection on the water or what is in the water. Then use the raw sienna and ultramarine to create a stretch of sand that can carry over the bottom edge of the canvas.

Adding cerulean blue to the top of the canvas creates more sky. Titanium white creates distance.

Smoke a cigarette. If it is very late, stretch, do a yoga pose while the paint dries.

Sip wine. Consider the sky.

Make a new horizon line with carefully mixed phthalo green and ultramarine blue and yellow ochre. Use masking tape if your hands are shaking – you need a straight line. Remove the harshness of the colours.

Phthalo green creates a lovely line right across the canvas. Add a wave and more depth where a shark could be hidden in the dark green water. The foam is simply titanium white blended back and forth. Keep adding depth to bring out the form of the wave. This is a series of wavy lines. Brush in more and more white as you approach the beach. This is very easy but it can take hours, and you can also hold your own hand still if you cannot blend properly. The shore is light but not white, and is full of patches of depth.

Wash brushes.

Cry and light another cigarette. If you feel you cannot paint anymore, you're wrong. If it is now dawn, look out the window and see the dark sea.

Here you add a tiny amount of red to the horizon line, but such a tiny amount that the viewer doesn't notice you have put it there. *You* know it's there but the viewer does *not*. Horizon is also whitish, blended grey. You paint that as well and the ocean's horizon becomes far more distant, and suggests an Antarctic Cape ocean rather than a tropical sea (Florida, Turks and Caicos). Ultramarine blue, green, ochre ... go over this a few times.

If natural light floods the room, that's okay. Your waves should be mostly phthalo green but use titanium white to make them hollow – don't be tempted to use ultramarine.

Stop thinking about the depth under the waves. Think about the see-through water as the waves approach the Cape shore.

Resist the urge to fleck the painting with cadmium red. Resist the urge to smear it across the surf. Do not under any circumstances deposit pools of red in the middle of the painting. Do not think about sponging red across the clean blue lines. Wipe the paint from your fingers. Stop thinking about your dreams of blood in the water.

Hide the cadmium red in the garage bathroom. Under stacks of toilet paper. Do not touch it again. Do not look at it. Also hide the primary magenta, quinacridone red and alizarin crimson. Close the bathroom door. Lock it.

The beach is done with rough strokes and then blended rough strokes. Make sure to scumble the brush along the canvas. Harsh scumbling will add white shapes to suggest rough sandstone under the water. Warning! Do not press the medium brush or the fine brush too hard to the canvas while thinking about those rocks or you will simply get smears that need to be roughed out.

Sleeping in front of the painting is okay.

Crying is okay.

Drinking wine is okay.

Spilling wine is not okay.

Cigarettes are not really okay.

The colours will come rolling in, line after line of depth, and the longer you paint these, the more you shade them together, the deeper and clearer the water becomes. If your forearm and fingers start to tire, you simply need to rest.

Your arm has done hundreds of paintings but maybe the arm is not as young as it once was.

At least you have an arm.

Consider losing an arm to a shark.

Use the palette knife to carve the horizon.

You can substitute the edge of the palette knife with a large shark tooth. Gently. Do not scar the painting as it is not a thing that should be scraped or stabbed. It is easy to do this. You can gently push the colour into the deeper part of the painting, creating bubbles and sea foam. The tooth has serrations so the effect is somewhat carnivorous.

Clean tooth.

Clean brushes again so they are not ruined.

Clean self so you are not ruined.

Admire your work. Note its incandescence. Note how you have not possessed such artistic fearlessness for a very long time. Try not to be afraid of it.

Email a picture of this painting to Demetrius.

Text your husband. Tell him good night, sleep tight. Only that.

Text Ben. Hope he will text back and prevent you from fetching the cadmium red and smearing it on the walls and across your body.

Notice that Demetrius's email has been returned as 'undeliverable'.

Sleep on couch next to empty wine glass waiting for the phone to ping. (It won't.)

Sicklefin Lemon Shark

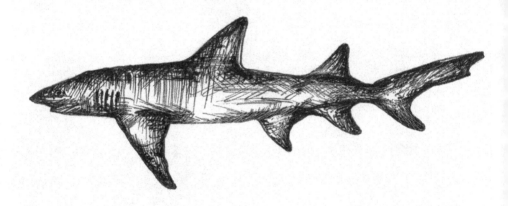

The sicklefin lemon shark ranges from South Africa to the Red Sea, including Mauritius, the Seychelles and Madagascar. Extremely territorial, it does not stray far from its home waters, and prefers bays and estuaries to the open sea.

This shark is usually shy and cannot be coaxed into human interaction, even when offered a reward.

India Ink Sketch from Artist's Private Collection, Cape Town

Days later I waited for Ben to come by the house – we hadn't settled on a time. I'd tidied up the living room and the kitchen. It was howling wind outside as usual. I was wearing a longish, heavy dress from New York. Sneakers. When the clock ticked past seven, I found myself wanting a glass of wine. I gave myself fifteen minutes to contemplate the darkening sea before deciding to open a bottle. *He probably won't come.*

Eight o'clock came and went and so did a second glass of wine.

Then the bell rang. It was so rarely used that I jumped, wondering if it was an alarm, some kind of warning before the sirens went off. I was already a little drunk ('lightly toasted', Jack would say), and when Ben rang again, I still didn't move, thinking he'd get the hint and come back the next day ... or later ... or never.

I heard rustling along the outside of the house, and then he was in front of the sliding doors, silhouetted by the pool light. Cupping his eyes, looking directly at me. He knocked, I feigned surprise, slid open the glass just enough for him to slip in, the sea air pouring in with him. Ben shook off the cold, squinted at the sterile light of my living room.

'Hey, didn't you hear me ring?'

'I was just coming.'

He had an animal vibrancy and I felt as if I'd let in something wild and predatory. He attracted all the energy in the room. Then he turned his attention to the paintings on the wall, slipped a hand into his battered jacket, and pulled out his pathetic mobile phone.

'You're a big deal. I didn't get it. You're like this huge deal in the art world.'

'Nobody is a big deal in the art world.' But he could probably see that I'd flushed, despite myself. I was a big deal to *him*. That was something.

He pointed at the scratched screen. 'I found an article about your work. Your work about the ocean.' He'd found an older piece on Artnet. A picture of me in Cape Town. He pocketed the phone, wandered around the room looking at the paintings. A sweet smell rose off him – a memory. Pot.

'I want you to show me,' he said.

'Show you what?'

'How it works. Why *this* is good.' He pointed to one of my paintings, another seascape, from just up this coast. 'I want to do this. I don't want to just fix sailboats and put down gel coat for the rest of my life.'

I could have told him that it took a lifetime of dedication to develop this sensitivity. Hundreds of hours practising your drawing technique, years in front of the easel. And, if you were lucky, the guidance of a passionate teacher in lower school and another in high school and another possibly in university. But I didn't say that.

He said, 'I'm impressed. I mean, your work is impressive, okay? My whole life, I wanted to do one thing that makes a mark, you know? And art, man. I kind of thought of it as a joke. But it's not. I mean, it's *real*. It's a *reflection*.' He approached the canvas I had hanging up at the door to the studio. 'So, what do you do first? When you start painting a thing like *this*.'

This was the lighthouse on Boca Grande.

'It depends. There's not a system, you know. It's intuitive. It depends what I'm painting, first of all.'

'Yeah?' His eyes measured me. 'Have you got back into the water yet?'

I was taken aback by the change in topic. 'No.'

'We could do it now.'

'What?'

'I told you. You have, like, the whole ocean in front of your house here. You can't keep painting it if you can't *swim* in it. It would be like painting from prison.'

'It's cold out there. Not to mention dark.'

'Oh, come on. Like you really care. I say we jump in and jump out.'

If I don't do it soon, I never will. I looked out into the dark, saw only myself looking back under the sanitary lights, my face hovering over the dead indigo of the pool. He crossed over to me, and suddenly he was very close.

'The ocean is *right there*. Fifteen metres out that door.' His blue eyes drifted over to the bottle of wine and my glass. 'Have another drink. I'll have one, too.' He looked at me, challengingly, opened the glass cabinet above the counter, withdrew another wine glass, and filled them both. 'To big, hungry sharks.'

I took mine. 'You shouldn't be doing that, you know. You're high. And I don't think drinking will help.'

'I'm not high.'

'You smell like a coffee shop in Amsterdam.'

'That doesn't mean I'm high.' He lifted the glass, polished it off in one gulp, his eyes shining.

I took a sip, tried to mimic his bravado. He pushed open the doors, walked down to the point. The endless water was almost flat. He stood illuminated by the moon, the stars, the lights of the city. He kicked off his ridiculous flip-flops (did he ever feel cold?), set his toe in the ocean, yanked off his top, threw it carelessly beside the pool. Like the kid he was. I stood in the doorway, cocooned in the light of the house.

He turned, looked at me quizzically. 'Are we going to do this? This is your sea, right? *Yours.*'

'I don't want you swimming out there, Ben.'

'Why not?'

'It's not safe. And it's dark.'

'You really think I'll drown out there? *Me?*'

'Listen. If you jump in, I can't save you. I won't even be able to *see* you.'

'You're jumping in with me.'

'I'm not.'

But I found myself walking to him. I told him he was reckless, we looked ridiculous out on this rocky ledge. And he ignored me, took my arm, pulled me to the sea's edge.

'We're doing this, and we're doing it now.'

He was not threatening me. We both knew I could leave him there and he could find his way off my property. I shook my head, but he reached forward, touched my dress, his fingers against my belly, and he pinched the fabric upwards.

'Take it off.'

'Stop it, Ben.' A whisper.

He took back his fingers, unbuckled his belt, wriggled the faded jeans down his body, stepped out of them. He looked at me, not in a sexual way but challenging, the way kids look at each other when they're daring each other to do something stupid. I forced myself to meet his eyes and ignore the planes of his shoulders, the convex turn of his stomach.

I could have told him to leave. Instead, I crossed my arms in front of myself, pulled my dress over my head. My thighs felt cool. I felt the wind across my chest, hoped he couldn't see my scar in the dark. I hoped he could barely see my body.

'Are you ready?'

I nodded and I closed my eyes. I thought he was going to touch me again, but he just turned and dove. Blood coursed through my ears; I barely heard his splash. I shut my eyes even tighter. Kicked off my sneakers and leapt into the impossibly cold ocean.

Water on my body both comforting and bracing, much colder than I remembered. I could see nothing and when I surfaced I was aware, first, of the lights from the house spilling out over the rocks. Then I noticed lights further down the beach, a glowing slash of sand under moonlight and stars. The ocean current felt strong, the wind whispering off the waves intense. Even the ocean spray sounded like a giant's laboured breath.

Ben had paddled further out. I heard him spitting water, wheezing, and I followed him beyond my point, felt the current lazily push us away from my house. I could not stop thinking about the teeming life all around me, below me. Things that ate things. A stray frond of kelp brushed against me and I almost screamed. Ben was striking out – in the dark, he was a white, glowing froth ahead of me. I bicycled my legs, thought about calling him back. I was out of breath from the cold. I lay on my back and looked up at the constellations of Lyra, the musical constellation, and then, beyond, Piscis Austrinus, the Southern Fish, then the constellation of Carina, the Keel, and Canopus. The keel and the fish – the story of my current life – spread across the glowing universe above me.

In months past I would have swum out to him. I certainly knew more about this section of ocean than he did. I'd spent my life unafraid of water, but now I had to get out. I began to panic and I found myself flailing back to the rocks, hauling my body out of the water. As I did, I thought of the shark coming from underneath, grabbing me before I could splash onto the rocks that dug into my skin. Once I was safe on land, squatting, hugging my knees, the water running off my legs in rivulets that dripped back into the sea, I realised I was shaking, frozen.

I looked out over the dark water and I could not see Ben.

He could have been hit out there and I wouldn't even know it.

Then I heard him splashing, saw him swimming easily back. He climbed out a few yards away, walked over to me in silence. He was breathing hard. He picked up his clothes, continued into the house.

When I caught up, he was standing in the kitchen by the counter. He'd pulled on his pants but was still dripping. His eyes glimmered. He'd taken the wine bottle by the neck – I imagined he'd already taken a swig. It was an expensive white wine, one of Jack's favourites.

'I made it out behind the break. The water was so cold – I never used to even notice it. All I could think was how cold the water was, and how sharks like the dark. That's what I was thinking.'

'It's called self-preservation, Ben. Did you notice I made it in for a minute or so too?'

'Don't pretend you don't know what I mean, Stella. I know you feel the same. But you – you can work through it.' He swept his arm at the paintings. 'You have all this. You have everything.'

I was taken aback by the bitterness in his voice. Or was it despair? He walked up to a new canvas I had stretched. He examined it, then glared at a jar of violet-blue paint that was sitting on a stool beside it. He twisted open the jar, took up a brush, jabbed it into the paint. I watched without protest. He held the brush the way one would when painting a wall, and made one long horizontal swipe across the canvas. He dipped the brush again, gave the canvas another, more confident sweep, and then again.

'How do you go from *this* to *that*?'

He pointed the paintbrush like a baton at one of my paintings. It was entitled *Depths*. I'd painted it in Nantucket. I was at a loss as to where to start, what to say. He was waiting for some kind of response, and all I could think was how much I'd like a hot shower and a warming drink. And to not have his eyes boring into me.

'Practice. You need a lot of canvases,' I said. 'And you need to feel comfortable with the brush, the kind of paint. You need to know the basic lines you are creating before you build on it. You may not even want to paint on canvas. There may be something else.'

He considered that, picked up the jar of paint and left the lid on the table (I wanted to take it up immediately, afraid it would leave a mark). He looked at the paint the way a man might admire a bottle of caviar, then walked over to the sliding windows beside me, close enough so I could smell the sea on him. He carefully dipped his finger into the jar, then touched the glass, smeared a blue stripe across it. He did it again, this time with more force, and I was thinking *now I really should stop him* because I'd be the one who'd have to clean up the mess with turpentine.

'You know what?' he said. 'That was a first step out there. We did it. You did it. We faced our fear.' He set down the paint, approached me, stood close in front of me. With his clean hand, the one that wasn't covered in blue paint, he unbuttoned the top two buttons of my dress and gently touched the top of my sternum, and I stood immobile. *I dare you.* And then he pressed his painted finger into my suprasternal notch. He drew a blue line downwards, over my scar, and left a mark, like a guarantee. And when I refused to move, he drew war paint on my face.

And for once in I had no idea how long I felt powerful enough to sink my teeth into another human being and bite until he pushed me away, the indent of my canines in his shoulder almost drawing blood. I was predatory.

I almost tore him apart.

Notes to self: On Water Consumption

Water required for one woman (artist), standing five foot six inches high and weighing one hundred and twenty-seven pounds almost exactly, (sometime) smoker, generally healthy, living in one seaside house:

1. One half liter for brushing teeth, washing face.
2. One half liter for coffee (non-negotiable).
3. One liter to wash cup, plate and wine glass I use every day. (Use minimal soap. Dry by hand. Never use dishwasher.)
4. Three liters to wash pot/s. (While living alone, eat from freezer, recycle packaging.)
5. One liter to keep kitchen surfaces clean (barely).
6. Two liters to drink. Use spring water. (Or drink Food Market-brand bottled water, kept in the refrigerator. Remind self to drink over a liter a day.)
7. Twenty liters to wash body (less than ninety seconds in shower).
8. Ten liters to clean house (scrimp on floors/washing sea fog from shatterproof glass).
9. Three liters every two days for potted plants on rocks by house and for small patch of grass between house and road above me.
10. Toilet uses 0 liters (use water from Nos 8, 7, 5, 4 and 1 to flush).

Total usage of water: 39 liters

NB. One above-described woman having sex with younger man will cause (approx.) 1.5–2 times consumption of Nos 7, 6 and 1. *Fix this!*

I awoke the next morning curled up in the center of my bed and I was once again mortal, human and hungry. I rolled over to the nightstand, picked up my phone and sent a message.

Are you coming back?

Within thirty seconds he texted back:

now?
Now.

I smelt like him, of my own fluids. I walked nude into the bathroom, stood in transgression beneath a trickle of water, felt it cold, then warm against my skin. I closed my eyes, counting. Today I would allow myself two minutes of this bliss. It was early, I thought. No traffic for him to negotiate. I stood hugging myself under the water and imagined him next to me, his arms around me, a small, huddled animal needing, always needing.

I shut off the water. Listened. Something was wrong. I grabbed a towel and wrapped it around my body. Strange sounds. I held my breath. Voices.

I'd turned on the alarm after Ben had left. Lasers covered all the doors. To get in, the bad guys would have had to smash the doors, or tear out the bars, or use a crowbar. I would have heard them.

Or not.

A sick feeling of vulnerability crept up my neck and I locked the door to the bathroom. That was stupid – the intruders would just kick it in before killing me. And that is how Ben would find me.

I unlocked the door quietly, pushed it open, saw my iPhone, tip-toed to it. I was dizzy with fear, couldn't breathe, my fingers shaking so badly I knew I wouldn't be able to dial. *Who do I call? Not 911. Wrong country.* I couldn't recall the emergency number in Cape Town, though I knew it was something similar. Then I remembered the number for the security company was in the phone's contacts, and I scrolled through all the names, listening. I heard a voice, then another. I couldn't hear what they were saying. It sounded as if they were simply chatting in my front room.

Another voice. A woman's voice. *That* I could hear.

I crept over to the door and there, right in front of my eyes, was the panic button. I'd completely forgotten about it. I could lock the bedroom door, press the button and the alarm would shriek. Then I could run back into the bathroom and lock myself in while they fled, as they surely would with all the noise. I gently turned the latch on the bedroom door and then I realised – it was an *American* woman's voice.

Every fibre of my body was tuned into hearing that voice above the outside wind and the ocean waves. When she spoke again, I was sure: somebody had switched on the TV.

I knew that robbers often drank liquor and ate things out of the fridge (which made sense, if you were housebreaking for survival). Did people literally *watch* TV while they looted a house? And if so, did they watch the news?

American news?

My fingers hovered over the panic button, and I held my breath. I didn't want the security guys to come here and find me naked, wrapped in my towel, frightened out of my wits by the television. Had there been an electric trip that reset the appliances? A power outage followed by a pulse of electricity that crashed computers and Wi-Fi devices and switched on the TV? Was that even possible?

I opened the door just a crack, silently, listened, and yes, it was the TV. Two American voices talking about American politics. Illogical finance. Both.

I stepped into the hallway, out along the catwalk, looked down into the living room and almost screamed.

It was Jack.

There he was, standing in the middle of the room, his suitcase, carry-on, briefcase and suit bag thrown on the couch. Hunched over his coffee in his thick terry robe, he looked like a comical, short-legged boxer. He was glaring at the TV screen, squared off as if he wanted to knock it down, though it seemed little more than a discussion about the price of gold ... Washington ... numbers tracking beneath talking heads. Jack's hair was wet, his suit, underwear and shoes were thrown in a pile on the chair next to the couch. I'd have to pick these up and have them dry cleaned. He treated his expensive garments like *gear*, things to be strapped on and buttoned down against his body, worn into financial combat. There was his towel on the floor next to the sliding doors. Outside, I could see where he'd splashed into the pool and where he'd risen from the water and dripped it all over the deck, walked to the outside shower and stood beneath it – the *outside* Biarritz shower, where people might watch him wasting litres of water in addition to what he had squandered as he heaved himself out of the pool.

The sun shone into the house, gulls screamed their welcome. I hadn't turned on the TV in weeks, was unsure how even to do it, but Jack had already located the remote, made coffee, used up our daily allotment of water. His computer was wide open on the coffee table. Despite his aversion to social media, Jack hated being offline. He was a midnight-shopper, a casual-checker-of-email, an obsessive texter, an adder-of-people-to-online-sessions.

And he had not even noticed me, standing almost naked, at once angry, relieved and infuriated.

Oh God, I thought. Ben.

I slipped back into the bedroom, picked up the phone.

>Don't come.

Tip-toed back into the bathroom, found my matching robe to Jack's, wrapped it around me, went back out to the ledge to call down to him, trying to sound pleased. Unfaithful Penelope hailing returning Odysseus from the white cliffs of Ithaca.

'When did you get in, Jack?' And: *Please check your phone, Ben. Do not force me to explain you.*

Jack looked up, sighted me, smiled, and suddenly I *was* glad to see him. Yes, it was good to see another adult. He waved his coffee up at me.

'Hello, gorgeous girl. Come down and drink my coffee. I bought some of those greasy croissants from that place in Camps Bay. Have one so I don't eat 'em all.'

'You didn't tell me you were coming back? I would have laid out something for us.' I gently trod down the stairs, careful not to slip. He granted me a quick kiss, looked me over, as if making sure of something.

'Charlotte found me a ticket and booked it. On one of those planes with the bar and the pyjamas and all that. She mailed you about it? I even emailed you from my seat. Did it come through?'

'No. Nothing came through. Not from you, not from Charlotte. You could have just called me.'

My iPhone buzzed in my hand. *Ben.* I slid him away with my thumb.

???

'Yeah, well, the other choice was a flight through London, and I didn't feel like that. The minute they know I'm in London, I need to go out to dinner, stay over and discuss the fund ... I needed to be incognito.'

'It's impossible for you to be incognito in First Class on a massive plane, Jack.'

on my way

'*Business Class.* I met some currency trader at the bar who'd heard of your work – gave me his card. Says he wants to buy a painting. He'd read about you. You're famous!' Jack searched in his discarded suit's pocket for the card but couldn't find it. His eyes drifted back to the TV.

No!

He pointed at the TV – there was a map of South Africa on the screen, just in case overseas investors had forgotten where it was.

'The banks in South Africa? They're toast. Toast on a rope. We're getting out in the nick of time.' Jack glanced at me. 'I was on the phone every day in New York. People are moving money out of here. I'm getting calls, texts, emails, people visiting the office. There are so many people running out of here with bags of money and gold and whatever they can carry. Stella? This economy? It's been junked. Totally junked. Half of my clients aren't even *allowed* to invest down here anymore. Institutional investors? No way, José.'

fine. wtf. i don't like games

He parked the subject of South Africa's imminent demise and looked up at me. 'Any takers on the house? Any buyers? We really need to get moving on this, Stells.'

'Nothing yet.' *But there have been calls.* Calls from the agent that I had ignored.

this is so messed up

'Yeah, well, it's all just a matter of cash. We might need to just drop the price. Somebody will buy it. People are fleeing here from Johannesburg.' He grinned. 'You know what my friends up in Johannesburg call moving to Cape Town? A "semigration". Get it? At least the Western Cape is still okay. Upcountry? Forget it. People have had enough. It's move out to Australia or freeze in Canada or move to the Cape. The lucky ones get into the USA. The engineers and the finance jocks and the doctors.' He raised his eyebrows. 'You haven't even started packing, Stella.'

'I'll start packing when *you* start packing. I'm *working*, Jack. *Painting* is my work. The teaching is my work.'

'We can hire people to help you pack. I'm not looking for a fight – sheesh, what a greeting.'

'I need a bit more time.'

'All I'm saying is ...' He took a breath. We had been to therapy. Jack had been told not to be repetitive and compulsive. 'All I am *suggesting* is that we get the house sold asap. We need to set the date when we want to move. Just so we know we have this nailed down. That's what I suggest.'

'People coming into the house, looking around, it's distracting, Jack. Invasive. I need to clean up. I need to make the place presentable. I need to be here for the agent. It's all ...'

Jack laughed, pointed at the windows, wriggled his fingers at the whitecaps skating toward us over the sea. 'With a view like this? Stella, people would buy this place if it was a murder scene. Speaking of which, what happened here? How did you manage to get blue paint all over the sliding doors? I hope that stuff's going to come off.'

Explain later Ben! Husband here.

I stared in distress at the incriminating blue stripes and Jack caught himself, decided against making a scene.

'Okay, I know you need, you know, solitude and everything. I'm not belittling your needs or opinions. It can wait, right? No biggie.'

I walked over to him and he hugged me. He smelt like the water outside and his own particular scent. Some kind of large cat.

'Let's go out to dinner later. Have you been looking after yourself? I'll make reservations down the beach, we'll have some wine. May as well enjoy the place? Come on, Stells, let me spoil you.' He glanced at his phone. 'I need to discuss some things with Thokwale later. Is it okay if he comes here? I can't handle going into the office yet – I'm jet-lagged – but I need to confirm some things with him.'

'Like what? What do you need to confirm, Jack?'

'There's business to wrap up.' He glanced at his computer. 'Look, there's other stuff. The Bastard, that Queensouth guy. He's bought more shares. He and his little band of thieves are living in a tax exile and they call themselves "activist investors", which in common terms means criminals. It's making it harder for me to pull all the money we can out of the country. And the clock's ticking. We need to be out before this currency crashes through the floor.'

'I'm not the one in a rush, Jack.'

'I know you're not. This is no biggie, right? No biggie. Just like, you know, housecleaning.'

'Doesn't Thokwale have an office?'

'Of course, but really, it's just as easy to do it here and do I feel like driving into town? No, I don't.'

'And it's more private here.'

'Yes. It's more private here. We can have a meeting, talk, figure out what's going to happen. Thokwale can make a house call, right? It's in his interest. He may bring a colleague. Some governmental person. Someone who represents the Reserve Bank.'

'Don't you want to stop and rest, Jack?'

'I rested on the plane. They don't let you use the mobile phone on those flights. I've been flying blind. I want to know what's happening now.' He tucked his chin into his chest. 'So, don't worry. I just need to sign off on some things.' He remembered something, went to his carry-on, tugged out a plastic bag from Kennedy, the cheery New York Yankees top hat emblazoned on it. 'Here. I found all the Yankees swag you could ever want. You know ...' He pulled a cap from the bag, perched it on his round head, held up a loud blue sweatshirt for inspection. Toasted me with an empty coffee mug. Then raised an empty red, white and blue beer glass. 'For that kid, over at the spring.'

Jack waited while I blanked.

'Your friend? The Yankees fan? They're going to lose to the Red Sox for the pennant? I even got him a fridge magnet. I could have gotten him a mini bat, but I was afraid I wouldn't get it into carry-on.'

Oh, yes. Vusi. 'He probably doesn't own a refrigerator. But he could put it on his Uber.'

'The kid drives for Uber?'

'No. Yes. It's a long story. Thank you, Jack. He will appreciate it. But I need to get to the university now. I would have made sure the place was tidy if I knew you were going to be here.'

'I'll call the service. Don't worry. It's tidy enough, right? The place looks great. The view here, wow. We'll miss it. Nothing like it.'

How could he not see the warped furniture?

Jack seemed to regard the sea as something he was also selling off, but which he could replace with another, better sea.

'Stells?'

The phone was in my hand and I tried not to look at the screen. Ben hadn't texted back and I couldn't even tell if he'd seen my message because his antiquated phone didn't seem to work like everyone else's.

'Yes, Jack?' *Please do not be driving over here.*

Jack's arms were around my shoulders. 'I didn't even mention the shark. Your experience out there. That was thoughtless. How are you doing?'

This is how the therapist had taught Jack to talk about things I cared about but he did not understand. Like art openings and missing meals and asking me to come out with him while I was finishing a painting. Jack was diligent and I had friends at home who envied this.

'I emailed a podcast to you,' he said. 'It's called *Surviving Trauma, A Beginner's Guide*. Plus I ordered a really interesting book on sharks. I mean, you look okay. Maybe this experience will be good for your art? Something that could be … um … processed?'

Processed. Being near Jack was comforting but overwhelming. He had completely taken over the space in less than an hour.

'I'm fine, Jack.'

'You look great.'

He gave me the once-over, and after ascertaining that there were no missing pieces, he turned his attention to his phone. 'You and me. Dinner, right? I'll make reservations.'

    nice

Copper Shark

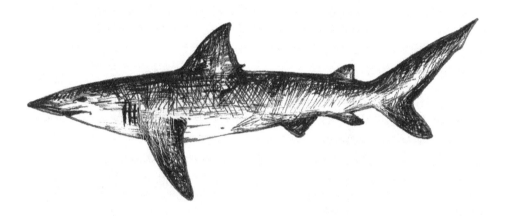

The copper shark is sometimes known to hunt in large groups but for most of its life it is solitary. It can be found worldwide with concentrations in the Mediterranean, Australia and New Zealand, and off the coast of Southern Africa. It prefers the surf zone but will move out as far as the continental shelf in the open ocean. It is highly migratory. The copper shark matures slowly compared to other sharks.

Conté Drawing from Stella Wright's Private Collection, Cape Town

None of this could be good for me. None of it. This was the epitome of stress. As I drove to the office, I had nervously glanced toward the public parking, terrified Ben would be there. He was not. He hadn't replied to my frantic texts checking that he wasn't going to just show up while I was gone. Jack was happily sitting on the couch, on the phone, the television keeping him company, the ocean spread out before him in supplication.

I tried to work at the university. I couldn't focus on the papers that had been handed in, or any kind of research, or the student creative projects that seemed to me like the artwork of some distant culture so I had no idea where to begin my critiques. I checked my phone, checked my email, thought about where I could find Ben. If he felt wronged or used, things could go from bad to worse. I sat in my office trying not to think about my phone, putting off the inevitable text as long as I could. I couldn't just leave things this way.

> Where are you, Ben?

Finally, he answered.

> working for living
> Where?

And he sent back a location. A boat yard, presumably where he worked. Perhaps an answer. Perhaps an invitation.

I abandoned the papers and the meeting I was supposed to have with Katie in the late afternoon. She had indeed been working, I saw, and she'd been sending me pictures of what she was doing in her home studio, which looked like a spare outbuilding on her parents' spread in the plush suburb of Constantia. It looked, in fact, like part of a barn and I wondered if Katie owned a horse. Horses seemed unreal to me now.

I drove against the traffic toward the quays, along the docks beside the slow-moving toy freighters. The afternoon Atlantic mist enshrouded the distant shape of Robben Island, former prison home to Nelson Mandela, current home to God knows how many seals and penguins and, of course, sharks. An unseasonal hot, draughty wind lashed my car. I was wearing my over-large sunglasses and drinking coffee and trying to prepare for whatever confrontation I would have with Ben. He must have known that what we had could never last. I was prepared for a tantrum but perhaps he wouldn't make a scene if there were others in the vicinity. This must end; it was the only thing to do.

I drew the Land Rover into his boat yard and yes, there was his little Beetle parked next to the gargantuan boat entrance, looking like it had slightly collapsed to one side. He hadn't replaced the roof racks, I noted. The windows of the car were gaping open. He left the windows down despite the crime; I wondered if he had difficulty keeping them shut, or if they had simply collapsed into the doors and he'd done nothing to fix them. The boat yard smelt dusty, dry – overly dry – and from inside the warehouse came the screech of a grinder. Beyond, the sound of banging: steel against steel, monotonous clangs three or four seconds apart.

A barnacle-encrusted fishing boat caught my attention. I stopped and marvelled that anyone would board one of these burly little vessels, work on it and live on it for months at a time. The boat looked like it should go to the wrecker, but somebody had already blasted off some of the barnacles and corrosion, leaving blue patches on a hull that would have to be sanded and sealed and then painted before the boat was launched out to Indonesia or India. The crew from this craft – the *Fuyuanyu* – would be crowded into the small, unspeakable restaurants close by the harbour, nameless, hole-in-the-wall places that served excellent Asian food, copious amounts of alcohol and were frequented by the latest generation of Cape Town prostitutes who for hundreds of years have specialised in lonely sailors far from home. One of my colleagues at the university had written a book on the subject; I'd attended the launch close to where I was standing. Jack found the culinary diversion fascinating, but I had patronised enough low-budget eateries and dive bars to last me a lifetime.

I peered into the gloomy workshop, where a yacht suspended in its cradle bathed in dusky late-afternoon sunlight. It was partially shrouded by huge tarpaulins, particularly the upper deck areas and the stern cockpit, probably so the dust didn't creep into lockers and spaces where navigation equipment had yet to be installed. The pedestal where the wheel would be mounted jutted out from under a tarpaulin, and as I made my way through the noise and the shadows I sighted Ben on scaffolding wielding a sander at shoulder level. He was wearing a bandana over his hair, which was pulled back in a ponytail, and a pair of plastic goggles with, incredibly, sunglasses underneath. A filthy paper mask sat over his nose and mouth. He looked like a surgeon for the damned.

I waited under the scaffolding while he worked at making delicate sweeps against the fibreglass, meticulously covering the expanse one yard at a time, subtly transforming the yacht's topography.

'Looks good.'

He wasn't expecting me, but he did not startle. He paused, lifted the sander, held it away from his face, flipped up the goggles, peered down.

'What are you doing here?'

'Ben, you just sent me directions!'

'You didn't say you were coming *now*.'

'I wanted to talk.'

'I'm kind of busy.'

'It won't take long.'

He clutched the scaffolding and clambered down, sliding part of the way. He must have climbed *up* the same route, I thought. He was strong enough to pull himself twelve feet off the ground. With a sander in hand.

Having him suddenly so close covered in dust was a slight shock.

'Are you going to paint that entire sailboat?'

'I can't just use paint. It'll affect the waterproofing. I've made an epoxy. They use it to fix larger boats.'

'Ben, I need to explain ...'

'You do. You definitely do.'

I couldn't see his eyes through the sunglasses.

'Jack flew in this morning. Very early. And unexpectedly.'

He looked impatiently at me, as if waiting for me to get to the point.

'I had no idea he was coming back. I wouldn't have had you over last night if I did. But he's here now and he's serious about selling the house and he's staying until things are ready for us to go.'

'When does that happen?'

'Soon. As soon as we can sell the house.'

He absorbed this.

'Ben, I did tell you I'd be leaving. And I just need to say that having Jack back, in our house ... it's made me realise that what we are doing is not right. For me, for you, definitely for him.'

'What are we doing, exactly?'

'Ben ...'

'I'm not going to go invite your husband for a pint at some larny banker bar to tell him. So stop worrying about it.'

'I'm also thinking about you.'

'What about me? There's nothing to think about. So, no problem.'

'*W*hat's no problem?'

'You and me, if we need to stop, that's no problem. That's okay.' He turned, pointed at his work. 'This is real. Right? *This* is *real*. I'm looking at it, and I'm thinking this is genuine.'

What a change of subject. 'Ben, maybe we should—'

'It's going to be incredible. But I don't think there are many people who will *understand*. You know?'

There was something in his voice that worried me.

'They'll understand it's a yacht that's been painted beautifully. That's the point.'

'Look at what I'm doing. You see that slight indentation? That colour? It's emerald-green marine topcoat.' He squeezed my arm, forced me to look up. He was excited, but he almost toppled me onto the floor. 'There's a big surfing competition down here. People come from all over the world to Hout Bay. Just like ten minutes from where you live ... Beyond the Heads, the waves are huge, some of the biggest in the world. It's called Dungeons. When it kicks it's a bigger break than Mavericks in California, or Jaws in Hawaii. It's heavier, harder, faster. And it's dangerous. You know? Big, meaty waves. Miles and miles of kelp. The ocean is cold too. Colder than northern California, way colder than Hawaii. And one year people started asking me, you know, was I going to try to compete at Dungeons because these big-name surfers were flying in from around the world, and maybe I would qualify. But there's a pecking order. And I thought about it and figured I could make it. I figured I could win at Dungeons, but I'm not on the circuit. I'm nowhere, man.'

'Couldn't you ... try out for it?' *Why are we discussing this?*

'You don't just sign up – it's not like the Argus bike race or the Two Oceans Marathon. It's this big sponsored competition and they put it on the Internet and TV and it only happens when the waves are peaking like eight to ten metres. It averages at three or four metres, and they come in fast. You're two kilometres offshore so they tow the guys out. In America that's like, what, twelve feet minimum, with waves rolling in at over thirty feet? There are seals out there so there are also sharks, and you can't see three metres down. They *invite* these surfers out to hack this. You know? They stay for weeks and wait for the swell, the wind, the current, the tide to come together, and then they do the competition. But we *know*, right? We know when it's starting to blow in. And by the time they get the cameras up and the Zodiacs out there it's usually misty and dark and the water is black and where it isn't black there's this white foam.

'Anyway. They start posting online how big the waves are, but there's a place you can just climb up and look. Actually *see* that the waves are big enough. And I was doing that. I was checking it out and they were saying,

"The big day is coming, get ready" and hyping it up, and one evening I just went up there and I could tell the next day they'd hold the competition. And I just sat up there, you know? Looking at those waves and thinking about those other surfers and all the gear they had, and the jet skis that would tow them out. And I was thinking, it's a kilometre and a half out and I feel pretty good and it was late afternoon. So, I just grabbed an overhead wave board I hadn't used since Hawaii. The guys call a board like that a rhino chaser, a big gun. And I paddled out. You paddle out through this area called Shark Alley. But back then, I couldn't care less. Now, I would. But *then*? No ways.

'And I told myself if I got too tired I'd catch one of the smaller waves and just ride it in and forget about it, but I managed to get out and the wind was kicking up and the waves were coming in way, *way* faster than I expected. I mean *really* fast, and the spray was coming off the crests and by the time I got out to where I thought they'd be staging the whole show, I was in this, like, canyon of waves. Like these giant troughs, and there was no backline, just these waves coming in and hammering me. And I thought, okay, well, I'll take the biggest one I can get and just call it a day.

'But I waited. I just rode the waves, paddled through them, managed to not get totally crushed even though I thought to myself, *I have maybe ten minutes and then I have to go back; getting out of this will be hard enough.* And it was getting dark, but I knew I could find my wave in ten minutes. I knew I just needed to survive in this ... I don't actually know how to describe it ... this huge *cauldron*. And the waves were coming in harder, against an offshore wind, which was making them stand up and get bigger ... and it was pumping the spray in my face, but I waited for it. Waited. Then, when I was almost out of time, I decided that what I was doing was letting fear rule me, and if I didn't try for one wave, just stand up, I was never going to do this. And the thing was ... I *knew* that if something went wrong out there, I was dead. Gone. So I just sort of took what energy I had and when this wave came in, it was like the ocean was folding in on itself, lifting me. When I looked down it was like standing on top of a moving building, and I just stood up and stayed low and just pointed the board downwards and I was falling with that board at my feet. I had to ride it with my heels, and for the first few seconds I was just pinwheeling my arms because the size of the wave was pushing me forward and it was already collapsing next to me, and I just thought I would make it if I could steer away from all that white water. It sounded like a train pulling up.

'I figured, *This is it, I'm dead.* There was no cool way out of this wave – I could keep riding this bloody thing but when it finally came down I'd be like an ant in a washing machine, you know? So, I just let it rip and kept riding, and there was no shallow spot out there, right? It's not like the waves get smaller, you just ride along and when you get off the crest all you can see in front of you is another wall of water.

'And I rode this thing and I was up for ten seconds. Longer. I have no idea – maybe twenty seconds, maybe more – and I was crouching on this wave and falling down the front of it, the board was making this sound like *takatakatakatakataka*, and I pulled out of the wave and it rolled over me, and I just let it go. I was underwater for a long time and I just kept pushing up and the back channel kept pushing me away, and the wave took forever to pass, but when I got up to the surface again I was almost dead, and I held on to the board and just floated there, and I knew I needed to kick out of that line if I could. But I got pulled up the face of another wave that didn't want to break. I was all alone out there with the birds and stuff, and I'd been dragged close enough to shore that I figured, *If I can survive this, if I can just ride this out, I can make it to the put-in place, get the board out of the water and make my way back up the path.* But it took a long time. Like, forever. I swam and kicked and it was getting dark and that heavy mist was hanging over the water, and then it basically *was* dark, and I knew what direction to go but I was tired. I just put my face down and pushed the board, kicked, swam, told myself I could make it. But what kept me going was thinking that if I just gave up and drowned, nobody would ever know I rode Dungeons by myself. So I just kept kicking and being dunked and rolled until I could hear the break, and then I kept paddling until I could walk out with the board. And I just sat there in the sand and looked out at the ocean and it was nightfall, but you could see it sort of brooding out there. It felt like I sat there for hours, and then I just chucked the board into the bushes and walked back up to the car and slept there, woke up when the sun rose.'

He sat down on the edge of the cradle strut, as if the memory itself was exhausting.

'People do it all the time. There are maybe a dozen people who've done it, but I've never told anyone. Until now. Because it's not about winning the prize or being a hero. It's about riding that wave and knowing I did it, knowing I survived. And, okay, it's nice if someone who means something to me knows about it too.'

'That's really … something, Ben. I'm glad you told me. I don't know what to–'

'If I can do that, I can get you back in the water. And myself. Manō has to give way.'

He towered over me in his painting gear, his intense eyes behind the absurd sunglasses, and I had told myself I'd be strong this time. He reached out, clasped the side of my palm.

'If we end this, I have nobody to tell. About surfing, about that Manō. Do you think I *want* to feel this way?'

'Please let go of my hand, Ben,' I said. Finally. But he didn't.

'If we lose the ocean, what do we have left? If we let that go, we let everything go.'

'We have life, Ben. Regular life. Okay? Being alive.'

'I want more. You do too. I look at those colours in your paintings, the brushstrokes – the way you press the paint into the canvas – and I think, with every painting I've seen, it's like this radical chick pushed down that paint. When I look closely, every painting is a … a kind of frenzy.'

'You haven't seen many of my paintings, Ben.'

'I have. And they're all over the Internet! You know what being with you is like?'

'Ben, I don't think I need you to—'

'It's like being out there in the waves – being ragdolled without a board – and you find the only other person in the same massive water and the two of you just hold on to each other until you're rescued. If either of us let go, we're both gone.'

'What happens if no one comes to rescue us?'

'We rescue ourselves.' He dropped his hand.

I rubbed my fingers, turned away and left.

I answered a handful of want ads that were within my *skill set*. I posted a resume on a website for artists needing work. These included: Museum curator. Concierge assistant. Art-supply salesperson. Other jobs artists could do:

- Waitress
- Bartender (needed a qualification from the state)
- Online B&B hostess (I could do this – I could check up on an apartment for somebody – until I thought about what people did in apartments, until I read some of the experiences others had had.)
- Hotel maid
- Art teacher (experience, state qualification needed)
- Online art teacher (teaching retirees)
- Stripper (Like being an artists' model – I knew of girls who'd gone into this kind of work from school. I could not imagine doing this.)
- Online stripper (Apparently taking off my clothes online could net me $10 000 a month from paid fans, though it was unclear how this worked. I needed a computer and a camera – I could get these, but I would also need privacy ...)
- Executive companion (One website promised $20 000 a month part-time for me to quaff champagne in limousines wearing sparkly, fish-

scale dresses. The girls in the ad were dancing with bemused-looking men; they were all younger than me, looking gleefully into the middle distance, living in an eternal night of debauchery.)

I finally found a job I could do without selling my soul or my body or all of my time. A small publisher was putting out a series of downloadable textbooks for children and they needed an illustrator. The publishing house was made up of a few people in an open-plan office space in Midtown. I emailed the editor samples of my work. She wrote back saying she was impressed but required specific illustrations in order to make a final decision: she needed drawings of a human torso showing the various organs, a cumulus cloud and a shark, my very first. I spent two days drawing by hand, with coloured pencils and ink. I ignored my own painting, and Demetrius was not subtle about his disapproval. He was purposefully distracting, clomping around his work, cranking aggressive, industrial music. A few times he came into the kitchen where I was working, stared disdainfully at my pad, my pencils and brushes, shook his head.

I left him to his resentment and walked over to a nearby coffee shop on Greenwich, where I finished the drawings sitting alone at a table with a latte they insisted on refilling, luxuriating in the warmth we did not have at The WorkHead. The waitress kept glancing at what I was doing, smiling shyly, approvingly. Another art student, I thought. Me, two years before.

I drew a cloud system. I drew the human torso (male), pink lungs with a heart nestled between them, a bright-red liver, an esophagus, a cluster of soft, cream-coloured small intestines nestled under a colon. I drew a mako shark from the sample picture they'd given me, spent time on the strange, aggressive proportions. Coloured in the flashing on its flanks, the gill slits with a crease of red underneath, the shark's mouth slightly open, looking as if it was mounted on the page.

I finished the drawings, took scans at a copy shop, emailed them to the editor. My first commissioned work.

The reply came via SMS within five minutes.

    These are fab fab fab! Let's meet?

Demetrius texted me:

    Where are you? U OK?

I texted back:

    I'm OK. More than OK.

Weasel Shark

Weasel sharks inhabit shallow coastal tropical waters from South Africa and the Red Sea to Japan. Although they live near beaches, their specialised feeding behaviours have never resulted in a shark bite.

Crayon Sketch from Stella Wright's Private Collection, Later Works, New York

I waited for Jack at a table set upon the faux-marble tiles of the restaurant he favoured overlooking the beach in Camps Bay, just ten minutes from the house. Our table was near the biggest window and it was dark outside, but if I looked carefully I could see the grey strip of beach before the darkness of the ocean, the jagged whitecaps. I considered asking the waiter for a pack of cigarettes and stepping outside into the lashing wind to smoke. When I'd returned home from seeing Ben, Jack was gone – summoned to the office after all, but he'd sent a sweet message asking to meet him for dinner and I had arrived on time because I am, at my most basic, a woman who is punctual.

I drank half the wine in my glass, wished I had something to calm me down. The waiter, suspiciously student age, paid careful attention to me. He probably recognised me from an opening or some lecture I'd given. Awkward, but flattering. Perhaps that was what I was: the kind of artist people almost recognised.

I finished the wine, ordered another glass. I hadn't bothered to reply to Jack because I knew he wouldn't text back; he tended to ignore personal calls when he was working. And now he was probably driving and he was scrupulous about not picking up calls. 'If you get in an accident while you're on the phone, insurance will not pay out,' he'd intoned more than once.

He was always warning me to stop fumbling with my phone while driving. To stop tearing open cigarettes with my teeth and lighting up in traffic. To stop changing my sunglasses to my distance glasses. To stop switching radio stations at speed. 'Your car says a lot about you, Stella,' Jack had scolded. My car was smeared with paint, smelt of linseed oil and turps, and filled with canvas rolls, rags, boxes, reusable shopping bags and milk crates. Jack vacuumed his car himself after long drives, and he dedicated a leather-covered door pocket to the small notebook in which he recorded his mileage. It was a purposeless task – he had no boss to claim it from – but it was one which he performed religiously.

So, I waited for my husband and worried a bit about him and worried also that somehow he'd figured out something about Ben. Or sensed it. I'd left Jack by himself in the house. There could have been evidence in addition to the indigo stripes on the glass door. Bottles, glasses, mugs? Silt in the bed? Human scents or traces of blood or the ghosts of Ben's handprints on the shower's sliding door? What of the smell of musth and rut? Traces of an affair that were hard to blot out. I felt as if I'd forgotten something, hadn't cleaned up the crime scene. Left spoor to be discovered by the sleepless sniffer dogs of matrimony.

But then Jack arrived. He saw me, waved hugely. He'd obviously already been drinking, which annoyed me. *Hypocrite*, my own second drink seemed to mouth. Jack kissed me on the cheek and flopped down into the plush chair, looked around the restaurant and then at me, sheepish. He was wearing the same crumpled blazer he'd flown in, beneath it a white turtleneck. 'Sorry, Stells. We got caught up. Thokwale and I have been going over the numbers.'

'You've already had a drink, or two, I see.' I couldn't help myself.

'Yeah, well, he opened a bottle of that incredible South African Merlot – can't pronounce the name of the estate. But, superb. Would have been rude not to have a glass with him. Better than anything from California.'

I straightened his collar. Jack shrugged me off, scanned the room again.

'Where's the waiter? We need a bottle of wine. Sorry for making you wait. And the traffic out there is still crazy-daisy.' He caught the eye of the waiter and motioned him over like a man gliding a boat into shore. 'The bank wants to buy one of your paintings, by the way. Did you know that?'

'No, I did not.'

'The piece in the Goodson Gallery. The one called *Sonic Location?*

They want it for the company collection. You know, your whale painting.' He ordered a bottle of red from memory and the waiter scuttled off, duly impressed.

'How do they know about it? Where did they see it? It's in storage.'

'They picked it up online. They've got a bunch of whale paintings at the bank because of their fund to save them, right? This coast is an important breeding ground.' Jack leant forward, took a sip from my wine glass. 'Guess how much they're going to pay for it, Stella. Go on!'

'I have no idea.'

'I don't want to discuss money at the dinner table but suffice to say, it's a shit ton. They have their own gallery at the bank. I'm telling you. A curator, the whole shebang. A *gift shop* even. Seriously.'

'I'm sure. I'm looking forward to hearing about it and seeing where it might be hung.'

'They've wanted it for a long time, and now is the right time to acquire it, apparently. Since we're leaving and all. I think it's a nice gesture. Whales are always a big hit.'

A bottle of red with an ancient-looking, comically unreadable label was placed in front of Jack, along with two large balloon glasses. He looked like a boy having a sundae. The waiter offered him a desultory splash. Jack whirled it, sniffed it, nodded, held the glass out to be filled, then dismissed the waiter. Then he studied the menu, pushed it aside.

'So. We may only have one little problem left before we can really say that our South African holdings are behind us.'

'A problem?'

'Legal snag. One big tax issue, really. It should be figured out soon. They say there are still ventures worthy of investment here. I don't know anymore, I really don't. This country is an enigma. I'm moving into a stage of my life where I'm looking for safety. Shelter from the storm, as the man said.'

'I don't understand the ins and outs, Jack, but I do think you need to be careful. No matter how attractive things may look.'

'I don't want to take risks. I don't want to buy gold. When the fund was started here, there was so much optimism.'

'Maybe there's more to living here than the *investment climate*, whatever that really is.'

'Not for us, Stella.'

'But maybe for me.'

'Look, I know you like it here. I'm *glad* you do. And I have a plan to make it up to you when we leave. Speaking of which, we really need to start talking dates.'

'I was hoping it would be more of a mutual decision. You haven't asked me about the status of my work here yet. My job. My teaching. My painting.'

But he wasn't listening. 'Have you ever heard of this American poet guy who says there's no such thing as change? Just *people* changing. I'm reading these investment gurus who say that safety is found in *embracing* change, not trying to avoid it.'

'I think you're speaking of Thoreau. Who actually said, "Things do not change, we do".'

Jack finished his glass, eyed the bottle. 'Yes, well, I think I'm turning into a person who doesn't like change.'

'That doesn't sound like you, Jack.'

'What? Not liking change? What's wrong with looking for investment security?'

'You used to love risk. You used to say that the real danger lies in not evolving.'

'Do you think I'm not evolving? I just bought a new office space in Midtown. And I need to look after you. After both of us. We're not getting any younger.'

'Why do you have this constant need to think for other people, Jack? It's sweet, but it's exhausting.'

'Because I *do* have to look after other people. After you. It's what I do. With all the love in the world, Stells, when was the last time you paid a bill? Or did taxes? Or balanced the books? I do all that, and I'm not against doing it.'

'That's hardly fair! It's not as though I'm incapable of doing those things. You always said it was *easier* if you took care of them. And I keep the house together. I make sure you have the food you like and the wine and the single-malt Scotch and that you don't leave for a meeting in a suit from the 1990s. I make sure your life is easy, Jack. It's not as if that just happens. And when you need to present your wife to the next set of customers, I dutifully listen to their tales of financial glory. All, by the way, while doing my own creative work and teaching. I do just as much for you as you do for me.'

'I know you do.'

'The Jack Barlow Show is a full-time profession. Not just making sure you eat three meals a day and take care of yourself. Jack ... sometimes being the supporting actor in the drama of your life requires a little bit of patience. Like packing up and moving to South Africa because just a short while ago you saw an opportunity that doesn't seem to exist anymore.'

'You *knew* when we came here it was just to pack up the fund. Not to look for other things to invest in. You *knew* this. I told you. Stells, there is nothing here I can't get for you in the USA. You like the ocean? We can move out to the Vineyard. You like beaches? We have them. Wine? I have a client in central New York who grows the stuff, or we can go to California. Restaurants like this? Boatloads of them in New York. And the art scene here is miniscule compared to back home. Face it, baby. You're a New Yorker. I am too.' He settled back in his plush white seat. 'I'm just not getting why you're so fond of this place. It's just another gorgeous – what do they call it? *Destination*.'

'That's just it, Jack. Sometimes what's attractive ... what is unique and strange ... is what you *can't* see about a person or a place. Isn't that obvious?'

'That's an odd thing for a painter to say.' He grinned.

'It's not, Jack. It's *exactly* what a painter would say.'

He reached into his jacket, extracted his phone, began pecking at it. 'I'm writing that down. I'm gonna take a picture of you and write down that quote and post it.'

'Where? You have no idea how to post anything anywhere, Jack. People even do *that* for you.'

'Fair enough. You can do it for me then. Post it on my Instagram.'

'No!' I laughed. 'Put your phone away. We're supposed to be having a conversation.'

'Okay, okay. You're right. Let's eat. I'm starving.'

Jack 'wouldn't think of' not having an expensive nightcap before leaving the restaurant. The truth is, Jack was not a great drinker, and he was still tired from the flight, but he was in an expansive mood. He texted his office and two people appeared to drive him and his car back to the house. I could handle alcohol better than him, so I drove myself home after we'd finished our crayfish pasta. When the driver arrived with Jack's Benz, he'd fallen asleep in the passenger seat. We both had to wake him up.

Revived, Jack jovially came into the house, poured us both a Scotch in the heavy lowball glasses I never touched unless he was here.

'I have something for you, Stells. I hope you like it.'

He snapped open his briefcase, an attaché case only Jack could carry off. He handed me a box, too heavy to be jewellery, I thought. Inside the flat box was a book, obviously carefully made, hardcover. High-gloss pages. *The History of the Hawsley House Print Building on Greenwich Street and Horatio Street* – the history of the building, stretching back to 1840. *Artistic Home of Stella Wright* – Jack had found somebody to reformat the original to include full-colour shots of what it looked like now.

And taped to the back cover was a gleaming key.

I felt my knees begin to crumple. 'Oh no, Jack! You didn't. You bought it?'

'I *reserved* it. I'd never buy it unless I knew you loved it. I just need to send them the word and it's ours. Yours.'

Page after page of the building's history. Its years as a warehouse, the gentrification of the area, its artistic origins, its days as a chopped-up party space – referred to in the text as 'its days of squalor', the very time I had been there. Its current manifestation as a high-end apartment. And the final pages showing it converted back into a studio – a fabulous kitchen with a fire-engine-red Viking range and discreet cream-coloured Sub-Zero bar fridge, bespoke entertainment area, a view of the river in the curated garden near the roof. My paintings Photoshopped into the studio area, to make it look as if I'd just stepped out. This was a proposal.

Summer in New York. Looking at the room I could almost hear the sound of the city, feel the afternoon sunlight flowing through the perfect push windows and skylights. The entire space had changed since I'd stood there at that party with Demetrius, and yet nothing had changed. *This is what artists dream of.*

'So, what do you say, Stells?' He was still more than a little drunk. He held up his iPhone. 'I can email the agent. Right now.'

'I still need to see it, Jack. It's a huge decision.'

'I know, I know, and I also know how much you love it here in Cape Town, by the ocean ... and I want you to know what's possible back home. As beautiful as all of this is.' He held up his Scotch to the glass doors, toasted the dark sea, then navigated his way across the room, wrapped his arms around me. 'Say yes. Let me do this for you.' He kissed me and he tasted like wine. 'I've missed you, baby. It's so good to be with you again.'

I hugged him back, found myself entangled in his arms and suddenly he was holding on for balance, and then we were collapsing onto the couch. 'God, you are so beautiful, Stells. Sometimes I look at you and I can't believe you're mine. Jesus Christ. How'd I get so lucky?'

I smacked his chest. 'I can't breathe, Jack.'

He shifted. 'If I buy you an art studio on Greenwich, will you let me have sex with you on this couch? Right now?'

I laughed. Only Jack could get away with such a proposition. 'On the *couch*? Are you sure? Will we *fit*?'

He pulled off his shirt, and his hair, greying and a little unkempt, stood up. His cheeks were flushed, his lips Merlot-rouged.

'You look like a Rembrandt, Jack.'

'Is that good?'

I had to laugh again.

Jack, the considerate lover, with a friendly body that fit mine. Comfortable. Familiar. Even on that unwieldy couch, with its leather that stuck to our skin and the inconvenient give and take that finally had him roll off me and almost onto the floor, his back unreliable upon the unfamiliar terrain of throw pillows. Lovemaking that was the affable, familiar ghost of what I'd had with Ben.

Jack dozed off while I went to shower. His phone rang just as I was drying myself, still feeling the animal warmth of his body. I walked onto the catwalk in front of the bedroom, naked, watched as he fumbled in his jacket for the phone, wearing only his loose linen boxers and, incongruously, a sock that hung off his foot like a deflated condom.

'Jack, leave it. It's late.'

He glanced up at me, winked, held up his finger. 'One minute. Promise.' Then he stage whispered, 'Bank.'

He collapsed into a chair, opened his computer, squinted at the screen. Jack's voice echoed around the house; he refused to lower it. A minute passed and I lay in bed waiting. I wanted him to remind whoever had called that it was after eleven here. That Jack's wife was lonely. That she knew she couldn't let him buy her that beautiful studio.

I tried to block out his voice, but it was impossible.

Then my own phone whirred beside me. Ben.

> hey
> No, Ben.

> OK
> Jack is here.
> who?
> My HUSBAND.

I waited for the reply, but nothing came. I added,

> You need to stop messaging me. Seriously.
> nah

In the days after that long night, what started to bug me was the way Jack walked around the house humming to himself. One afternoon he was sitting in the main living room, papers spread out before him, dressed as if he was at his club in Martha's Vineyard: wide-wale corduroys, bright red, with cheerful smiling whales embroidered into them. An open Brooks Brothers shirt, a loose V-neck casual sweater. Bare feet. Frayed belt, glasses pushed up on his head. Music was blaring through the wireless speakers, and I could smell something simmering – the lights were on in the kitchen, bright rows of them he never bothered to shut off. A bottle of wine was open on the kitchen island, and a half-full glass set on the floor by his chair. When he saw me, he gave one of his friendly waves, as if seeing me walk into my own living room was a pleasant surprise. This was Jack's charm, his unique ability to make everywhere his private berth. Jack filled every space until there was room only for the bit players in the great drama of his life.

I stood next to his chair, cleared my throat. Outside, terns played against the breeze.

'Jack, I need to ask you a question.'

He set the paper down. 'Sure. Shoot.'

'I want to know what you're planning on doing about that man in England.'

'Which one? There are lots of men in England.'

'You know who. Queensouth.'

'You mean the pirate activist investor, aka The Bastard? Why do you care about him?'

'Because you don't discuss him anymore, and that worries me.'

Jack stood, theatrically shielded his eyes, looked out over the rocks into the twinkling Atlantic. 'We're on the lookout, partner. And I gotta tell you, he's been quiet. Maybe too quiet.'

'I'm not joking, Jack.'

He sighed. 'Queensouth and his friends are the last thing on my mind right now. They seem to have given up. They need more funding to keep getting up to their bullshit and the gold price just fell out of the crib. Might not be worth their while. There might be easier pickings. Who knows how people like that think?'

'Jack, you need to do something for me.'

'For you? Name it.' He took a sip of wine.

'Promise me that nothing will happen to that man.'

'I'm really surprised you'd say something like that. I don't know whether to be flattered or not. This is boring investment stuff. This isn't, I dunno, some kind of mob movie.'

'I want you to promise.'

'Promise *what*? What's going on?' Annoyance.

'That nothing will happen to Queensouth.'

'Oh, for crying in a frozen bucket, Stella. What are you talking about? He could slip in the shower tomorrow morning. He could be hit by one of those big red London buses. He could choke on a crumpet or whatever they choke on over there. Not that I would care.'

'I just want to be sure you're not even *thinking* of—'

'Are you being serious?' He gave me a bear hug, and breathed into my hair, smelling faintly of a cologne I'd given him for Christmas. He smelt masculine, but old. *Not like Ben Hume*. Then he said, into my hair, just loud enough for me to hear, 'You have to be kidding me. What gives?'

He was a shade shorter than me without his shoes on. He tucked his chin into his neck and bobbed and weaved, then smiled, spread his hands and tap-danced across the room, his bare feet beat a staccato on the tiles. He was slightly out of breath when he placed his hands on my shoulders, concern rather than mirth, in his eyes. 'Are you really okay, Stells?'

'I just want to know that man will be all right.'

A brief silence was broken by the insistent tones of his phone on the table next to us. Jack let it ring.

'I really have no idea why you would *ever* think I was capable of anything … *anything* … like you have just insinuated. It's beyond me.' He kissed me and I drew him toward me, hugged him. He stroked my hair. 'What's this all about? Huh?'

I dug my fingers into his shoulders. I needed a moment before telling him that something life-altering had happened to me and there was no going back. That I was dreaming of a shark's eye. Of blood. Of Ben Hume.

How would I start?

'Stells? Ouch?' He began pulling my fingers from his biceps, like a man extracting himself from a snare. The phone burbled once more. He picked it up, looked at the screen, flicked it, told whoever it was to hold on for a moment. 'This is New York. I won't speak to them until I know that we're good.'

I nodded. We were good.

'You're sure? We'll talk later, okay?'

That night Jack lay next to me on his stomach. He slept deeply, his breathing was erratic, and it was comforting to have him near me, not least because he wasn't snoring. He'd strewn his clothes around the room, and a half-drunk tumbler of Scotch was on his nightstand. He'd been on the phone with New York for an hour and I had studiously ignored him afterwards. We'd not said anything more about Queensouth, and a blue-lit article on my iPhone had informed me that I was 'reflecting my own trauma upon my partner'; I was 'seeing violence where there wasn't any'. Just because my life was awash with violent clashes with death didn't mean Jack's was.

Nevertheless, that night I dreamt of Queensouth. I knew what he looked like from some online pictures Jack had found of him, part of an arrogant interview he'd given to a business journal in London. Jack had been enraged. Queensouth was a short, pouty man with childish pink cheeks. In my dream he was resplendent in his raffish, double-breasted, striped banker's suit, the collar too wide for his narrow shoulders. He was underwater, upright, his eyes open, contemplating me, the filaments of his hair standing up in the gentle current. Seeing him didn't frighten me, although I knew we were both deep under the waves. His arms floated up beside him, a dancer in adagio. He saw beyond me, into the undersea vastness.

I wanted to reach out and touch him, but he was sinking from the photic zone, where light could penetrate, where life was possible. His toes, clad in perfectly tied black leather brogues, were pointed. He began to drop in mid *assemblé*. When he finally disappeared into the bathypelagic darkness, I found myself swimming upwards, the salt water getting warmer and warmer, until I woke wrapped in my sheets.

Tears were running down my face. They tasted of the depths. Of guilt and shame.

And Jack was gone.

'You're taking the job? You're actually going to spend your time illustrating *children's books*?' Demetrius found this to be hilarious. 'Animals and clouds and mountains and all that?'

I was. I would be paid per illustration. The editor's name was Giselle and she loved my work. We'd spent an hour in her office creating a brief and drinking cappuccino. I'd be working on a series of junior encyclopedias. She'd given me a list with sample photos: sheep, fence, cloud, horse, bull, barn, fish, whale ... shark. I could send in the drawings as high-resolution scans, and the work was seemingly unlimited. My first six submissions would pay my share of that month's rent, if they were accepted. I could complete them in a week of focused work. Less.

Demetrius watched me colouring in the outline of a box turtle, shook his head. 'This isn't *you*, Cat. If you do all this ... *drawing* ... you're not going to have time for your *art*.'

But I was happy.

I would eventually create over a hundred drawings for Giselle's encyclopedias. Demetrius refused to let up on his derision and the tension between us became unbearable. I was in the middle of another project for Giselle, a travel guide to Prague, when I finally found the courage to tell Demetrius I was moving out of The WorkHead.

On the way back from the university, I drove over to the spring, always in search of water. I stopped the Land Rover at the top of the road, strangely devoid of fellow seekers. I toted my plastic container along the narrow lane. The people walking up and down the sidewalk had disappeared. The police van was gone. I was alone.

Where there was once the fountain was now simply a flat, bricked-up area. A sign said the spring had been closed indefinitely; the water flow had been diverted. A new collection point would soon open elsewhere.

It was eerily quiet. I trudged back up the road to the corner, then began walking toward a church where I'd often parked. The church parking lot had only a few cars. A car guard was sitting by a tree, wearing a bright vest. He looked at me solemnly.

'There was a boy here. He helped at the spring.' I pointed down the road. 'I'm looking for one of the boys who used to help there. He was just a small boy. He had a water Uber.'

The man raised his hands in the air, perhaps in acknowledgement of the unpredictability of the universe we shared. I continued.

'His name was Vusi. He liked the Yankees. Do you know him? Do you know where I might find him?'

The man smiled, made a placating, negative sound that might have been 'no' or it might have been 'I'm sorry'.

I thanked him, turned back to my car. The Yankees shirt and cup and hat I had for Vusi were in the back. I drove away, past the spot where they said the new spring would be, but I saw no people anywhere. The new spring would be more efficient, if it ever opened, but I would miss the old one. The quaint ceremony of it.

I drove back toward our side of the town in silence. I had no idea what I was going to do with the baseball souvenirs Jack had brought for Vusi. Maybe I'd see him at the new spring ... I really hoped I would. It was important to me to make good on my promise. Then I realised there was nothing substantial for Jack and me to eat in the house; in his absence I'd been subsisting on meals at the university, food I ordered in, frozen things and whatever I could pick up at the convenience shop down the road. Without Jack, mine was a feral existence. In the two weeks he'd been gone, I'd been living like a survivor of some minor catastrophe, eating through our last rations. I needed to stock the fridge so we could eat some decent meals at home. Jack liked to cook. I drove through the darkening evening to the plaza near the beach, parked the car, entered the achingly perfect Food Market, its rows of fruit lined up under the incandescent brilliance of a hundred artificial lights.

I pushed my shopping cart through this eerie perfection, trying to remember the last time I had actually shopped for myself and bought daily things like dishwasher soap and oil and butter and bread. These things were usually delivered – I had trouble locating them. South Africans had nowhere near the selection of grocery items we had in the US, but they made up for it with beautiful packaging. There was none of the dingy disarray of a New York market. Here, items were offered as if in a museum to consumables. A pop-up African sushi chef toiled behind a shiny glass counter lining up glistening caterpillars of California rolls. The wine was displayed as if by a Chardonnay algorithm for the well-heeled, a consumer who represented only one percent of the population.

And I found myself dissected in the neon light. Here I was, possibly buying food for the last time before my house was sold, before I left my manifestly imperfect home by the sea, where I had made my own mess, my own art. In the last weeks, secrets had piled up, secrets of an imperfect life becoming even more so as I pushed my plastic cart through the aisles, avoiding the German and American tourists in their bright shirts and shorts and loafers and dock shoes. Into the cart I threw bags of salad, trays of muffins, plastic tubs of cottage cheese, crackers, squares of fish, steaks, chicken kebabs, vegetable packs, hummus, pitas, wholegrain bread, two jams, bottles of red wine bearing the Food Market tag. Kids followed yoga-toned mothers down the aisles past me, grabbing tubes of sunscreen and packs of spring water and sandwiches in triangular plastic shells. I was guessing at what we needed; basically everything.

That same feeling from the day I'd met Ben washed over me, the feeling of being lifted and dropped, of being in water displaced by something huge and pitiless. For a terrible second I thought I was going to faint in the store. I steadied myself, held on to the shopping cart like it was the side of a lifeboat, and suddenly remembered my father in Florida, pushing a similar cart along in Publix, realising that a supermarket shopping cart can hold you up, keep you steady, give perfect lines of direction, even when you are too frail to let go.

My phone buzzed. I scrabbled it out of my bag.

> hey
> I am busy.
> u ok?
> Not sure.

thinking bout u
I'm scarred.
and me. got lots of scars. also almost got chomped by Landlord
I am serious.
me too ☺

I switched off the phone. *What am I doing? What on earth is happening to me?*

There I was in an oceanfront Food Market, my purse in the cart before me, pushing a mound of food wrapped in plastic.

I abandoned it and walked out into the bright setting sun and toward the rolling ocean. I walked past tables of people drinking wine, past the beach stalls, across the busy road and then over the strip of grass before the long white expanse of beach, still dotted with unlikely winter sunbathers soaking in the final rays.

I kicked off my work shoes, black Italian sneakers; I owned a row of them in different colours, most flecked with paint. I walked through the sand toward the water and stood in the surf, at the very end of the ocean, breathing. Even in that moment of loneliness I saw the colours of the endless sea more sharply than ever. I felt the water reaching for me and I wanted to wade into it. Swim in and dissipate, like a single drop of living blood. I was weeping.

I'm sure I caught no one's attention.

Kitefin Shark

The kitefin shark lives so close to the sea floor that it is not deemed a threat to humans. It is the largest luminous vertebrate in the world. The purpose of bioluminescence varies, ranging from defense and communication to warning and illumination. Bioluminescence is widely regarded as a means of sexual attraction, although the kitefin shark does not normally utilise it in this way.

Pen and Ink Illustration by Stella Wright for Children's Encyclopedia Series, New York

When I appeared at work, Katie was waiting for me by the office door. I tried to remember if we had a meeting scheduled. We had not, this was an impromptu visit, and she was beaming.

'I finished the first figure.'

'That's encouraging.'

'Would you come to the studio and take a look?'

I paused. The students' studio was two floors up, four long flights of stairs. Would I make it? But she led the way and I followed. The wind was more intense today, cold weather that would perhaps bring rain – the city was braced for it. I noted that Katie was wearing heavy denim, and a baseball cap. Other young women were wearing trendy leather pants and boots, some with scarves. I felt dowdy following her in my shapeless barn coat, ancient cargo pants and T-shirt, the clothes I wore to the studio when I didn't have meetings or teaching.

We climbed up the wide industrial stairs and I felt my heart begin to thump. I took long, careful breaths as we ascended to the second landing. Students waved at me as they passed, but by the next landing it was no good, I was tired. I took Katie's arm and she looked at me quickly, and I removed my hand.

'I'm sorry. Give me a moment, okay? Just a little out of breath.'

Katie was startled. 'Oh god, can I get you a chair? I don't ...'

'I just need a minute.'

She waited, gamely. 'I think you'll like this.'

I took my time answering as I steadied my breathing. 'It's ... more a question of ... do *you* like it?'

'Yes.' She smiled. 'I think I do. Working with leather is much harder than I thought. You were right. I got some help, though. I took lessons, and somebody from a shoe factory in town came and helped me.'

'There are still shoe factories in Cape Town?' Big breath. Normal breath.

'Yes. Like, yes.'

'Onwards. Upwards.'

We summited the last set of stairs and I entered the studio. Students had set up curtains and sheets to give themselves privacy, dividing the room into ghostly sectors. Today the place was almost empty, and I followed Katie to her worktable in the back of the studio where she'd set up something that looked strangely familiar yet not at all familiar.

It was not an entire woman, as promised. Instead, it was a leather arm. Exquisitely feminine. Somehow Katie had folded the leather over the hand and forearm so that it looked like it was encased in a long, violently elegant, shoulder-length glove. The hand itself had been painstakingly formed, as if it was not covered in leather, but was reaching away from the glove and leather itself. She'd set it on a stand, palm faced up. The fingers were slightly curled, inviting the viewer to come hither.

I had an intense vision of her creation as an arm floating by itself, deep in the sea, torn off and abandoned. It smelt of leather and glue and some kind of softener. I felt like touching it.

'What do you think?' she asked nervously.

'Beautiful.' I realised that Zulu and Van Staden were in their gowned cubicles; they could hear me. I found myself reaching out to Katie, hugging her gently. She felt warm, young, strong. I am not a hugger – she knew this and was unsure what to do with my praise. I let her go and she stepped back, looked at me as if I might be drunk. I turned to the piece. I put the leather fingers in mine. It felt as if I was touching something that was just about to live. The leather was soft, and as I pressed down I found that what was inside the leather was firm, resilient.

'Please be careful, Prof. I'm not sure how strong this is, okay?'

I withdrew my fingers. I was jubilant.

'It's perfect.'

And then I felt that strange dizziness, but I knew it was a small elation.

I turned and left her. The others remained silently immobile as I departed the studio and groped for the handrail and the stairs. I was smiling. Beaming, and I did not know why.

After the radio had finally announced the strong possibility of impending rain, I found Mandla standing on a ladder near the pool. He was looking up at the eaves of the house, the overhang of slate and tin roof, and he seemed to be touching the rafters. I walked out by the pool, shaded my eyes, watched him work. He was pounding nails into the eaves, supporting them with what looked to me like raw two-by-fours.

Gravely concerned, he climbed down the ladder to stand beside me and opened his hand. Inside was a mound of rotted wood he'd scratched off the inside of the eaves.

'This is too, too bad, Miss Stella.'

'Where did you get that? Which eave?'

'Listen. Wait. You must listen.'

I heard the ocean, of course, and the infernal wind, which whined from across the beach. And then something else. A whistling. A creaking and a groaning, very faint, that started up and ended with each heavy gust. It was the sound of trusses and rafters, of braces holding fast a roof that was pulling away from its skeleton. It was the sound of wood straining against steel. I climbed up the ladder and looked, saw where the rafters sticking out of the superstructure, jutting out of the house itself, had worked their way loose, and the wood had already started to give. I leant against the house, put my ear to the trusses and the fascia, and listened to the sound of movement.

Ours was one of the originally tiny bungalows that had been built along the coast decades ago. It had been expanded over the years, siding had been added. But ultimately it was a house not designed to withstand coastal gales forever. How many of these houses around me – painted in fresh pastels in anticipation of vacations – were so fragile? How many could be blown away in a real storm? It seemed as if in one stroke everything we clung to would explode into flinders.

As it was, the house's rafters and blocks were grinding against the trusses; the wind was howling under the roof overhang and pushing upwards. The metal braces holding the trusses to the rafters, as far as I could see, were painted over in white, but huge builder's bolts had driven right through the paint, discoloured in sections. Mandla was bracing these using more wood and long nails. He would have to paint them, but I doubted this would do much good – somebody would need to come up here with smaller bolts, a drill, metal supports, do work that was beyond one man and a ladder, certainly beyond Mandla's strength. Someone would ideally have to go into the roof and set up supporting rafters, a job for four or five men, a team. Something for the next owner to deal with. These braces might hold on the fascia, might be of some use, but the sound of the rafters grinding against their anchors rose out of the foundation of the house, a heavy viola groan, the harmonics of wind and land.

The corrosion here was deep. It made me helplessly enraged. I did not want the next owner to tear it apart and build something else. I leant against the house on top of the ladder and felt like I was on top of a mast. Behind me the ocean twinkled. I turned and looked out at the water, then at the other cottages dotting the shore. 'My' beach could be deserted for hours, even on the clear days. Deserted enough that a woman and a man could be tracked by a shark a hundred yards offshore, stagger through the gentle break to the sand, and nobody would see. And now a storm was coming and most of the shuttered houses were already battened down.

Ours was the most exposed. And if the incoming storm destroyed it, Jack, Mandla and I would be the only witnesses.

In the next few days the wind really picked up and with it the noise of the house increased. The rattling of windows was sometimes enough to sway the pots and pans hanging over my kitchen island. It gusted into my bedroom and caused ghostly cold spaces throughout my house.

Beyond my walls, the wind was a tantrum that began hot and wound up cold; it pumped through the city like bellows, blowing the smog, the litter, the rats, the bottles, the grime, the birds into the sea. It expelled poisons and toxins in angry gusts; it blew away the cigarette smoke, the smog, the dust and the dry mountain topsoil that found its way into the crevices of the city. Exhaust from late-night taxis, angry trucks, vans ... all blown away so furiously one could watch it disperse. Nature's way of detoxing.

As it found its way around buildings, down streets and through alleyways, the wind made it difficult to walk across campus, to ride a bicycle. It caused whirlpools of confusion in the City Bowl. Shopkeepers snapped at customers. People drove faster and more recklessly.

At the sea it mercilessly kicked up whiteheads. On deserted winter beaches, the sand turned into a vicious haze of swirling angry devils. Patrons in coastal restaurants played a grim game of wait-and-see: looking out at the water, waiting for the wind to ease, but barricaded behind windows and doors closed against the offensive.

And so the wind built a storm through the week.

I came back from the university one day and Mandla had performed another miracle.

In the garage he'd discovered a crate full of strong shroud wire and another crate of holds. Shroud wire was for yachts – when I'd discovered it could be layered into forms, I'd bought some from a nautical store for students who might want to sculpt with it. Bound in bunches like thin rope, it was medieval-looking, almost frightening. Sinister. But Mandla had cut the shrouds into varying sizes, added the holds and used nautical bolting to make neat lines. Each shroud-held set and corresponding bolt was lined up on the garage floor.

He'd climbed into the roof, and it was there that I heard him drilling. I looked up into the trap door, called his name. He didn't hear me. The ladder reached the one-and-a-half stories upwards from the studio. I made the climb, and the ladder gave slightly with each step, bowed inwards, and when I was almost to the trap door I looked down at the furniture, at the kitchen, the hard, tiled floor. I had never been afraid of heights, but I really was very high up and falling from this height would be deadly. I poked my head into the crawl space, and there he was, balanced on one of the ceiling joists, drilling into a rafter. It was dark, and it smelt musty and damp up there; rotting wood and sea salt. Light shone through chinks in the roof. He had a flashlight pointed at where he was working.

Mandla turned, smiled widely. He set down the drill, turned the light away from the crossbeam and I saw what he had done.

The holds and shroud wire were bolted from the rafters to the joists. Mandla had used dozens of heavy-duty bolts, each shroud wire and hold carefully placed to allow for the pitch of the roof. I was in a small forest of wires holding down the roof; he'd drilled in over two hundred bolts and there was much more to do. I crawled on the joists beside him, checked the tension of the wires, and then amid the exhalations of air through the roof I heard a new sound; an eerie humming, wind through the shrouds of a yacht at sea. Gusts of air pressed and released the roof and thus the wires. I felt as if I was inside a giant harp, hearing the music of redemption and salvation.

He had laid out yet more wires to be attached and I picked up the drill, which held an eight-millimetre bit, extra-long. With one of my metal rulers he had marked where the next shroud would go, a neat X. I pointed and he nodded encouragingly. He was covered in sweat and sawdust. I applied the drill, set the trigger and the drill screamed and burrowed into the soft wood, the sawdust not dry, but living. The drill finally poked through the wood; it was difficult to remove it from the rafter. I was dizzy. Mandla crawled over to me, took the drill, set it on a joist. And so we worked upon drifts of pink, foaming insulation.

Securing one shroud took me twenty minutes and by the end I was exhausted. I carefully climbed down the ladder, and Mandla followed. I could hardly trust my footing. I stopped midway, and Mandla waited patiently, the soles of his sandals just above my head. When we reached the floor he looked at me expectantly, then up at the trap door.

'I have as many of these wires as you need, Mandla.'

'Many. I need too many.'

'Can you do this by yourself? I don't think I can help you. I'm afraid I'll fall through the ceiling.'

He laughed. 'I can put these in for you, Miss Stella, yes.'

'This will make a good support. Thank you.'

He nodded. Like me, he seemed willing to try anything to save my house. I watched him as he scrambled back up the ladder, quickly, effortlessly, and lifted himself through the trap door.

He worked until dark. I was below, in the kitchen, and I could hear the drill screeching again and again. When he finally came down, I served him a dinner of pasta and pesto and bread, which he carried outside and ate looking at the fortresses of dark clouds over the sea, the end of a cold front. He was whipped by the wind, and when I asked him to come in, he shook his head, returned the dish and fork to me, picked up his bag.

'There might be rain soon. I must come tomorrow and keep working?'

'Yes.' I paid him a great deal extra and he took the money without comment. As he turned to go I asked, 'Do you think the wires will hold up there?'

He smiled. 'I think maybe.'

Jack and I settled into a routine we could both live with. Jack got up early in the morning, drank his coffee and disappeared into town. He would call during the day. Every call was about the agent. The impending sale of the house. Our return to the USA.

The morning after Mandla began work in the roof, after I'd told Jack about it, he'd insisted that we stop doing repairs to the house – that was for the new owner to worry about. We needed to focus on the sale and on moving out. Over a series of increasingly exasperated texts, I received

another text.
From Ben.

> want to say good-bye
> We did that already.
> no, for real. leaving Cape Town. this job is finished

He sent me a picture of a smooth, jewel-green yacht's hull. I could see his gloved finger in the frame. I touched it, held my breath. *This is how I lose Ben. With a text message. Well, of course.*

> come to Noordhoek

He wanted me to drive to the long stretch of beach, a half-hour drive from my house. Finally, I replied:

> It's very cloudy, windy. Huge storm brewing!
> that's why you have to come
> ?
> sea is wild, it's now or never, bring yr suit

I didn't reply. But I did drive out there with a bathing suit and a thermo top.

I parked in the huddled parking lot overlooking the rolling breakers. My car was one of only a few; his Beetle was nowhere to be seen. I picked my way down to the sand and then along the surf. This beach was ringed with dunes. It became more and more lonely as I walked away from the cluster of houses and the one small restaurant, leaving the mountains sloping into the sea at my back.

He was a lone figure looking out at the ocean in his surf gear.

It was cold. The incoming waves were large enough to be terrifying. The roar of the sea and the hiss of the foam at our feet made speaking almost too intimate. He glanced at me, registered my presence.

'I answered an ad for a job from a shipyard in Perth. I think I've had enough of Cape Town.'

I didn't answer.

He pointed out to the water. 'The break is actually closer than it looks. The water is shallow for quite a while. The real waves are over there ...' He pointed further down the beach, toward a jutting point. 'It's a bit of a swim, but then you turn and look up and down the beach. You just need to get through the chop.'

'That's not "chop". That's big surf.'

'You can do it. I'll be there.'

'I don't want to.'

'I don't either, but we'll be fine. We'd better do this before the rain comes.'

I waited.

'I think I'm going to miss you.' The spray from the ocean was wetting his face and hair. 'We need to do this together, Stella. Next time I swim will be on Cottesloe Beach.' He waited a moment, while I ran my fingers over my goosefleshed arms. He was exasperated. 'Listen to me, right? You *paint* the sea. You *live* next to the sea. If you want it back, we must *take* it back. This is it – your last chance, because I'm out of here.' The wind picked up, pushed me forward, but he braced himself against it. 'And I'm not leaving you like this.'

'Like what?'

'Scared. Of painting, Cape Town, the ocean, the beach. Don't let Manō take all that from you.' He began walking toward the water.

I forced myself not to hesitate and followed him into the churn.

The waves smashed into us but we were both able to dive under them, into the icy water that sounded of reverberations and spin. And he was right. I could reach down with my toes and touch the sand for quite a while before the ocean floor disappeared and then I was pushing myself through the water, under the waves, and then over, Ben close beside me.

The sea was flattened from time to time by the wind, the sun weak above us, backlighting the clouds. He reached out and touched my shoulder, a reassuring human touch in a limitless expanse of ocean – we were in this together.

Perhaps we shed our fear like outgrown carapaces. We swam toward the horizon, past the last line of waves. I stopped and he tread water beside me. The ocean spray was now mixed with a fine intermittent rain.

Rain I had not felt in months. *The drought is breaking.*

We looked up to the sky as pockmarked waves swelled and began to curl in front of us. I turned and looked around me at the heaving grey ocean, full of life, some of it deadly. I inhaled the wet, salty air. Punched the water, and screamed. And he watched me, and then howled, and the two of us called out to the infinite expanse, lost, vulnerable mammals. I plunged downwards and shouted into the depths, heard my own watery voice. Who knew how far it could carry? Underneath the surface was grey-blurred silence. The current and tide pushed my body out of the friendly gloom toward the break, and still I shouted, demanded to be heard, until my lungs were empty and I broke the surface and smelt the sea and the fresh scent of rain.

There he was, almost close enough to touch, laughing. Our laughter must have echoed to the strip of beach. *Scream it out, shake it off.*

We had reclaimed the sea.

It was Ben who decided to turn back, and when we did the beach was far away. And as I swam into the rising land-borne surf I felt an exultation that would have frightened me if he hadn't been there. When I caught a final wave with him, we rolled downwards with the same childish exhilaration as we would on a roller coaster, until the reassuring sand was beneath my feet and we were navigating our way to the beach, returning to the embrace of the land.

It was a revelation. I wiped my eyes and turned to face the spray and the wind and the lonely gulls who had witnessed it all.

He was standing knee-deep in the receding waves. Smaller now.

I breathed in the dense fragrance of the ocean awaiting rain.

'I'm going home.'

'We did it. We rescued ourselves.'

I kicked through the cold surf to him. My heart beating, thriving.

'Thank you.'

I sunk my nails into his chest and scribbled him out. I left marks on his body. Snarled red trails around his throat. I turned and walked out of the water to the comforting sand and the lonely wind, and I never saw Ben Hume again.

By the time I reached the Land Rover, the weak sun was gone and the clouds had darkened ominously. Just as I reached the car, the first real rain began, stinging droplets, then fat splotches against the window. I sat in the quiet confines of the car and pulled on my warmer clothes, tried to towel-dry my hair. Suddenly the wind gusted hard enough to rock the vehicle back and forth, and I started the engine. It was later than I thought; I needed to get home. On my phone, an accusing green line of texts from Jack waited to be opened.

As I pulled out of the parking area the rain began in earnest, the storm pouring over the mountains to the west. I squinted at the beach. Ben was walking in the opposite direction, toward the town of Kommetjie. I thought of him in his yellow Beetle, navigating his way to his apartment, where I would never meet him again. Driving away from the beach I gritted my teeth into my sadness. *Some things have an end.*

My phone rang. Jack again. I clicked it off and he immediately called back.

'I'll call back in a moment, Jack.' *I'm busy mourning a man I will never see again, and trying to drive in very hard rain.*

'Stella, listen. We have a major problem. The wind is tearing this house apart and I'm trying to get your things out of the living room. You need to stay wherever you are.'

'Wait, what?'

'Where the *hell* are you, Stella? We're being hit by some kind of, I dunno ... *hurricane* ... and the pool is already flooded, the roof is tearing itself apart.'

The wind churned into the car. I began to feel the first twinge of anxiety. 'All of my work is sitting in the studio–'

'We're getting it out. Stay where you are, Stella. I don't want you driving in this. I can barely hear you.'

'Jack. Do *not* leave that house ...'

'Just don't come here. Mandla is with me. We'll figure this out!'

'I'm in the car. I'm twenty minutes away. We can't just leave the house to the elements.'

'Stella, the roads are crazy. I don't think you quite understand what's–'

'I'm coming to help. And Jack?'

The phone crackled. We were disconnected.

The water against the windows was now a drumbeat. The road might be closed soon if I didn't hurry up. I flicked on the brights and hunched over the wheel, and the car struggled to stay in its lane. Soon rain was hitting the windshield as if the Land Rover was in an AutoWash, the wipers barely coping with the deluge.

The rain in Cape Town – when it does rain – is Mother Nature having a nervous breakdown. Every Southeaster is another chance for Mother Nature to tear the Cape away from Africa once and for all, and try she does. The traffic becomes confused and suicidal as drivers smash into lakes of collected rainwater and hydroplane – just as I did as I drove back toward the house, dodging the stalling and honking cars, and fighting an increasing panic.

Closer to the city water spouted over the coastal barricades, and people huddled together holding up mobile phones to film the impressive spray. Ragged, forsaken homeless souls hunched over in search of shelter. A taxi full of sodden riders and their driver still screaming for more passengers managed to stall in the middle of the road. On the coastal road, past the condos standing up to the onslaught, the abandoned shoreline now looked like the site of a military landing as the ocean boiled against the rocky shore. On the approach road to my home there were fewer cars, so I parked in front of the pathway to the house (the public parking was already hopelessly flooded). Sliding and slipping down the path, I came around to the front and noted that seawater had flooded the pool. The outdoor furniture and several large potted plants had been tossed around like toys. The wind screamed into the land from the ferocious sea.

But worse, one of the sliding doors had been blown in, smashed by a chair flung by the gale. As I entered the house, Jack was trying to move a box of canvases.

'I told you not to drive in this, Stella! Jesus,' he shouted above the roar, stressed and annoyed. 'Help me with these paintings, now that you're here.'

'Where's Mandla?'

'He's in the roof. He's trying to fix it. Or something.' Jack glanced at me, then behind me. 'I'm going to nail these doors shut. There's wood down the side of the house. Stuff in the garage.'

Outside, the storm hammered against the house; if I stood still, I could almost feel the house sway. The wind outside rose to a screech and Jack looked at me, puzzled.

'Feel that?'

I waited. I felt as if we could be ripped from the land at any moment.

Jack said, 'The floor just rose up and down.'

Then he was in and out with the wooden boards, piling them in the middle of the living room and then doing his best to cover the windows while I moved paintings through the back door to the garage. Looking into the gathering gloomy dark, I realised we should have sealed up the house days ago. The side windows were at least closed and locked, the shutters facing the beach pulled shut.

The lights flickered.

As we tried to cover one of the side doors, Mandla shouted down from the trap door. 'Mr Jack, Miss, please come now, you must please see this.'

Jack clambered up the ladder and I followed into the rafters to where Mandla was sitting beside a camp light in the twinkling array of sea cables. Viciously cold air poured in where the tin roof met the house.

'You must be quiet,' shouted Mandla incongruously, and we tried to be, but it was impossible to escape the roar of the wind and the rain against the metal of the roof and the dull, industrial groans of the ocean. But then we heard it.

Mandla grinned. 'The wires. They are singing.'

And so they were. The wires were vibrating at different octaves. The eerie, hollow, metallic sound reverberated through us all and we were briefly transfixed, as if in a church. What flowed through us was the same holy resonance one hears after the hardest notes of an organ have melted away and all that remains are the sonic reverberations.

Then the electricity cut and we were plunged into darkness. The sounds were much closer. Outside, grey skylight peeked in as the roof panels wobbled and shook. The wind huffed against the roof, the rain frantic. Raindrops hitting the roof became smaller and sharper, as if the wind itself was lifting them back into the clouds.

The foundations are struggling to hold on to the rock.

Jack looked up at the roof, and then at me, and I tried to discern his face before turning away. In the close, singing darkness I felt the clear sadness of betrayal.

And then I heard the first tear. It was a quick grunt of wood and then a loud ping of a bolt ripping out of the sodden rafter and swinging free in the dark.

Then there was another one.

Jack turned to me. 'We need to get out of here right now. There's nothing we can do.' As he said it, another rip and another ping. 'This roof is not going to hold.'

Mandla said, 'Mr Jack, you can get down first, please. I'll help Miss

Stella onto the ladder.'

Jack hesitated for a moment but when the next bolts popped, he started to make his way to the lip of the trap door.

It was almost too late. All around us I could hear the metallic ping of bolts starting to give in the sodden wood. What kind of wind could tear off a roof? I began crawling to the dark opening. Below, Jack was directing the weak light of his mobile phone. Mandla took me under my arms and gently held me as I found my way onto the ladder and then down, my heart pounding in my throat. Jack helped me off and when my feet reached the floor I saw we were standing in two inches of water, which was pouring in under the glass doors, slamming around the windows and leaking down the white walls.

When Mandla reached the bottom, he looked hopefully upwards at the roof. And then the storm paused a beat – a legato in the cacophony – just before I heard a massive 'pop!', as if a giant child was playing with oversized bubble wrap. In the darkness above, dozens of bolts jerked out together and clanged into each other. What was left of the wires pinged and banged until in one moment I heard something greedily slash open the top of the house.

We looked up through the trap door to a sky full of clouds.

Jack pounded me on the shoulder. 'Your paintings!'

The garage roof was still holding, and we loaded everything we had into the cars, all the things that would fit. It was a long, arduous job, nerve-wracking as we heard the torn remnants of the roof slamming up and down. Every time we ran back into the house the wind and rain intensified. When the cars were loaded, we worked on getting what was left onto tables, covered in tarps and tied down. My painting gear, my tools, my paints, easels, unpainted canvases, frames and brushes we piled up just inside the front door. Electronics were covered in plastic bags and stored in the downstairs bathroom.

We lost another door at around 3am. The frame simply tore out of the walls and then the whole glass door fell down with a splash into the flooded lounge, exposing the living room and the kitchen to the pitiless ocean. A single sheet of water lay over the pool, the terrace, the living room. The outside furniture was submerged. Water ran furiously down the stairs. The house rocked back and forth. Jack and I climbed up to the bedroom, him with plastic bags. 'Put in whatever's valuable. Papers, passports, whatever.'

'I'm not leaving.'

'Look at this place, Stella. *Look at it.* Don't leave important stuff in the drawers. We have to get it all downstairs. We might not get another chance.'

And so we shoved my jewellery and iPod and computer and Jack's watches and even the bedside clock into the bags, along with Jack's computers and electronic gadgets and endless documents. We threw bags full of clothes and papers over the stair railing and they splashed down into the living room and were spirited into the garage by Mandla. Every time I went into the garage, I looked to the ceiling but somehow the roof held. As we fought our way downstairs with the last of our important belongings the house grumbled, and another strip of roof flew off. It was clear that everything would have to be replaced; the electrics were gone.

And still the rain pummelled us.

The three of us finally stood in the crowded garage, with the camp lights flickering on and off, the paintings piled on trusses and in the cars. It was then that Jack looked up and listened, took my hand and pressed the button to open the garage door, which thankfully still worked on battery power.

'Out! We need to get the hell out.'

We had keened our ears to tell-tale signs of destruction, and now something sounded different, like a groaning, as we fled out onto the path leading up to the street. The groaning turned into a howling wail and I turned around just in time to see a chunk of the remaining roof wrench itself off the building, hesitate over the exposed, torn trusses and beams, and come crashing down onto the rocks.

Jack looked at me. His eyes were wild, his hair was clinging to his gaunt face; he looked like a shipwrecked sailor from centuries ago, one of the first damned mariners to stagger up to these shores.

He looked up into the ferocious sky and laughed.

I found myself laughing too, next to Jack, next to Mandla, who watched us, and then also began to laugh: three hysterical people at the end of everything in the dying rain and the perplexing gale.

Whale Shark

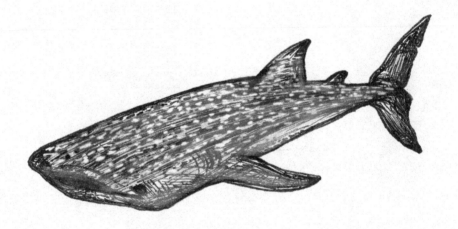

The whale shark is the largest known shark, growing to a maximum length of 62 feet (18.5 meters). Whale sharks prefer warmer waters and are reliably found in Australia as well as Mexico, the Maldives, Indonesia and off the eastern coast of South Africa. Whale sharks can live to 130 years with some specimens reaching 180 years. First identified in Cape Town's Table Bay in 1828.

Pastel from Stella Wright's Gifted Private Collection, Cape Town

The storm reached its coda at dawn.

There was extensive damage all over the city, but especially along the coast. Houses and roads were flooded. Trees had fallen over onto vehicles and walls and fences. Ripped-off branches were everywhere. Power and phone lines had collapsed. There were several bad accidents. Clean-up was going to be costly and would take time.

The drought was over.

We had spent the night huddled in Jack's car with my paintings, pulled safely away from the house and away from any trees that might come crashing down. Jack even nodded off just before the early dawn, while the wind shook the car. I did not sleep. Neither did Mandla, who sat behind us in rigid silence as the water raged against the windows.

Once the rain completely stopped, we walked around the house surveying the gaping holes that used to be sliding doors. Many of the homes near us had damaged roofs but none were as bad as ours – a definite downside to being the most exposed house on the point. We sorted through towels and clothes salvaged from upstairs and changed into whatever was dry.

We found dry clothes for Mandla, who did not want to stay. There *was* nowhere for him to stay. The place now offered only crude shelter from the wind and the tentative birds. Jack found him a trench coat, boots and one of his duffels, and as much food as he could carry, and Mandla walked up to the road in the weak morning light. He'd need to attend to his own home, which was probably much further inland, but possibly also flooded. He turned at the top of the road and waved. Was he laughing? I don't know.

I still see him there, tall, impervious to the weather, outlined against the grey sky, hatless. A herald. *Wanderer Above the Mist*.

'Power's out. We can try and find something to eat in the fridge, before it all goes bad,' Jack noted.

The inside of the house itself was ruined. Some of the rafters had crashed into the floor. Wearing an incongruous blazer, jeans and a white sweater – his only dry clothes – Jack stalked across the puddled floors like a doomed admiral, and discovered the wine cabinet. He opened it theatrically.

'You'll be pleased to know the wine has been spared the wrath of Neptune.'

'I think we could use coffee more than wine at this point.'

'On the contrary, there's no electricity so we may as well have a drink. This is an excellent bottle of wine. Really superb. And keeping wine by the sea, as you know, is difficult.' He located two glasses from an unopened cupboard and handed me one.

'Jack, don't be ridiculous,' I said, taking the wine.

'After the night we've just had, Stella, we surely need a drink.'

Above us the cormorants were discovering the beach again, circling over the house and calling to each other. I could see them through the torn hole in the roof over the living room. Water dripped in furtively from somewhere, and trickled down the stairs. And there was my husband, ankle deep, pouring himself a drink from a hundred-dollar bottle of Syrah.

'I'm not participating in this, Jack,' I said. 'I'm going to find more towels and a sweater. There must be some more suitable warm clothes for you too, somewhere. We need to take stock.'

Jack took a large sip of wine, ran his wrist across his lips. 'You're right. We do. In fact, now seems like the *perfect* time. Do you have something to tell me, Stella? Specifically, I'd like to know if you've been having an affair?'

Such a stark question, on such a stark day. I was completely taken off-guard.

'What? Jack, I–'

He looked through the torn maw that was the front of our house toward the calming sea. Then turned the full force of his gaze upon me.

'Please don't lie to me. I could tell the minute I came back. You've been completely ... off. Preoccupied. Distant. Jumpy. Withdrawn. Paranoid, even. Checking your phone all the time. It's obvious you're seeing somebody. I can feel it. I'm guessing that's why you've been putting off selling ... this?' He waved the glass at the carnage around him.

I took a sip of wine after all. 'Jack, I'm sorry.'

'Who is it? You owe me that, at least.'

'It's not important.'

'Not *important*? It is to me.'

'It's not. And it's over, Jack. I–'

'It's just so *unlike* you, Stella. I can't believe it.' He looked at me. Drank. 'It's somebody at the university, right? Some professor? Wait ... not a *student*?'

'No. Of course not. It wasn't even an affair, Jack. I promise you. It's over.'

'It wasn't an *affair*? Did you sleep with him?'

I nodded.

'Then it's an affair, Stella! A big, fat fucking betrayal.'

'I know, Jack. And I'm sorry. I truly am. That's why I ended it.'

'I want you to know, I have never cheated on you.'

'I know.'

'I've had my chances, too. I've had many.' He took a long gulp of his wine, finished it. Threw his glass with some force against the wall.

Somewhere above us, the wind caught some of the remaining roofing, released it, and it thudded down against the joists.

'So how long has it been going on, Stella? Are you leaving me? I mean, what exactly do you expect me to do here?'

'Jack, this is not the place ...'

'*This*, this wreck of a house, is most definitely the place,' he shouted. He hoisted himself to his feet, splashed over the tiles and carpets, poured himself another drink in a new glass, then theatrically flopped back down on the chair in the middle of the living room. Water rushed out from under him, poured onto the lake on the floor.

My teeth were chattering and I waited. Jack set down his glass on the coffee table.

'Stella, I need to understand why you've done this to us.'

I made my way over, sat on the coffee table in front of him. Like I was teaching a child a gentle lesson.

'I wanted to talk about this in a better place. I wasn't expecting to have this out here.'

'Well, you can't always get what you want, Stella. I need to know *now*.'

'Fine. It was the day of the shark attack. I was swimming as usual in the ocean like I told you, and there was this surfer–'

'This part you omitted to mention, I recall.'

'And he spotted the shark, and the shark ... attacked ... him, and we helped each other get out of the water.'

'And?'

'And it was so terrifying, Jack. I can't explain the horror, the fear. I really thought I was going to die.'

'And? I don't understand, Stella. If you were so scared, so ... affected by this, why didn't you tell me about it?'

'Because you weren't here, Jack! If you remember–'

'No, no, no, Stella. If *you* remember, you didn't even bother to tell me when this happened to you. You told me two weeks afterwards, *two weeks*. At least now I know why ... And when you did deign to mention this life-changing event, what's the first thing I said, Stella? The *very* first thing? I immediately offered to fly back here and support you. And I meant it. And you know it. And you said *no*! You said you were fine.'

'Because you wouldn't have understood, Jack. You just wouldn't have understood. I had a near-death experience and the only person–'

'I'm sorry, you had a *what*? You didn't nearly die, Stella. That shark didn't even touch you. You had a bad scare – sure, I get that. I'm not downplaying how frightening it must have been, but nothing actually *happened* to you–'

'You just proved my point, Jack. When I was next to that shark, I thought I was going to be eaten alive. I really and truly believed, with every fibre of my being, that I was going to *die*. So, for me, it *was* a near-death experience even though I didn't have a scratch on me. And Ben felt the same way. We *both* thought–'

'Oh, Ben is it?'

'Yes, Ben, okay. His name is Ben. We were so shaken up. It felt like we needed help getting over it. We needed to help each other ... heal.'

'I see. And has the get-over-our-almost-shark-attack sex with Ben helped you, Stella?'

'Jack, please don't be crude. I'm trying to explain like you asked. I didn't just hop into bed with him, okay? We talked. We just talked at first. We connected over our fears of the water and our nightmares. And the sex ... just happened. But it wasn't about that. It wasn't a relationship. At all. We were just trying to get over this traumatic event–'

'Here's what I don't understand, Stella. You actually *have* had a near-death experience. With your heart. You could really have died without that surgery. Why weren't you traumatised by *that* brush with mortality? That's what I'd like to know.'

'I don't know, Jack. I *was* affected by it. Of course I was. But not like this. I can't explain it to you.'

We both sat in defeated silence.

'I'm tired, Jack.'

'I'm tired too. We've been up all night. Maybe we should go upstairs, see if there's anything left up there, just go to sleep for an hour or two, even if there's no roof. Even if there's no *bed*.' He grimaced. The wine was in his system. He had no tolerance.

'No. I mean I'm *tired*, Jack. My heart is damaged. And I've realised that I lost something years ago, before I met you, and now I think I've found it again.'

'What? What did you lose?'

'Myself.'

Jack sat slumped in the chair. His eyes were just a little glazed in the new morning light. 'Don't understand that.'

'I don't either.'

'We've all lost parts of ourselves along the way, Stella. It's called getting older. We have a great life. I've given you everything. You want for nothing.'

'You're right, Jack. I'm not denying that. But I'm tired of apologising.'

'*I'm* the one who's been wronged here, Stella!' He stood, shivering. Wobbly on his feet. His teeth were maroon.

'You should go back to New York, Jack.'

'No! We need to go back *together*. Look, Stella, we can fix this. I'm willing to forgive you. God knows I'm not the best husband in the world. I can see past ... whatever happened. As long as it's over. You're obviously suffering from post-traumatic stress. I just didn't see it. You can work through it with a specialist therapist. And we can go to counselling to deal with ...'

'I don't want to go back to New York, Jack.'

'Fine. We'll book into a hotel for a couple of weeks while I wind up the business. You can salvage what we can from this place. We'll sell it as is – I don't care if we make a loss. We need to get back home, Stella.'

'You're not hearing me, Jack. I don't want to go back. I want to stay here.'

'What are you talking about, Stella? Our time here is over. My business is in the States. Our homes are in the States. Our friends. Our family. Our lives ...'

'I know, Jack. I said *I* want to stay here.'

He blinked, finally comprehending. 'You want to stay here without *me*? For how long?'

'I don't know.'

'If I go, Stella, that's it. I'm not coming back.'

I nodded.

'I'm not kidding, Stella. I thought you said it was over with this guy, that you didn't love him.'

'It is over. And I don't love him. I don't want to stay for Ben. I want to stay for *me*. I like it here, Jack. I like my job. I like the art I'm making. I like this house. This ocean.'

'So, what, you want me to wait around for you in New York? Until you come to your senses? Until you *find yourself*? What are you saying, exactly?' He looked at me, pained. 'I can't understand this. This is crazy. This is *insane*. I love you, Stella. You know it. I love you.'

'I know you do, Jack.' I took him by the shirt. 'Listen to me. You didn't do anything except be exactly the man you have always been. You're kind and you're funny. You're generous and you can cook and you have great taste in art even though you know nothing about it. Blame all this on me.'

'How does that help me, Stella?' He gently pushed away my hands. 'What now? What do you want from me?'

'Here's what I want from you, Jack. Listen carefully. I want to stay in this house, and I want my paintings and my other artwork. That's it.'

'You want the house? *What house?* Look around you, Stells!'

'It can be rebuilt, Jack.'

'I dunno,' he said glumly. He picked up his glass, poured in a last splash of wine, and downed it, set down the glass.

'Jack, I know this is my fault.'

'I'll ask again. I'm begging. We go to sleep and when we wake up it'll be like a thing that just only *maybe* happened. A bad, whaddyacallit? A bad dream.' He picked up the wine bottle, waved it at the wreckage of the walls, at the rocks, the screaming birds, the swirling waves, the receding clouds. 'All of it. Gone. Poof. Big mistake. We can have a do over. A *mulligan*. Like in golf, right? I'll grant you a mulligan.'

'We're not going to do that.'

'No? What do we do right now?'

'You leave the house. I rebuild.'

'I'm supposed to just walk away and leave you here? You're really going to blow up our lives like this? Throw me away, and everything we have together? You're being irrational. What happens when you wake up and realise what you've done? What then? You're going to regret it, Stella. And I tell you something. I'll be far away and long gone.'

'One of the perks of living on the moral high ground is your responsibility for the other person falls away, Jack. I'm not ready to go back. I want a quieter, simpler life. And your world is anything but simple. It's fast-paced and competitive and stressful. I just can't do it anymore.'

Jack was picking his way toward the back door like a man walking out of a casino, his savings gone. As he stepped up to the higher level of the kitchen, his boat shoes squished on the tiles.

'I have no idea where to go.'

'Go to a hotel, that big one on the water, just down the road. You need to, Jack. You have work to do. I'll call you a taxi. We'll talk again tomorrow. I'll bring you some clothes ...'

'Who the hell is on the road now? Nobody. I'll drive slowly.'

'No, Jack, you're drunk. You can't drive.'

He grunted again. 'This is Cape Town – nobody gives a damn. And we don't need to do this. You can take it all back and I'll take it all back and we can start cleaning up this mess. Or we can leave it and you can come with me to the hotel and we can have a warm shower together and order room service and wear big white, fluffy robes and get drunk and fuck and sleep. Start again.'

'I'm sorry.'

He splashed clumsily toward me, enveloped me in a hug. 'Come with me. Let the ocean have this place. All of it. I'll find you another one.'

'No, Jack.'

Jack pointed at the house, at me, then swept his arm around us. 'Are you saying you're going to leave me and just stay here ... in this ... *beach cottage*? Think strategically for once, Stella.'

We faced each other one last time like the couple we once were.

'Listen to me,' I said. 'You never listen. You *look* like you're listening. But really *listen*, Jack. Life is more than just an investment.' I wanted to shake him but he was too solid. 'Anything can happen to us. The things that affect us most are not announced on the financial pages. Things change in a second. The world is full of the sharks you don't expect. That doesn't make it a bad world.'

Jack was with me now. He nodded, an admiral stoically accepting the cost of battle. He gazed out over his lost sea. He looked at me and nodded curtly, a final resignation.

Paint this memory, I thought. Title: *Knowledge of Defeat.*

Once Jack had left for the hotel, a diminished dark shape hunched over in the back of the taxi that came to fetch him, I sank into the surprisingly dry couch. I felt depleted, and allowed my emotions to wash over me along with the sounds of the ocean and gulls and wind and dripping water. There was tremendous guilt, but not shame. A deep, deep sadness. Heartache; a new kind. I didn't like to think of the pain I had caused Jack, the look of bewilderment on his face. My tears flowed for a long time. I was hollowed out. I needed to sleep.

Upstairs I discovered a section of my closet that hadn't been completely doused. Above the bedroom, the sky was starting to clear but the ocean wind was beginning to make itself felt inside the house. I slipped on the heaviest sweater I could find, found the last dry blankets, took them downstairs. The house was terribly exposed and vacant. Above me, a piece of the roof creaked in the breeze. I lay down on the couch, looking out at the water, closed my eyes. Title: *Exposed to the Elements.* I was easy prey for anyone curious enough to venture onto the point to survey the wreckage. I reached into the bowl on the coffee table, extricated the shark tooth, dangerous and sharp in my hand, and ran my thumb over the serrated edge. I held it tightly as I drifted off to sleep.

I dreamt, but only briefly. I was floating again. I opened my eyes under water and there was the eye, larger than ever, suspended before me, but this time I thought I could see my reflection. Or at least the outline of myself. I was not possessed of that cold, foreboding feeling. Or the terrible fear. Just a warm acceptance.

I woke up and the tooth was still in my hand. I carried it with me as I gingerly walked around the house and took stock. The furniture sat in pools of water, the ocean breeze prying through the doors and sending ripples right there in the center of the living room. Submerged carpets. Moisture running down walls. Outside a tired sun shone over the spent Atlantic, over the waves like a giant hand pressing downwards. The water was deep cerulean, the clouds were stacked like white, billowing castles with grey bottoms. Gulls searched for the leavings of the storm. The only thing to do now was to bail out the bottom floor.

I went to the kitchen, higher than the living area and spared the brunt of the storm, hopefully spun a knob on the stove, waited until the gas burst into life. Flames cheerfully rose in a ring and soon there would be coffee. I could take a mug and bring it out to the point, sit and watch the ocean. It was still early; I had the entire day.

I set the tooth on the counter and began.

Mandla appeared that afternoon from around the back of the house, looking like someone who'd survived a bomb blast in the remnants of a long sweater, soccer shorts and flip-flops. I was sitting cross-legged next to the pool, once again regarding furniture at the bottom. Plastic bags. Leaves and a sea sponge. A layer of dust swirled into the middle of the water; ripples fed across it. Mandla stood by the doors and waited until I waved, two survivors hailing each other over the wreck. He glanced into the house, shook his head. Then he stood inside, looked up at the tears in the roof. We looked in together, and I said, 'If you hadn't put those links up in the attic, the *entire* roof would have come off. *Much* more damage.'

He nodded.

'I'll make you coffee. There's no power, but the gas works. I can cook us something to eat.'

'My house is gone,' he said.

'It's not gone, Mandla. It's damaged, but it's not gone.'

He drummed his chest. 'My house. My house. Not *your* house. My house. It is gone.'

'Your house? It was blown away?'

'Yes.'

'I'm so sorry, Mandla.'

He shrugged. 'I must get some of the things.'

'Of course. Can I help? I have the Land Rover. My big truck?'

'Yes, the truck would be good.'

'We can do it now.'

In the garage we pulled my paintings out of the Land Rover. I slipped in behind the wheel and Mandla hopped in next to me.

'Where to?'

He pointed. 'This road.'

We drove up the coast road to where, unbelievably, street sellers and vendors were setting up for the day; business as usual despite the wreckage of the storm. Jack would still be sleeping in the hotel, I thought. He'd be sprawled across a double bed, by himself. I'd call him later. We had a lot to deal with.

White horses twinkled in the morning sun as Mandla piloted us along. Did he live in the settlement in Hout Bay? And how could I not know where he lived? This was how we all existed on this side of the city. Cocooned. Oblivious. Our decisions affecting people we never saw, people who were invisible even when they were right in front of us.

We were only two miles from my home when Mandla pointed just ahead, on the water-darkened dirt shoulder of the road.

'Here. Here.' I slowed, looked at him and he pointed furiously. 'It is here.'

I stopped the car. Mandla was squinting over the waves. There was nothing except rocks, the ocean, the mountain to my left jutting up, covered in scree. The wind gently rocked the car.

'I don't understand? There's nothing here, Mandla.' I pointed at the sea. 'This is not where people live. Nothing. There's nothing here.'

He opened the door, jumped out. I hesitated only for a second before I stepped out to stand next to him, looking out at the ocean.

He shaded his eyes. 'The storm took everything.'

He moved away, to the edge of the shoulder that plunged down perhaps thirty feet into the water. I'd seen people stop around here before. Surfers picking their way to the ocean. Divers seeking crayfish and mussels and whatever else they could find. Mandla leapt over the lip, made his nimble away across the rocks, turned once and waved me down.

'Come, come.'

I followed clumsily as he hopped from flat rock to flat rock, over spreads of gravel and stinking kelp and an orange-and-white sixty-gallon drum. I tried to follow his feet, put mine where he'd put his. After just a few more steps we arrived at a small hump of rocks against the water, and when we crested it I realised I was looking at the remains of a human dwelling. Mandla's home.

A twisted piece of corrugated iron sloped into the lapping water. Pieces of weed sagged beneath it. A tarp, part of a sail, a bench ... these were a jumble on the rocks, but his other possessions were still afloat. A kerosene lamp, bottles, a crate, clothing, papers, folders. A purple suitcase rocked in the tide, mostly submerged. Strewn across the rocks were sun hats I recognised. I had given them to him; one was from the Edgartown Yacht Club. Beyond the corrugated roof was what for all intents and purposes was a flooded cave, the water breathing in and out of it. A military blanket and a greyed duvet coated the rocks. The barest measurements of human survival against the elements. I could see where he had built a fire, close by where I might have simply adjusted my thermostat. Pieces of firewood floated in the outgoing tide, some whole, some blackened. The entire place had a fecund, living smell: a smell of the ocean, of life lived against the odds. He stood looking at it, shaking his head, and I stood in shocked silence beside him.

I took his hand in mine. It was rough, calloused, heavy with bone and tendon.

'This house is finished,' he said, and shrugged.

'Is this where you lived, Mandla?'

He nodded, looked at it all, this assortment of sea trash that within hours would be swept away.

Tears were running down my face, despite the spray. 'I don't believe it. A *cave*?'

He shrugged. 'Gone.'

'You can start again. Do you hear? You must stay at my house and start again somewhere else. I can help.' I added, 'You must rebuild somewhere better. Safer. It is *wrong* that you had to live here.'

'It was my place. I choose this. I do not live near other people. If I live in the township, they will kill me.'

'I'm sorry, Mandla. I am so sorry. I … I don't know what to say.'

He lived here because he was the kind of outsider who feared for his life. And I was just like thousands of other people like me, who had no idea what lives and struggles were lived by the people I saw every day. As far as I was concerned, Mandla vanished into thin air as soon as he walked down the road from my home, only to magically materialise when he came to work.

'I want to help,' I said. 'We can salvage a few things; replace the others later. Don't worry.'

'Mr Jack is coming back?' He looked doubtful. 'Maybe he will not agree.'

I shook my head. Waved my arms. 'He has left. Gone away. You know?'

Mandla laughed, flapped his arms, too. His laughter echoed off the water, echoed out of the cave. I am not sure I have ever heard a man laugh so freely.

'Miss Stella made him fly? Will he come back?'

'I don't know, Mandla. I really don't know. And please, I am just Stella.'

Mandla flapped his arms again, his back to me, still screeching and hooting in mirth, waving his arms like some magnificent, resilient bird bracing its flightless wings against the wind, perched alone on an unforgiving shore. His arms and his laugher a defiance against the stubborn rocks, the destruction, the hatred, the end of everything.

Egg Case

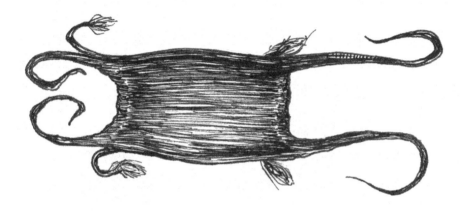

Some shark species are oviparous; they produce eggs in capsules (*Chondrichthyes*) that develop and hatch outside the maternal body. People often find egg cases (colloquially known as mermaid's purses) on the shoreline or underwater. If you see a capsule underwater, *do not* remove or disturb it as it is likely to still contain a developing creature.

The brown shyshark and its egg case, endemic to the shallow coastal waters of South Africa, is often referred to as 'plain happy'.

Charcoal Drawing from Stella Wright's Private Collection, New York

I would see Demetrius one more time, about a year after I left The Work-Head to join the Manhattan artist migration to Bushwick, where I rented my own, smaller studio. I somehow paid the rent with illustration work and a trickle of painting sales.

Demetrius came to my first real exhibition at a new artist-owned gallery on West 25th Street. It was a collection of my wildlife paintings and my first beach drawings. The gallery was moving with the times: it had its own online magazine and its website touted an 'artist's social media program', 'social media marketing services' and online 'advice for collectors'. My publisher had underwritten the snacks and had promoted the exhibition online, Giselle insisting it was a great place to 'create an authentic buzz for our series' and sell our books, which hung in discreet baskets near the entrance along with a collection of bright postcards of my paintings. We'd branched out from children's encyclopedias (*My First Guide to Mammals*, *My First Guide to Sharks and Rays* ...) to *Beaches of New York State* and *Oceanside Rentals of New England*. We sold seventy-five books that evening, all carefully bagged by an intern in a severe purple dress and heavy black glasses, who vanished at the end of the night with our waitress.

Demetrius didn't come to the reception, even though I'd emailed him the details. The show went for a week, and the day before it ended I opened the gallery door to a grey late afternoon in New York, the wind rushing down 10th Avenue, the bright jollity of the interior lost to the sudden dark angularity of the city. The downlights from inside the gallery room shone weakly through the window – the gallery was, after all, a slick-looking former shop. By then I had sold almost everything. A review in the *Chelsea Art Weekly* described my work as 'careful, accomplished and evocative'. I was going out to dinner with a friend from Yale who'd driven down from Connecticut just to see me and to buy a painting she'd seen on my Instagram page.

I would meet Jack two years later. When I was finally coming into my own, surviving off drawing and painting.

I didn't notice Demetrius standing beside the next shopfront, a dilapidated, closed coffee shop, perhaps one of the last casualties of the rise of Starbucks.

'Cat.'

I turned and it was him, smaller than I remembered, in his black-leather motorcycle jacket, his spattered jeans, his boots, his hat, looking at me challengingly, his fingers stuffed in his pockets. I gasped, not so much because I missed him, but because at that cold moment he looked so very alone on that endless sidewalk, standing there as if he had paused on a much longer journey into downtown. I rushed over and tried to hug him but it was awkward. Things had not ended well between us. But then he smiled. I held him by the shoulders, as if preventing him from falling forward, and he'd taken part of my coat in his fists, and we stood like that for a moment in that cold street. Two people clinging to each other in an endless sea of time and sadness and disappointment.

'Do you want to come in? I'd love you to see. The gallery closes the show tomorrow.'

'I came this morning and checked it out.'

'You don't approve. I know. It's too *commercial* ...'

'You didn't show *Big Blue*.' For a moment I wondered what he was talking about, and then I remembered. *Blue, Blue Sea*. Still in my new apartment. Still wrapped up. 'Guess it didn't fit with the showing?' He smiled.

'I didn't want it to sell.'

'I'll buy it.'

I laughed.

'For real ...'

'I have no idea what to ask for it.' That painting was something from another time. Another me.

'After that,' he said, pointing to the gallery, 'you can ask a lot. More than I can for any of my work. You can ask for *something*.'

'I know you think I'm a sellout. Using paintings to sell books. Beachscapes, animals, sea life. Definitely not your thing.'

'Maybe. At one time. But life has a way of kicking your ass. I've grown up. Maybe you have, too.'

'Let's see each other again. I need to be somewhere now.'

'Yeah, me too.'

'Coffee, okay? Or a drink. We're going to do this, Demetrius, right?'

He nodded, that sage nod of his I remembered so well. He turned, began walking away. The taxi I had summoned rolled up beside us. I finally called to him.

'De?'

He turned.

'I want you to have it.'

He shrugged, not understanding.

'The painting. It's yours.'

'You want me to have *Big Blue*?'

'Yes. It's just as much yours as it is mine.'

He narrowed his eyes. 'How much? You're going to be big time now, Stella. I'm just a struggling artist over here.'

'I want you to have it.'

'It's big. It's a huge painting.' He beamed.

'You have the room for it.'

'Yeah. I guess I do. Well, you know where to send it. And I haven't rented out your room to anyone else yet.'

I laughed and he turned, crossed the street, as I opened the door to the cab. I waved but he was already down the street, almost out of sight. And then he was.

I would indeed send the painting to him. It would be picked up and would traverse the city in a truck, travelling through time and place to where we used to work. I know he signed for it, and he would send me a picture of it on the raw brick wall of The WorkHead, that familiar light from the Hudson River falling against it.

I would email him a number of times. Text him. Invite him to lunch, to dinner, to breakfast. There'd be no reply.

I finally took a cab to the West Village and knocked on the door to a nondescript studio whose occupant had left no forwarding address.

He'd taken *Blue, Blue Sea* with him.

Renovations were already beginning in the hallway.

Adaptive reuse, Cat.

Weeks later, against my better judgement, I drove back to Ben's place and found it locked. I searched around for the landlord, who had no idea where he'd gone. Ben had disappeared and left behind some clothes, the mattress and a few utensils and, as the landlord prosaically put it, 'heaps of his bloody rubbish, wood and plastic'. Ben's tools had also disappeared. I was offered the rental of the studio for a cut rate, almost nothing, if I was interested. I wasn't.

That day I stood in the empty space, looking at the empty workroom, the kitchen that was not a complete wreck but simply a small room with a tattered sink, and the empty bedroom without its mattress, the windows shut against the wind. I tried to scent him, like an animal finding its way back to its territory. But he was long gone.

One morning I received a letter from Perth. Inside was a creased photograph of Ben standing on an incandescently white beach grinning at the camera. A real photograph. He had the beginnings of a beard, his hair long and wet. He was wearing surf trunks and had a surfboard. On the back was written, simply 'Ovahimba Point', which I discovered via Google was a surf spot north of Walvis Bay in Namibia that was so inaccessible that he must have hiked there after somehow driving up north with his surfboard. Perhaps someone had given him a lift. Perhaps he'd bought a car and left it when the road along the Skeleton Coast turned into sand.

He had scrawled beneath, 'Paint these waves for me.' Endless waves disappearing into a brown swathe of desert. I would indeed paint them. Those waves would be the first things I would paint once I had rebuilt my studio.

I traced his face with my finger, closed my eyes, held the picture to my fragile heart. I imagined him surfing that ocean as it hurtled into the desert, alone again, and sleeping on the beach under the endless stars. Finding his way out of the country and then the continent. I am comforted thinking of Ben in Perth, Jack in New York. I am between – I don't know for how long.

I sometimes think I see him: sun-bleached, lean, shaggy, walking among the crowds, his thin denim shirt hanging off his shoulders, grinning at me from thousands of faces that are not his. I've painted him, the Ben in my memory and sometimes in my dreams.

I would dream of a shark one last time. It was the same shark I had met, somehow smaller than I remembered. I was very sure it was the same shark, with its unique markings and colouring I had not noticed in my fright. I was underwater once again, close enough to touch the animal that regarded me, unmoving. It wasn't on the eternal hunt sharks require to stay afloat, the constant movement they rely on for buoyancy. It was very still, watchful. The water was blue and clear. Golden beams of sunlight broke through the surface and shone all around us and on the gently waving kelp, bustling fish, tiny octopi, bright coral, plants from another age, billions of particles of swimming life in the swirling currents.

The blue eye facing me reflected the teeming sea like a lapis lazuli set deep in the shark's misshapen head. I reached forward to touch its face and it dispersed into tiny shimmering droplets. Then I was alone, swimming up toward the air.

I am becoming more and more part of this place. I have claimed the surfboard Ben never took back, and that survived the storm. On some mornings I float on the ocean waves without fear. I sit behind my break on the very hot days, and the seabirds scream and circle above me. They crowd the rocks. The sea heaves and sighs. Below my vulnerable, naked feet are miles and miles of kelp. Countless fronds sway slowly back and forth in the tides, and fish play within them.

On some days, the sea is dark and cloudy. It can be brooding, and it's always cold. But it is also marvelously indigo, beckoning and endless. I am aware of how close the sharks might be. Perhaps only a heartbeat away, as they always have been. Of all the dangers in this world, they are the most unlikely and the most necessary.

I have long ago stopped imagining another kind of existence. Sometimes I lie face down on the surfboard and hear life teeming beneath me. Then I paddle with cupped hands toward my point. Sometimes I stand. Sometimes I am carried.

Each time I reach the shore, I'm aware that this is the life I have chosen. Me, alone, whatever the consequences. I no longer dream of sharks, or blood, or New York and the life I left behind. I have chosen to make art here, in this space of brilliant, endless colours. I can stand on my tiny beach and gaze out over the ocean, shade my eyes and look into the mountains of snowy clouds that pile over the teal horizon – toward Jack in America and Ben in Australia. Draw the outlines of the dark breakers out there curling into cobalt waves as they roll into the shore, then ripple into foam tinged with living green upon the wet-ochre sand. The white beach house sits exposed and precarious upon its point.

Colour this sea blue and grey, turquoise in the morning and indigo in the evening. Checker the birds riding the wind above. Shade in the brooding rocks that jut from the shore and under the water.

Paint this tiny woman standing alone in the wind, alive, her hair white-and-yellow-bleached by the sun and the salt. Title it: *My Side of the Ocean*.

CPSIA information can be obtained
at www.ICGtesting.com
Printed in the USA
LVHW040313200723
752981LV00006B/156

9 781770 108332

Accomplished American artist Stella Wright's beachside home in Cape Town is perched on the edge of land and sea, safety and vulnerability, the domestic and the wild. When Stella takes an afternoon swim, she is unprepared for the drama that unfolds. She and a nearby surfer are tracked by a giant great white shark that swims close enough so she can look it in the eye, leaving the two of them deeply traumatised.

The surfer – Ben – is a waterman who paints trawlers for a living. There is an almost instant attraction between them, but Stella is married to wealthy American financier Jack Barlow, and she and her husband are preparing to leave the country.

Stella and Ben begin a passionate affair. The two of them must face their fear of the water; Stella because beaches and oceans form the basis of her art, Ben because surfing is his passion. Into this situation Jack flies in from overseas to tie up their affairs and bring Stella back to New York.

Stella must make a choice between the man who has reawakened her original passion for art, and the man who can give her everything else the world has to offer.

My Side of the Ocean is a novel of great empathy and insight, exploring essential questions about what it means to live, and love, when the secure foundations of a life have been ripped away.

'This novel grips you and doesn't let go. A thoroughly enjoyable re
— PAIGE NI

'Imbued wit
sea, *My Side*
powerful no
empathy ab
love, emigra
your fears.'

'A compelling love story with a twist. An engrossing and thought-provoking read that highlights the fragility of life and love, and the power of the choices we make.'
— JASSY MACKENZIE

RON IRWIN is a senior lecturer in the Centre for Film and Media at the University of Cape Town. His debut novel, *Flat Water Tuesday* (2013), was Book of the Month for *The Buffalo News* and the Target Book Club, and has been optioned for film.

Fiction

ISBN 978-1-77010-833-2

Also available as an ebook
www.panmacmillan.co.za